DARK CORNER

RON FISHER

Fisher, Ron. Dark Corner (J.D. Bragg Series Book 2). Published by MysteryRow.

ISBN-13: 978-1-949073-04-1 (Kindle)
ISBN-13: 978-1-949073-05-8 (epub)
ISBN-13: 978-1-949073-06-5 (paperback)
ISBN-13: 978-1-949073-07-2 (hard cover)

“Every murderer is probably somebody's old friend.”

Agatha Christie

This book is dedicated to Chip, Mike, and Mackenzie.
My life's bragging rights.

ACKNOWLEDGMENTS

I'd like to thank all the people who helped me so much with DARK CORNER, the second book in my J.D. Bragg mystery series. First, my Beta Readers, Jeff Upshaw, Patrick Scullin, Joanne Wanciak, Joyce Crowe, Tom Douglass, and Elona Smith. THE FISHER GROUP—Hal, Mary Ann, Travis, and Wil Fisher—for all their design and production wizardry. My Tasmanian friends Jason and Marina Anderson at Polgarus Studios for their excellent formatting work and advice, and finally, my incredibly smart and talented family—sons Michael and Chip Fisher and daughter Mackenzie Fisher Squires and her husband, Jamie. You guys are the greatest.

PROLOGUE

Northwest Spartanburg County, South Carolina.

Jamal Johnson walked down the deserted two-lane blacktop, mad as hell, and getting madder with every step. The only light along this stretch of the country road was the full moon in the midnight sky above, but the spreading limbs from the thick stand of hardwoods on either side of the road arched over him, blotting out even that. He could barely see the tarmac beneath his feet and was having to straddle the center stripe just to keep from walking into a ditch.

Damn you Willie Tee, Jamal thought, I can't believe you went off and left a brother like that. I come with you, and you knew I expected to leave with you. Did you think I wouldn't mind walking home? It's five freaking miles, bro. You and me gonna have a 'come to Jesus' meeting when I see you again.

Jamal thought back to the dinner party he and Willie worked tonight at the rich folk's house on Hunting Club Road, just over the line in North Carolina. He'd stayed a few minutes afterward to help clean up, and when he came out to leave, Willie was gone. He probably went off with Della Wiggins, the water girl, Jamal thought. Willie was hitting on her all night, with her giggling and swinging her little round butt and flirting right back. For a second, he wondered if he would have gone off with her if he'd been in Willie's shoes. Della Wiggins was hot.

But he knew he wouldn't have. First, he was going steady with Monique, and even if he weren't, when Jamal Johnson said he'd do something, he would do it. Unlike Willie Tee, who he'd learned the hard way, wasn't a man of his word.

Jamal wished he could have called his mom to come and get him, but she was visiting her sister in Charlotte. He was glad he was seventeen now—his birthday just a week ago—and his mom could now sign for him to get his driver's license. Somehow, he'd find a way to buy a car, even if it was a piece of crap—as long as it got him around. He was saving up for it, but it was hard to juggle working with school, as it limited his job opportunities.

He had held an afternoon and weekend job at a stable, but he got let go. The man told him he didn't need him anymore, said he had enough full-time stable hands. Now he was having to find odd jobs to do, like tonight, waiting tables at the parties the wealthy horse people threw at their big houses. He liked horses, and hoped he could pick up another job working at a stable, or when there was a horse event at USEC—the Upcountry Steeplechase and Equestrian Club—where they held the big Upcountry Steeplechase every year, which was coming up soon.

He occupied himself thinking about dumb things, mostly to pass the time as he walked—like a question he had about USEC. With the "US" tacked on the front, it sounded like a government thing. Not an exclusive club for horse lovers and Steeplechase racing. He'd expressed that thought to several people in the past, who, if they were the rich white folks who were USEC members, looked at him like how that could be any of his business. He finally decided to keep his mouth shut about it. They were rude, but they were right. It wasn't his business, and it wasn't like he'd ever be a member there, anyway.

Jamal looked up at what few small patches of sky he could see through the cover of tree limbs spread over the road. People called the part of South Carolina where he and his mom lived, the "Dark Corner." Well, it certainly was dark tonight, he thought.

He was hoping he could make it into Landrum before the Pizza Shack closed. That was probably where Willie Tee was. It was where most of the kids hung out. If Willie wasn't there, maybe he could find someone else to give him a ride the rest of the way home.

He had tried to flag down a couple of guests leaving the dinner party, but they drove right by him. He could serve their food, wash their cars, and work in their stables, but he wasn't one of them, and never would be. But it wasn't just because he was black, he thought, with some irony. Most of them were color blind. It was because he was poor—which to them, especially some of the ones he'd heard called "trust fund babies," being poor was worse than being black. They looked down their noses at the poor white locals the same way they looked at him.

The headlights of a car suddenly appeared behind him, and he moved over to the shoulder to try to wave it down. He was surprised when it actually pulled to a stop behind him. He tried to see the driver behind the wheel, but the headlights blinded him. He could tell that the car was a big SUV, like a Chevy Suburban, but that didn't say much. Big SUVs like Suburbans, Tahoes, and Yukons were the choice of automobiles for almost every horse person in the area. He didn't care who it was, as long as they would offer him a ride.

Suddenly, the driver floored the vehicle and came speeding directly at him. The unexpected move shocked him so that he was a moment late jumping out of the way. The automobile hit him squarely, knocking him into the weeds and underbrush beside the road.

He lay there in shock and pain, the coppery taste of blood filling his mouth. Breathing was a struggle, and his ribs felt like they were on fire.

He heard the car door open and close, and through blurred vision, watched a shadowy figure come up and stand near him. All he could see was a pair of all-weather duck boots, but he couldn't lift his head high enough to see who was wearing them. They were like the ones he wore to muck out stables, and common with all people, man or woman, who spent time around horses. Whoever it was brought a shovel with them. It was resting, digging end down, on the ground by the shoes.

Jamal tried to speak, but the sound that came out was indecipherable to his ears and unrecognizable as his own. He watched as the shovel lifted out of view, and he heard what sounded like a grunt of effort, then a terrible pain exploded in the side of his head. It was the last sensation Jamal Johnson would ever have.

CHAPTER ONE

Atlanta, a couple of weeks later.

When I heard the name Jamal Johnson, it was on a late Sunday evening, when Kelly Mayfield, the love of my life, asked me what I thought happened to him. I was lying on the sofa in my apartment with my head in her lap, thinking about trying to persuade her to move the arrangement into the bedroom. Although the name had a vaguely familiar ring, Jamal Johnson, or what happened to him, was the last thing on my mind.

"John David Bragg," Kelly said. "Do you even read the newspaper that bears your name as publisher?"

She thunked me on the head using her thumb and forefinger like she was checking for ripe melons at the supermarket.

"If you did," she continued, "you would know that Jamal Johnson has been the *Clarion's* front-page headline for the last two weeks."

The *Clarion* was the weekly newspaper in Pickens County South Carolina I inherited from my late grandfather, Garnet Quincy Bragg, who had owned and published it for most of his adult life. The paper was now seventy-five percent mine and my sister Eloise's, and twenty-five percent Kelly's—which I sold to her for much-needed funds to pay off debts, keep the financially troubled paper afloat, and provide my sister and niece with an income. Kelly, who was already working as the editor, bought her share a year ago, after my grandfather died.

Kelly was still the editor—and, truth be told, the *real* publisher. I was publisher in name only, and an absentee one at that. My sister Eloise was the CFO, office manager, and head of advertising sales. Even Eloise's teenage daughter Mackenzie was on the staff as a cub reporter.

The *Clarion* was making a small profit now, unusual in the era of the shrinking printed word where so many newspapers were having a hard time or going under. The success was due to Kelly's move to a digital publishing version, and my sister's new-found talent for procuring advertising—something my late grandfather abhorred.

I couldn't claim credit for any it, other than having enough sense to leave them alone to do it. I was an investigative reporter and feature writer with an Atlanta-based national sports magazine called *SportsWord*, with no interest what-so-ever in working at a small-town newspaper, especially one in the place where I grew up. Luckily, neither my sister nor Kelly needed or wanted my help with the *Clarion* any more than I wanted to give it to them.

The only problem with the whole thing was that Kelly and I were trying to carry on a relationship while living a hundred and forty miles apart.

"My mailman is always delivering my mail to the wrong apartment," I said. "Sometimes I don't get my copy of the paper." That was a lie. She knew it, and I knew she knew it.

She thunked my head again.

"Jamal Johnson is a teenager from over in North Greenville County who went missing. The police believe he shot someone's thoroughbred horse as an act of revenge because the owner fired him from his job as a stable hand. They think he's run off because of it."

"The look on your face says you don't buy that," I said.

"You're right," she said. "I don't. Everyone I've talked to who knew the boy, including an old friend who lives over there, has convinced me he's innocent. They all say Jamal is a sweet kid who would never shoot anyone's horse. They believe it's a case of 'blame it on the black kid.'"

I suddenly remembered how I knew the name, Jamal Johnson.

"Do you know if this kid's mother is Millie Johnson?" I asked.

"How did you know that?" she said, surprised.

"I know her oldest son, Taylor. We played college football together."

I sat up and leaned back against the sofa, a memory of those days filling my head and throwing a wet blanket on any fire I may have had about shuffling Kelly off to bed.

She saw the sudden change in me.

"What's wrong, J.D.?" she asked. "You look like you've seen a ghost."

"Maybe I have," I said. "Taylor Johnson got badly hurt in a game and I was responsible for it."

She gave me a hard look, her dark eyes boring into mine.

"You're going to have to explain that one to me," she said.

I would have preferred not to, but I brought up the subject of Taylor Johnson, so I probably owed her the story.

"It was my junior year, toward the end of the season," I said. "I'd won the starting quarterback job by then and Taylor was one of my wide-receivers—and my friend. I called a passing play, with Taylor the target. It was a crossing route pattern, a physically tough pass because the receiver must be prepared to take a hard hit from the secondary the instant the ball touches his hands. Taylor knew what was coming, he'd done it many times, and was as tough as any receiver I'd ever seen, despite his smallish size. I took the snap, faked a handoff to a running back, and threw the ball to Taylor, but it went high. Taylor made a leaping catch, which put him in the air and off his feet as their cornerback hit him from behind like an oncoming train. They both went down in a heap, and Taylor didn't get up. I stood and watched as they worked on him until an ambulance came out on the field and took him away."

I took a deep breath, and paused before the next part of the story—the part I'd never get over, the moment indelibly etched on the walls of my memory.

Kelly sat patiently, waiting for me to continue. By the look on her face, she already knew the worst was yet to come.

"After the game," I finally said, "Coach gathered us all in the locker room for an announcement. He told us Taylor had suffered a spinal cord injury. Early diagnosis was, he was paralyzed from the neck down."

"Oh my God, J.D.," Kelly said, grabbing my hand and squeezing it tightly.

"To this day," I said, "he's lying in a bed in a facility in Greenville South Carolina, with someone having to feed, bathe, and help him with the bathroom necessities. His paralysis was so severe, his phrenic nerve stopped stimulating his diaphragm, and it quit functioning. A doctor explained this to me at the hospital later. He needs 24-7 assistance with his breathing and has a breathing pacemaker surgically implanted in him. It has an electrode in it that stimulates his phrenic nerve and causes his diaphragm to contract. Otherwise, he couldn't breathe at all. It gives his speech a start-stop effect with sudden short gasps of breath. It's heartbreaking to listen to him try to talk."

"And now the younger child is missing," Kelly said. That's too much for one mother to take."

"Taylor won't take it too well either," I said. "He's crazy about that kid. He's always bragging about his younger brother Jamal—how good he is at running track, how smart he is in school, what a great kid he is. It's like Taylor is living his life through his younger brother now. If something has happened to that boy, it will kill Taylor."

"So, you still see him?"

"Not as often as I should," I said.

Kelly fell silent. "I interviewed the mother," she finally said. "She told me she is a maid and a cook for a wealthy family. Maids don't make a lot of money, and don't usually get insurance from an employer. I wonder who pays for Taylor's care. It must be terribly expensive."

"A moneyed-alumni started a nonprofit organization called the Taylor Johnson Foundation, which raises the money to pay for his care. I've never been too broke not to donate something to it every year."

"Did you ever meet her?" Kelly asked. "Mrs. Johnson?"

"Yes, I did. Several times before the accident when Taylor and I shared rides home for holidays, and a few times since, when she's been there on my visits to see Taylor. I'm ashamed to say, though, I haven't visited him in months."

"Is there a father in the picture?"

"When we were sharing rides home from college there was. I gathered that Jamal, who was just a baby then, was an unplanned surprise, there is such a gap in his and Taylor's age. But the father died not long after Taylor got hurt, leaving Mrs. Johnson, a widow."

"Mrs. Johnson doesn't believe Jamal would just run away like that without telling her," Kelly said. "They appear to have a close, loving, relationship."

Most mothers would think that of their children, I thought, but I didn't voice it. "I liked Mrs. Johnson. She was always sending Taylor these terrific peanut butter cookies, and he would share them sometimes. The first time I met her, I told her how much I liked them, and she began sending them to me, too.

She didn't stop when Taylor got hurt. I kept getting those cookies until I graduated."

Kelly looked at me silently for a minute.

"You blame yourself for Taylor's injury, don't you?" she eventually said. "But I don't see how it was your fault. Football is a dangerous game."

"I try to tell myself that," I said. "But it doesn't work. After all, I called the pass, then made the bad throw. I'll always wonder how things would have turned out if I'd been more on target with it, and not over his head. I made him expose his blindside to the hit."

I needed to derail this conversation before it put me into a permanent bad mood. Playing "what if" wasn't going to change a damn thing.

"What proof do they have that Jamal killed the horse?" I asked.

"There were no eyewitnesses to the shooting. All the authorities have, are accusations from the horse owner. Jamal worked part time as a stable hand for him and the man recently fired him. He claims Jamal threatened to get even with him. And of course, there's the rifle."

"*Rifle*?" I said.

"They found the rifle that shot the horse in a shed out behind Jamal's house," Kelly said. "Mrs. Johnson swears Jamal didn't own a firearm, and never had. She says someone put it there."

I remembered that shed. It was a small wooden building out back painted white like the house. I'd supposed they used it for storage.

"How do they know it's the rifle that shot the horse?"

"The bullets matched. The police said it was definitely the gun that shot the horse."

"You mean they ran ballistics on a horse shooting?" I asked. "Do the cops up there not have enough to do?"

"The horse was worth millions," Kelly said.

"Jesus," I said. "What horse was it, Seabiscuit?"

"My friend Natasha, who lives over there, said it was a champion steeplechaser. A famous stud horse now. That whole area is big 'horse country.'"

"Natasha? How do you two know each other?"

"We were roommates at Smith. Her family moved down years ago and built a huge horse farm and stables in that beautiful border area of Tryon North

Carolina and the South Carolina part they call the Dark Corner. They're horse and steeplechase enthusiasts."

"What does Natasha do for a living?"

"Nothing," Kelly said. "She's never worked, and neither has her parents. I don't think her grandfather ever worked either. They all live off a huge trust fund left by a great-grandfather who rubbed shoulders with the Carnegies and the Rockefellers. She's a descendant of American royalty, you could say."

"Or robber barons," I said. "Don't they call her kind of people 'trust fund babies?'"

"They even call themselves that. In their circles, I think it's a badge of honor. There's a whole clique of them over there. They're all into horses, steeplechases, fox hunting, and raising pedigree dogs. Quite a close-knit group. Almost incestuous in a way."

"Doesn't sound like a group I would fit into."

"Natasha isn't bad. She isn't snobby at all. Wild, but not a snob. She just divorced her third husband."

"With her money, I guess she can get a new husband every year."

"Oh, she doesn't need money to get a husband, she's drop-dead gorgeous. Natasha stole every boy I dated in college. She's a man thief. She can't help herself."

Kelly stared at me as if she had a question. She did.

"You're a native South Carolinian," she said. "Why do they call it the Dark Corner?"

"Looking for a history lesson?"

"Yes, I am. Enlighten me."

"Well, they call it 'corner' because it's the far northeast corner of Greenville County, but for some, it has come to include the little town of Landrum next door in Spartanburg County, and even the Tryon area just over the North Carolina line, too. The 'dark' part came about before the Civil War when it was the only area in the state that voted against the nullification act, which gave South Carolina the right to ignore federal mandates—the argument that eventually led to secession and civil war. A politician was making a pro-nullification speech on Glassy Mountain there and was physically pulled from the wagon bed where he was speaking. He shouted out that 'this was a dark corner where the light of nullification could never shine.' The name Dark Corner stuck."

"Am I boring you yet?" I asked.

"No, I'm impressed," she said and motioned for me to continue. "You're quite the history nerd."

"I minored in history," I said before continuing. "There are some who think it's called the Dark Corner because of how backward and poor the area has always been," I went on, showing off. "Not everyone there had electricity until the fifties. There was a time when the biggest crops up there were corn and peaches, grown mainly for the numerous bootleggers who lived in the hills and hollows. The corn was for the whiskey, the peaches for brandy."

"John David Bragg, the history professor," Kelly said.

"Here's more history," I said. "The Bragg family, next door in Pickens County, was involved in that business a couple of generations ago, too. Still Hollow, the old family home where my sister still lives didn't get that name because it's so quiet and lovely. It's called Still Hollow because there was always a liquor still up some hollow on the property."

"I knew there was something illicit about you," she said. "I like it."

"But I digress," I said. "The Dark Corner stayed poor and dark until those trust-fund-babies like your friend Natasha started coming in and buying up the beautiful countryside for a song, dispossessing the people who had owned the land for generations. They replaced the small farms with their mini-mansions and large horse farms. The old folks are mostly gone now, either dead, or in a condo in a town somewhere, purchased with the money they received for their land, and probably sorry they sold so cheaply. The natives who stayed either have commercial peach orchards or work for the new elite who have taken over the Dark Corner, helping them raise their thoroughbreds, organize their fox hunts, and work as their servants—like Millie Johnson."

Kelly was smiling at me.

"What?' I said.

"You sound like your grandfather. You're a reverse snob just like he was."

"I guess that's only natural," I said. "Where do you think I learned it?"

Since his death, Grandfather was never far from my thoughts. He raised my sister Eloise and me from childhood after both our parents were killed when a jack-knifing eighteen-wheeler swept their car off a rainy highway one night. He was an undemonstrative old man, with stern ways and unyielding moral principles. We had our disagreements over the years. Unfortunately, I didn't realize nor appreciate that his harsh methods were for my own good, and that he loved me, which I guess I'd never believed—until after he died. Kelly was right. Grandfather and his high-minded principles shaped my life, and my greatest regret is I never got to tell him that.

"You're starting to look too serious again," she said. "Let's change the subject."

She was right.

"Steeple chasing," I said. "Do they ever catch the steeple?"

"God, you're a hick," she said, laughing. She then gave me another look as if I might not be kidding.

"Seriously, are you not familiar with a steeplechase?"

"I'm in the sports business, darling. Of course, I know what a steeplechase is. It's also called 'jump racing.' As you probably know, there are two kinds: one run by people, as in a track and field event, over hurdles, the other with horses and riders. It's obviously the latter we're talking about."

"Have you ever been to a race?" she asked.

"Can't say that I have. Nor a fox hunt or a dog show."

"That's where it got started," she said. "Fox hunting. In Ireland or England, way back. I've been to a race. I went with Natasha once. It's more exciting than regular horse racing and more dangerous, I think. They jump over hedges and rail fences, some surrounded by sand and water, and with the horses and riders bunched together running full out, sometimes they stumble and fall coming over a jump. Horses and jockeys get hurt, some of them very badly. That part I don't like. I don't think I could ever become a great fan of the sport."

"I couldn't either," I said. "I'll stick to football where only about four players per team get a concussion in each game."

"Or become paralyzed from the neck down," she said, solemn again.

Dammit, I thought. I'd brought us back to that subject.

"On that note," she said, "I'm going to bed."

When I joined her in the bedroom, she was lying under the covers, naked.

I shed my clothes and joined her.

She was lying on her side; her hair spread across the pillow like an open Japanese fan. I held her and kissed her, always amazed that someone like this actually loved me. But we played our long-distance relationship like some complex game, cautious in the use of the love word, neither of us wanting to be the one to push things so far that the other one had to make a decision that might tear us apart: like, who gives up their job and career and relocates? Me to South Carolina? Her to Atlanta? It was a decision neither of us was ready to address because neither of us knew what the outcome would be. So, we made a silent agreement not to talk about it. But it was a looming question we would one day need to face.

We made love tenderly, but for the first time since we'd become intimate, my mind drifted. I couldn't stop thinking about Taylor Johnson.

CHAPTER TWO

We were up early Monday morning. Kelly made oatmeal and toast while I made the coffee. We sat at the kitchen table eating and not talking much. She read the *Atlanta* newspaper which came with a thump outside my apartment door, and I sat tossing around an idea that had come to me in the night.

Finally, I said, "Why don't I follow you back and stay for a couple of days?"

She looked at me as if she thought I was kidding.

"That would be terrific," she said. "What brought this on?"

"Well, for one thing," I said, "I didn't get enough of you this weekend."

That was true, but it was also true that I kept thinking of Taylor, and wondering how he was handling his little brother's disappearance.

"What's the other thing?" she asked.

"I want to go see Taylor. I want to know how he's doing, and if there's anything I can do for him or his mother."

"You're a good man, John David Bragg." Kelly stood up and kissed me on the top of my head like I was a child.

"I need to get dressed and get going," she said. "When you get there, come by the *Clarion*. Eloise will want to see you, and maybe we can have dinner with her tonight."

I agreed, and while she was getting dressed, I called Joe Dennis, my boss at *SportsWord* magazine. Joe was my old editor there, and now the new publisher of the magazine. I still answered directly to him, which was great, because he was a good man and my friend—unlike the former publisher.

I told him I was going away for a few days on family business, but would email him a piece I'd written about suspected kickbacks in the building of a new billion dollar NFL stadium in a major city out west. A council member and a team executive were suspected, and it made a juicy story. I promised Joe he would have it in less than an hour. The story would keep him satisfied until next week's edition neared deadline. Joe was okay with that and knew I wouldn't let him down.

I was finishing up the article on my laptop when Kelly came out ready to go. "Are you coming?" she said, seeing me still sitting at the kitchen table.

"I'll be along later," I said. "I've decided to go straight to Greenville and see Taylor first. Go ahead and make plans for dinner with Eloise, and I'll meet you at the *Clarion* when I can get there. We'll go to my sister's together."

She placed a hand on my shoulder and leaned down and gave me another kiss. This one, she would never give a child.

"Okay," she said. "I'm off. Drive carefully."

"You too," I said and watched her pull her rolling overnight bag out the door, admiring the way she moved. I never tired of looking at her. She was a tall and graceful woman who bore the high cheekbones of the Cherokee in her bloodline from generations back. Her hair lay straight and long over her shoulders, so black it had a blue sheen to it. I would be looking forward to a couple more days spent with her. I emailed the Word file to Joe and went to pack a bag myself.

For a second, I toyed with the idea of driving the vintage 1959 Cadillac Eldorado I'd inherited from my grandfather, but decided against it. It was his pride and joy, and he'd been obsessive in the care of it. I tried to carry on the tradition, and only drove it around town to show it off, and on Sunday drives when Kelly was down. It was still in pristine condition, and I left it under the tarp to keep it that way. I threw my bag into my trusty old hard-top Jeep Wrangler and took it instead. It was a dozen years old, and another accidental scrape or dent would be lost among the many.

Two and a half hours and a hundred and forty-five miles later I walked into Taylor's room in Greenville. He was in bed, as usual, watching the news on a TV on the wall. I didn't try to count the number of tubes and lines running into and out of him. His eyes were sunken into his head, and he looked like he'd lost even more weight since I'd last seen him.

He cut his eyes toward the door and saw me. He grinned, but it came out more like a grimace. The only thing that still looked like the Taylor I knew was the spark of life in his eyes. He hadn't given up when most other people would have.

"J.D. . . . my man," he said. "Good to . . . see you." The breathing pacemaker showed its effect on his speech.

"Hey bud," I said. How are you doing?" It was a dumb question.

"You hear . . . about . . . Jamal?" he asked.

"Yeah," I said. "I came to see if there's anything I can do to help. How's your mom?"

"She's awful . . . broken up. Jamal . . . didn't do . . . anything. Cops got it . . .all wrong. He's . . . a good kid. Didn't . . . kill no horse."

He lay there looking at me for a long moment before he spoke again, Wolf Blitzer's voice on the TV the only sound in the room.

"I knew . . . you'd come," he finally said.

"I'm sorry it's been so long," I said. "I meant to get over here before now."

"I've got . . . a favor . . . to ask," he said.

"Anything, Taylor, you know that."

"Find . . . my brother. Clear . . . his name."

It took me a moment to realize he was serious.

"Please," he added, desperation clear in his face.

"Taylor, I wouldn't know where to start. I don't know anyone in the Dark Corner. I think we should let the cops do their job. They'll find him."

"No!" he said, as close to shouting as he could probably get. "Cops . . . aren't trying. They don't care about . . . some black boy . . . going missing. Busy . . . with more . . . serious things. I saw on . . . TV last year . . . when you proved . . . the cops wrong. You . . . caught that . . . guy. You . . . can do this."

He bored his sunken eyes into mine, a message in them that said if he could, *he* would go looking for Jamal. But he couldn't, so I must do it in his place. He was calling in a debt he didn't even believe I owed—but he knew *I* believed it, and would pay it to assuage the guilt I carried for my part in his injury.

"I guess I can at least try to build a fire under the cops," I said, "and look in on your mama, but I don't know what else I can do."

He looked exhausted from the effort it took to talk. In good conscience, there was something I needed to say to him before I left. Something I'd been thinking all night.

"Taylor," I said. "If Jamal is innocent of killing that horse, why would he run away?"

"He didn't . . . do it," Taylor said, raising his voice again.

"That's not what I mean," I said. "If he didn't run away, then something—or someone—caused him to disappear, and he may not be coming back at all. You need to prepare for that."

"You think . . . I haven't . . . thought of that? But even so . . . I got to know . . . for Mama's sake . . . *and* mine."

"Would he take off if he heard someone was going to pin it on him?"

He seemed to think that over for a minute.

"Don't know . . . about that. Maybe. But he would . . . tell Mama . . . he was going."

He closed his eyes and lay silent for a while. A nurse came in and checked his pulse. She turned to me, "He's exhausted, so maybe it would be better if you left and let him get some rest. He's had a turn for the worse since his brother went missing. He loves that boy."

I know," I said and turned to see him looking at me.

"I'll do what I can," I said.

"Thank you . . . J.D.," he said, so quietly I could barely hear him. He closed his eyes again, and I left.

CHAPTER THREE

A half-hour later, I was in the little town of Pickens, the namesake of the county where I grew up. I went straight to the offices of the *Clarion*. Doris Mozingo, my late grandfather's long-time administrative assistant (and rumored paramour) was at the reception desk and greeted me when I came in. The crusty old lady agreed to stay on when we took over the *Clarion*, to remain the mother hen of paper and the stanchion that held it all together.

She was also the closest thing I had to a mother after Eloise and I went to live with Grandfather. Mrs. Mozingo—no one called her Doris, she commanded that much respect—still treated me like a ten-year-old, and I loved her enormously for it.

She came around her desk and gave me a big hug, squeezing me against her ample breasts, then stood back and looked me over.

"You've lost weight, John David," she said. "Are you eating right?"

"I've upped my workout regimen lately," I said. "Soon to be lean, mean, and handsome again."

She laughed. "Well, be careful you don't overdo it. The car won't go if there isn't gas in the tank."

"Good advice," I said, gave her another hug and asked her if Kelly and my sister were in. They were, and I went back to see them.

I found them both in Eloise's office going over what looked like circulation numbers.

After hugs all around, Kelly gave me an expectant look. "Well, how did it go?"

"As well as could be expected," I said. "Taylor isn't looking too good."

"What have you been doing, little brother?" Eloise asked. "I want to hear about it, too."

"Nosy as ever, big sister," I said. We laughed and hugged again. The Braggs were big huggers. "I went over to see Taylor Johnson," I said.

"That poor man," Eloise said. "How's he taking the news about his brother?"

"Not well," I said. "We'll talk about it later, but first, how are you? It's been a couple of weeks since I've seen you."

My sister, as always, said she was fine, which she would say even if it weren't true. Eloise was not one to dwell on the downside of life, even with all the loss she'd experienced. First our parents, then her husband, Billy, who drank and drugged himself into an early grave, and more recently, our grandfather. She grieved of course, but she always bounced back. She was better than me at handling tragedy.

My sister never held a regular steady job until now. From the moment we came to live with our grandfather as children, she stayed home and took care of grandfather and me. I flew the coop after college, but she remained the mistress of the household of the hundred and fifty-year-old farmhouse everyone called Still Hollow. But this new job at the *Clarion*, for which she was responsible for heading up business and advertising, suited her. She had a rosy color to her cheeks, a spring in her step and she looked particularly lovely today.

It was funny, but I rarely thought of my older sister as pretty. She was, well, my sister. But she *was* pretty. I wondered if she was seeing anyone, something she rarely did, although I knew of several eager suitors, one of them the bachelor Sheriff of Pickens County.

I asked about my teenage niece Mackenzie. Eloise said she was still at school. Mackenzie was working part-time at the paper until summer break, and then she'd be full-time until the fall when school started back. She was a special kid, actually a young woman now, and I tried to be a male presence in her life, given the fact that all the other men she'd ever known were no longer there for her.

I never knew if I was any good at that or not. I wasn't trying to be a surrogate father for her, just family and a friend. She treated me more like an older brother than an uncle, which I liked. She was about the same age as Jamal, I suddenly thought, and a wave of heightened empathy washed over me for Taylor and his mother. I couldn't imagine Mackenzie suddenly going missing like Jamal.

"How is she working out?" I asked Eloise.

"She's doing great," Eloise said. "She loves the job, and her grades haven't slipped a bit for all the hours she puts in here. She's developing into a good little reporter. A nose for news is certainly in her genes. I'm very proud of my baby."

"You should be," I said. "All that and good looks too."

"Oh God, I know," Eloise said. "I lose track of all the boys that call the house."

"So, are we on for dinner tonight?" I said, looking to both of them for an answer.

"Does the Pope live in Rome?" Eloise said. "I'm making chicken and dumplings, especially for you."

She knew it was one of my favorites.

"And I've got blackberries I canned last summer," she added. "I'm making a blackberry pie, too."

"Mrs. Mozingo will like that," I said. "She thinks I'm too skinny."

"Oh, but you're just right for me, big fella," Kelly piped in, draping an arm over my shoulder.

"I'm looking forward to it," Eloise said. "It's been a while since the whole family has dined together."

Her words took me by surprise. I had never heard Eloise refer to Kelly as *part of our family*, and it was probably silly, but I wasn't sure how I felt about that. Eloise was automatically taking my relationship with Kelly a step farther than I had. There wasn't anything wrong with it, I supposed, I was just a bit taken back when she threw the issue out into the cold light of day.

They went back to work, and I went downstairs to the paper's morgue to read the issues of the *Clarion* with Kelly's Jamal Johnson stories in them. The headline on the first one was, "Teenager sought for shooting prize horse."

There was a picture of Jamal, a typical high school annual photo, showing a clean-cut kid with a broad smile and looking nothing like a horse-shooting thug. He didn't have Taylor's physique or once movie star good looks, but there was a definite family resemblance.

The story went on to say Johnson was suspected of killing a horse belonging to a Wilson Kroll, a wealthy horse breeder and stud service operator in North

Greenville County. According to this Kroll, the horse was the prize stallion of his stables and valued at several million dollars. There were no witnesses to the shooting, which happened late at night, and they didn't find the dead horse until the next morning when the stable-hands showed up for work.

Kroll was out of town at the time of the shooting, but upon his return, he told the Greenville County Sheriff's department Johnson had worked for him up until a few days earlier when he fired him for unsatisfactory performance. He stated that Johnson had vehemently disagreed with the charge and threatened to get even. Wilson Kroll believed Johnson made good on his threat by killing his horse.

Sheriff's deputies searched Johnson's home and property, where he lived with his mother, and found a bolt action 22 rifle hidden in a shed out back. Tests proved that this rifle, recently fired, was the weapon that killed the horse. The Authorities said they believed Johnson ran away to avoid capture.

I wondered if the cops would have done a ballistics test if Kroll had been some average Joe with a dead saddle horse?

The article ended by asking for anyone with knowledge of Jamal Johnson's whereabouts, to give the Greenville County Sheriff's office a call.

The *Clarion's* next issue began as an update to the first, stating that Jamal was still missing. Where it differed, was this follow-up story was more about Jamal, and less about the crime. I could read between the lines that Kelly had come to believe in his innocence. Here she deliberately chose not to convict the boy with her story. Admirable, but arguably not in fitting with a journalist's imperative to stay neutral. I'd have to rib her about that.

Kelly wrote that as far as the authorities could determine, Jamal went missing sometime after eleven o'clock on Saturday night, the night after Wilson Kroll's horse was shot. The boy was last seen leaving a dinner party where he had worked as a waiter. The location of the party was a private residence in the Hunting Club Road area of Tryon, North Carolina, just over the North and South Carolina state line from Greenville County, where the boy lived.

There was an interview with Mrs. Johnson, who claimed passionately that her son was innocent. She said he had never owned a gun, and didn't like them. As far as she knew, he'd never even fired one. He didn't hunt, and was too soft-hearted to kill any animal, especially a horse. He loved them. She insisted that someone planted the gun.

She was grief-stricken and worried, claiming Jamal would never run away without telling her, and that something bad must have happened to him and the police weren't doing anything to investigate that.

So, she and Taylor were both fearing the worst.

Others interviewed described Jamal as a good, gentle kid who studied hard, had high hopes for college, worked odd jobs saving for it, and was liked by everyone.

Evidently, Wilson Kroll wasn't one of them.

Another story on the front page of the Clarion caught my eye. There was a serial killer loose in the upstate. His victims were all prostitutes, it appeared. The latest was a young woman in the neighboring city of Anderson, and the specifics of her death matched other unsolved murders in the Carolinas over the years. So far, the police had been unable to prove the killer raped these women, but they all had a similar modus operandi: strangled to death, with their faces disfigured post-mortem, mouth, and lips mutilated by a hammer-like object. They all had two-gallon clear plastic zip bags placed over their heads—to avoid the blood splatter, the police speculated. The news media had dubbed the killer the 'Carolina Stalker.'"

If this story had made the news in Atlanta, I must have missed it. I couldn't remember a serial killer in this part of the country since Wayne Williams and the famous "Atlanta child murders case" back in the early eighties.

The article was particularly interesting to me on another level. It showed Kelly and my sister were expanding the coverage of the *Clarion* to include bigger stories than just the local news. They picked this one up, I saw, from a news service. When my grandfather ran the paper, he rarely did that. He focused strictly on local news. I was glad to see this happening and gave Kelly all the credit. She continued to show what a savvy newspaper woman she was.

I took no income from the *Clarion* except for the peace of mind that Eloise and my niece Mackenzie would have a stable financial future, and insure the upkeep of Still hollow and keep it in the family. I was happy to see them bringing new life to the paper.

I went to a computer and tried to find anything I could about this Wilson Kroll. I came across a story of him on an equine website. He was described as the son of a wealthy Lake Erie shipping magnate from Cleveland Ohio, now deceased, who had moved to the upstate of South Carolina a few years ago to breed and raise horses. He sounded like another one of Kelly's friend Natasha's trust fund babies.

Most of the story was about a prize stallion Kroll owned, named Emperor. The horse was a great steeplechase champion, now a sought-after and highly profitable stud horse for Kroll's stud service business. Emperor sounded like the horse that was shot.

Shooting a horse for the insurance was nothing new to me. Some time back, I did a story about a big-time horse owner in Kentucky who killed several of his race horses for the insurance money. My story led to his arrest. This kind of insurance fraud was so typical that the first person the police usually looked at was the dead horse's owner. But here, the alleged threat from Jamal, the rifle found in his mother's shed, Kroll's alibi, and the kid's timely disappearance pointed the authorities away from Wilson Kroll and directly on Jamal Johnson.

If someone *was* framing the kid, the most likely candidate was this Wilson Kroll, the dead horse's owner. The insurance on this horse had to be big bucks.

I sat and thought about it for a minute. The biggest problem with proving Jamal's innocence was the rifle they found in his storage shed. As to everything else, the shooting and the threat, there were no witnesses. Just Kroll's word. A "he said, he said" situation, usually hard to prove. But the police said they had no reason not to believe the man. He was a reputable and upstanding citizen of Greenville County.

And he was white and rich.

Kroll aside, everyone seemed to think this kid walked on water, but Kelly was the persuader for me. She was a damn good journalist who knew that even the good could go bad. Kelly wouldn't buy into Jamal's innocence easily. She would approach this with an amount of skepticism, as would I. But something had convinced her Jamal didn't do it, and in the absence of additional information, I tended to come down on her side.

So, I would go into this thing giving the kid the benefit of the doubt and assume he was innocent. By taking this approach, however, I was presuming he didn't run away because he'd killed the horse. As I saw it, the most likely reasons for his disappearance were: one, he knew someone was framing him and didn't think the police would believe him, or two, he didn't go missing by choice—

whether connected to the horse shooting or for some other reason entirely. The latter didn't portend good things for Jamal or the Johnsons.

An idea had been rolling around in my head since I'd made my promise to Taylor. I gave Joe Dennis my NFL Stadium story to tide him over while I was away, with nothing else on the burner. So, why not write a story about this Dark Corner community of horse lovers and steeplechase enthusiasts? I wasn't out to horn in on Kelly's coverage of the Jamal news. I would never do that—and she would never put up with it. Jamal would still be her story. Mine would be more of a human interest piece. If I turned up anything newsworthy about the dead horse or Jamal's disappearance, which I'd obviously try to do, I would pass it on to Kelly so she could break the story. I wouldn't be working against her; we'd be working together. Only, no one over there would know. The upside was I would have a legitimate reason to poke my nose into things in the Dark Corner and ask my questions. The downside was I could end up with the most boring story ever written.

Maybe Kelly was right, and I was a reverse snob, because the thing about a story like this that stirred my interest the most, aside from the business of trying to find Jamal, was the prospect to bring a comeuppance to whomever in this elite little wealthy clique deserved it. I found myself setting my sites on the dead horse's owner, Wilson Kroll.

CHAPTER FOUR

Kelly and I showed up for dinner at Eloise's at 7:30 and we all sat around the table small-talking and enjoying Eloise's chicken and dumplings, topped off with her homemade blackberry pie. I'd need to double my running and workout regimen while I was here, or I'd end up the size of an NFL offensive lineman.

I kept thinking about the comment Eloise made earlier at the *Clarion*, calling this a family gathering and casually including Kelly. The thought was like a fly in the room buzzing around my head, distracting me. I knew why it disturbed me; it was that old fear of commitment rearing its ugly head. I thought I was getting over that. Kelly was like no other woman I'd ever known, and I knew I loved her. But whenever I thought of a permanent future together, I still broke out in a sweat. Old emotional hang-ups die hard.

During a lull in the conversation, Mackenzie made matters worse by asking when Kelly and I were getting married. She asked it jokingly, but the look Kelly gave me across the table held more sadness in it than humor. It reminded me again of our conversation-in-waiting, the one we were putting off for practical reasons: living a hundred and forty miles apart. But what did that say about our relationship if it was driven only by practicality?

After dinner, Mackenzie went to her room to do her homework, and Kelly, Eloise and I went into the den with after-dinner cups of coffee. I told Kelly and Eloise the details of my visit with Taylor, and his asking me to find his little brother.

"What did you say to him?" Kelly asked.

"I told him to leave it to the cops as they can find him better than I can."

Kelly was looking at me closely. "But he didn't accept that."

"Taylor doesn't trust the police," I said. "He says they aren't giving it much effort, and he's probably right. Finding a kid who shoots a horse can't compete with other, more serious crimes on their plate."

"That doesn't surprise me," Eloise said. "I hear that every policeman in the upstate is looking for that serial killer they call the Carolina Stalker. So what are you going to do?"

"He's going to try to find the boy himself," Kelly said, answering for me. "J.D. feels he owes Taylor for the part he played in Taylor's injury."

She knew me too well.

"Taylor's my friend, and he asked me to do something for him he can't do himself. I can't turn him down."

"That's my John David," Eloise said, her expression somewhere between smiling with pride and tearing up.

Kelly came over and kissed me on the cheek. "He's my John David, too," she said. "True blue. That's why I love him so."

"The key word here is 'try,'" I said, pulling her down on my lap. "There's no way I can find that kid. I don't know a soul over there but his mother, and if she knew anything, she would have already told the police."

"So what are you saying?" Kelly asked. "You promised poor Taylor you'd try, but you'll just go through the motions? Maybe you're *not* my John David," she said, but smiled when she said it.

"Of *course* I'll try. I just can't guarantee how far I'll get. I can help Mrs. Johnson out wherever I can, and bug the cops to do their job, but beyond that, I only have one idea. I can write a human interest piece for *SportsWord* about that little community of wealthy horse owners, which will at least give me a reason to talk to people. Jamal Johnson is your story, not mine. I'm not out to scoop you, but to find Jamal. Any news I find concerning Jamal and his disappearance, I'll feed to you."

"We'll be working together," Kelly said. "I like that. The timing is good, too. Next Saturday is the Upcountry Steeplechase, the big race they have over there every year. Twenty thousand people will be there, with the locals partying every night leading right up to race day—which is just a big party in itself. Everyone you need to talk to will be there, probably even people the cops didn't question, but might know things."

"That offers possibilities," I said, "but other than crashing these parties, I'm not sure how I wrangle an invitation to them."

"I have an idea for that, too," Kelly said. "Natasha Ladd."

"Who's Natasha Ladd?" my sister asked.

"She's a rich friend of Kelly's," I said. "Can she get me into these parties?" I asked Kelly.

"If *anyone* can, it's Natasha."

Kelly excused herself and went to call her old college friend. She came back twenty minutes later and said Natasha was excited to play a part in finding Jamal.

"She said she would meet you at noon tomorrow at her place if you can make it."

"I can make it," I said.

"She has an idea to pass you off as a new boyfriend. I'm not sure how much I like that, but she says seeing her with a boyfriend du jour on her arm is a familiar sight to her friends, which would make you easier to explain, and for them to accept."

"Is that really necessary?" I asked. All I need is an introduction to the right people. I'll do the rest."

"That's Natasha," Kelly said, sending Natasha's address and phone number from her cell to mine. "I learned long ago not to argue with her and to just go with the flow. But you can take it up with her tomorrow if you want. And J.D.? You watch out for her. She's a terrible flirt, unashamedly outspoken, and is probably on the lookout for husband number four."

"She won't be interested in me," I said. "I'm not husband material for someone like her. I don't have any money."

"That doesn't mean she won't look at you as an appetizer for the main event." She laughed and added, "I don't think a country boy like you has ever met anyone like her. She's a man thief. I learned that in College. But If she messes with you, I'll smack her silly," she added.

"I know you will," I said. "You even scare me."

"You remember that," she said and laughed.

Kelly and Eloise got up to clear the dinner table and wash dishes. I went to help them.

Later, Kelly and I went back to her place. There was a lot to do tomorrow, but nothing as pleasurable as what Kelly and I did later. Not once did my mind drift to Jamal or Taylor Johnson.

CHAPTER FIVE

Kelly made an early breakfast for us on Tuesday morning. In the world of calorie counting, it was the polar opposite of the dinner at Eloise's the previous night. This morning, the menu was a grapefruit half with sugar substitute, a slice of whole wheat toast with low-fat butter, no jam, and a cup of black coffee. The complete breakfast had fewer calories than one bite of Eloise's blackberry pie. My brain told me this was the right way to eat, but the rest of me would always want the pie.

We sat at the kitchen table and talked. Out the window, a couple of early-bird golfers drove their carts around the golf course. Kelly wasn't a golfer, but she leased her home in the Pickens Country Club neighborhood for the open spaces and the view. A perfectly manicured rolling fairway lay just outside her windows. Leasing a house and not buying one was another reminder of the unanswered questions about the future of our relationship. I rented my apartment in Atlanta, too. Both of us seemed to be living in a holding pattern.

"So, how do you feel about your 'horse country' story?" she asked.

"I'm liking it," I said. "Beyond helping me access people who may know what happened to Jamal, it offers a potential literary theme that readers like. If I can put some teeth into it."

"And what might that be?"

"Exposing the dark underbelly of a spoiled, wealthy clique and their foul deeds always make a cracking good story. People love to hear bad stuff about rich people. You know what they say, if you're rich you couldn't have gotten that way honestly."

She laughed. "Who says that?"

"People who aren't rich."

"There you go, sounding like your grandfather again."

"I don't have anything against rich people. Unless they got there dishonestly, or on the backs of the less fortunate. Neither did Grandfather. It was hypocrisy and phoniness he didn't like. He would often say 'a principled man is one who does the right thing when nobody is looking.' Being principled has nothing to do with how much money you've got."

"And that doesn't describe you to a T?"

"I wish. But I'll never be the man he was."

"Stop selling yourself short, J.D.," Kelly said and smiled at me.

"I don't know if I'm principled as much as I'm just an avenger of the unprincipled. I enjoy meting out justice a little too much with the stories I choose to write."

"Well, whatever you are, I love you for it," she said.

I stood up and kissed her. "I need to go if I'm going to meet your Natasha at twelve o'clock, and I have something else to do first. I'm going ask the cops where they are on finding Jamal. I suddenly realized I didn't know who had police jurisdiction over that little corner of Northeast Greenville County. The closest towns were Tryon, over the line in North Carolina, and Landrum, in South Carolina, but Landrum was in Spartanburg County, the next county to the east. Mrs. Johnson's mailing address was 'Landrum,' but I didn't think the city police from there came over to Greenville County. I asked Kelly.

"Greenville County Sheriff's Department," she said. "I have the card of the chief investigating deputy." She went and got it for me. "I hope you have better luck than I did. All he would tell me is Jamal did it and he'll turn up eventually."

I took the card and said, "We'll see, I said. "Maybe the cops have made progress since you talked to them."

"I hope so," she said. "Give me updates if you discover anything, and say hi to Natasha for me," she added, and left for work.

I called the number on the deputy's card and man answered after a couple of rings. "Deputy Randy Waldrop," he said.

"Deputy Waldrop," I said, "my name is J.D. Bragg, and I'm a friend of the Millie Johnson family. I was hoping you could spend a few minutes talking to me about Mrs. Johnson's missing son, Jamal?"

There was a pause as if the Deputy was taking his time forming a response to my request.

"What would you like to know . . . Mr. Bragg, was it?"

"Yes, J.D. Bragg. I'd rather come in and talk to you in person if you have a few minutes this morning."

Again, he paused before he spoke.

"I'll be at the Sheriff's Department northern area command center at 4900 Old Buncombe Road until eleven. I can see you any time before that if you can make it."

"Where exactly is 4900 Old Buncombe Road?" I asked.

"Do you know where Furman University is?"

I said I did.

"The Northern Command Center is just south on Old Buncombe Road just before it joins U.S. Highway 276 north. It will be on your right."

I knew exactly where that was. It was nearer the city of Greenville than I'd guessed—the designation *Northern Area Command* suggested it might be further north, nearer the Dark Corner, but I could easily make that and still be at Natasha Ladd's by noon if I hurried.

"I'll see you there inside thirty minutes," I said and hung up.

CHAPTER SIX

The Sheriff's Northern Command Center was hard to miss. Several Sheriff's cruisers, dark blue Fords with a yellow stripe down their sides, sat in the parking lot next door. Deputy Waldrop was waiting for me in a small office inside the one-story flat-topped building. He was about my age and wore a dark blue uniform. He had Marine Corps short hair and the fit look of someone who worked hard at it. We shook hands as I introduced myself. He gave me an apprehensive look and pointed to a metal chair across his desk. I took it.

"So, what can I do for you, Mr. Bragg?" he asked.

"I was wondering if you could give me some details regarding Jamal Johnson, the missing teenager who's supposed to have shot the horse up in the Dark Corner. What he's charged with, what evidence you have, and what progress you're making."

It was a moment until he spoke. Deputy Waldrop seemed to be overly deliberate in his actions.

"Tell me again what your interest is in this," he replied.

"I'm a family friend, and I've promised the Johnsons I would help them stay informed of your efforts to find Jamal. You probably know his mother is convinced he's innocent and doesn't know where he is or why he's missing. You can understand how worried the family is."

"You need to understand this is an ongoing investigation and there are some things I can't tell you."

It sounded like standard issue cop-speak. "I understand. I'd just like to have some details to give them."

He's still in the wind," Deputy Waldrop said. "We haven't found him. We're checking with known associates and relatives, and we have a missing-persons out on him."

"What are the charges against him?" I asked.

"Malicious Injury of Property over $10,000, a felony. He could face up to 10 years in prison, and a possible fine. He's on the cusp between a juvenile and an adult, so that could go either way. This horse was worth a lot of money, so I'd advise his family to get a lawyer and prepare for the worst."

"You found the rifle that killed the horse in a storage shed out back of the Johnson's house, I understand," I said.

"That's correct," he said. "Ballistics prove it's the same gun."

"If you went to the trouble of a ballistics test, did you check for finger prints too?"

"The weapon was wiped clean."

"Mrs. Johnson has sworn the rifle didn't belong to her boy," I said. "She claims he's never owned a gun of any kind."

"It's not exactly unheard of for a teenager to keep secrets from his mother," Deputy Watson said. "He could also have borrowed it. A cheap rifle like that is basically untraceable."

"Since the shed was kept unlocked, couldn't anyone have placed the gun there?"

"It's possible, of course, but given the threats Johnson made to Mr. Kroll when Kroll fired him a few days earlier, the rifle, and the suspect's lack of an alibi, give us motive, means, and opportunity. The fact he ran also makes him look guilty."

"But, you only have Mr. Kroll's word for the firing and the threat, right? Are you aware Jamal told his mother and his girlfriend that Kroll let him go because there was insufficient work for him at his stables, and Jamal held no animosity toward the man?"

"We've heard that," Waldrop said, "but the suspect, of his own actions, isn't here to give his account of the incident."

"In fact, there were no other witnesses to the threat . . . or to the shooting of the horse, was there?"

"No, there were no witnesses to either event. A stable-hand found the horse dead in a stall early the next morning."

Waldrop sat and stared across his desk at me. "We're doing our job, Mr. Bragg. Now if there's nothing else, I have other work to do today."

"What if you're wrong," I said, remaining in my seat. "What if Jamal Johnson didn't shoot the horse? Would he run away then? Was it because he knew someone was framing him? Or, did he go missing for an entirely different reason? Like someone *making* him disappear?"

"Do you have any evidence we don't have?" he asked, unsmiling.

"Not beyond the many people, family *and* friends, who believe the kid didn't do it," I said. "When that many people stand up for the kid, it makes you want to believe them."

"As I've said," Mr. Bragg, "All the *real* evidence we have says he shot the horse and ran away to keep from getting busted. He'll turn up eventually if that's the case."

"I just want to know, for his family's sake, that you're looking at this from every angle, and are not just taking the horse owner's word for it. It's been my experience that the most likely person to dispose of a horse is the owner—for the insurance money.

"Mr. Kroll has an iron-clad alibi. He was in Kentucky at a horse auction when the horse was shot on Friday night, and didn't return until late Sunday."

"That well may be, but Mr. Kroll didn't have to shoot the horse himself, he could have had help."

Deputy Waldrop looked at me, his lips pressed into a thin line.

"What *is* your experience in things like this, Mr. Bragg?" he finally said. "I thought you said you were just a friend of the family?"

"I am," I said. "But I'm also an investigative journalist, and I have prior experience with equine insurance fraud."

"You should have identified yourself as that," he said.

"Why, would you have said anything different to me?"

"I might not have said anything to you at all. As I told you, this is an investigation in progress, and we're careful about what we say to the press."

"I'm not the press," I said, "I work with *SportsWord* Magazine."

"I used to subscribe to that magazine," he said.

Used to. I fought off the petty urge to ask him why he no longer subscribed, hoping it wasn't my fault, but I didn't.

"Look, Deputy Waldrop, I just want to make sure you're covering all the bases. Jamal's mother is convinced something bad has happened to him."

"You're that guy, aren't you?" Waldrop said, pointing his finger at me. "That sportswriter who solved those murders over in Pickens County. You caught the guy who killed your grandfather. I thought your name sounded familiar."

He studied me for a minute longer, then leaned over and opened a desk drawer. He took out a business card and placed it toward me on the edge of his desk. I picked it up and looked at it. It was for a Brandon Wise, Investigator, Olympic Equine Insurance Company. I noticed the company headquarters was in Louisville, Kentucky, with branch offices in Virginia, Maryland, and Tryon, North Carolina. The area code for Mr. Wise's number was 828, which was the same as Natasha's, so he worked at the Tryon office.

I looked up at Waldrop, and he almost smiled at me.

"You and this guy have similar suspicions," he said.

I gave him a two-fingered salute, got up, and left.

CHAPTER SEVEN

From the deputy's office, I drove north to upper Greenville County, turned east on Highway 11 for a few miles, then headed north again on Oak Grove Road through the area called the Dark Corner. There was a faster way to where I was going, but I decided to check out the area; it had been a long time since I was there. I wound my way through the rolling terrain past peach orchards, pastures, horse farms, country homes both large and small, and a Baptist church with old tombstones covering the neighboring hill. The hump of Hogback Mountain loomed on my left the whole way; it's heavily forested summit appeared close enough in the clear morning air to almost reach out and touch it.

With a few twists and turns, I crossed over the North Carolina state line into the border town of Tryon and the heart of the area's horse and steeplechase country. I quickly found Hunting Club Road and headed east, where Natasha Ladd lived. The GPS directions on my cell phone lying on the console of my Jeep showed I would find her house approximately two miles ahead. The total driving distance from Kelly's house was about forty-five miles, and I was right on time for my twelve o'clock appointment.

Hunting Club Road was a perfectly landscaped two-lane blacktop lined with brown or white rail fences, emerald green rolling pastures, tall trees, and country estates that would put clubhouses at most country clubs to shame. All the houses sat back from the road, surrounded by impressive stables, many with jumps and training rings near them. The houses were spaced far enough apart to illustrate the sizable acreage on which they sat.

Magnificent horses grazed and frolicked in some of the pastures. Everywhere I looked was a Country Living magazine cover. The neighborhood was truly an enclave of the very wealthy. I couldn't help thinking that just a couple of miles away in any direction, people lived in rusting doublewides and small two bedroom homes, and happy to have them. *An island of rich folks in the middle of tobacco road*, I thought. Income inequality illustrated.

As I neared her house on Hunting Club Road, I stopped for a group of horseback riders crossing the road in front of me. The riders were clad perfectly in fox-hunting attire. They wore black hacking jackets and hard bowler hats with white riding pants and shiny black knee boots. They followed a man dressed in the same way but in a *red* coat. He would be the "Hunt Master" if my memory of what little I knew about fox-hunting served me. A dozen yapping hounds led them into a grassy meadow. I rolled down my window to see and hear them better, and an attractive young female rider saw me and smiled.

"Tally ho," I said in my best British accent and smiled back at her. *Where the hell am I? The North Carolina hills, or Bramham Moor in Yorkshire?* The woman broke from the rest of them and rode over, still smiling at me.

"Are you J.D.?" she asked, looking down at me from her perch atop a large brown horse. The animal looked like it might stick its head through my window and take a bite out of me as if I were a shiny red apple. I had ridden horses, and even a plow mule belonging to a childhood friend's old man, but I was just a tenderfoot compared to these people.

"Yes, I am," I said, "and you would be Natasha." Kelly didn't exaggerate. Natasha Ladd was a striking woman.

"We're heading in from a morning hunt that ran a little long," she said, "but they usually do. So, go on up to my house and wait for me, if you don't mind. It's the next driveway on the left. My little bungalow is to the right of the big house. I'll be along as soon as I put Cherry away. It should only be a few minutes."

Cherry might be the horse's name, but it fit as a description for both horse *and* rider. They both looked to be in mint condition.

I took the next driveway and drove up to her "little bungalow." While it was only about a fifth the size of the large estate next door, it was still five times as big as my apartment in Atlanta.

Architecturally, it was the same as the big house; a steep wood-shingled roof and sharp gables, and built with the same dusty-rose-colored brick. It was as if they tore off a wing of the big house and pushed it about fifty yards away. A stable with some of the same trimmings and big enough for a dozen horses sat behind everything.

I cut the engine and waited. Two landscapers worked the flowers and shrubs at the big house, another one edging the walk that dissected the perfectly manicured lawn. I could smell the sweet aroma of gardenias blooming somewhere. The occasional whinny of a horse and the song of a distant Mockingbird, the only sounds of a quiet, peaceful morning in paradise. I didn't hate the rich; I envied the hell out of them.

A few minutes later Natasha Ladd came around the corner of her house, hat and hacking jacket in her hand.

"Who lives next door?" I asked.

"My parents, but you won't get to meet them. They're in Europe. An overdue vacation. It will be the first Upcountry Steeplechase they've missed in years."

Natasha made motions for me to follow her in, and as I did, I noticed her front door wasn't locked. Clearly, here in paradise, no one worried about home intruders and burglars.

After some small talk, Natasha excused herself and went to take a quick shower and change her clothes. She told me to make myself at home, so I took the opportunity to scope out her bungalow. She wasn't a girlie girl, I noticed. Dainty knick-knacks and lacy doilies shared no part of the well-appointed, but not overly-done country-rustic décor. Dark wooden furniture with bold colored cushions dominated the room, with a large native-stone fireplace the center focus. The place wasn't necessarily masculine, but it did give off the air of a bold type-A personality, someone who was probably accustomed to running things her way.

Pictures of Natasha on horseback, jumping hedges, and hunting foxes formed a gallery on one wall. I went over and studied them. Not one of them showed her with anyone who looked to be an ex-husband. Out of the marriage, off the wall, I suspected. One photo was of her standing with an attractive elderly couple dressed in a lot of tweeds, whom I took to be her parents, the occupants of the big house next door. Her father was a distinguished-looking gentleman wearing a brimmed hat that only needed a feather in it to mark him as the squire of the estate. Her mother would have been attractive at any age. I could see where Natasha got her looks.

Natasha finally came out wearing brown slacks, with matching belt and shoes, and a beige collared-blouse open at the throat. Small gold studs in her ears seemed to be the only jewelry she wore. She had pinned her hair up in a purposely tangled way that gave her an elegant and an outdoorsy look at the same time. If she'd put on makeup, it didn't show, but she didn't need it. She was a naturally beautiful woman.

"How about some lunch?" she said. "I'm famished."

"Sure, if it's not too much trouble," I said, thinking of the sensible but unsatisfying breakfast Kelly made.

"Oh, it's no trouble, we're going out," she answered. "I'm a terrible cook. I have someone to do that, but I gave her a paid vacation this week. If things go as planned, we won't be here much anyway. I'm going to keep you busy. So, we'll go to a restaurant in Tryon, have a leisurely lunch, and get acquainted."

She handed me an uncorked bottle of Cabernet Sauvignon. "The place we're going is BYOB, and I like a glass of wine with my lunch."

The wine was French, and to my untrained eye, looked expensive.

"I'll drive," she said, once we were outside. "I'll give you a tour of the area after lunch, and we can go meet some people."

I followed her out to her car, a dark-blue Chevy Suburban, and climbed in. She smelled as nice as she looked. Not perfumy, but fresh, like a forest after a rain.

As we pulled out of the drive, she looked at me and grinned. "Kelly sounds like she's madly in love with you and I can see why. You're hot."

"And she said you were outspoken," I said, giving her a quick look.

"I speak my mind. Does that bother you?"

"It depends on what's on your mind."

She kept her eyes on the road, but a tiny smile curled the corners of her mouth, like she had a comment on that but didn't make it.

"I'm excited about this," she said, instead. "I minored in drama in college, and this will give me a chance to flex my acting chops."

"Do you think it's really necessary for us to pose as a couple?" I said.

"Absolutely. To get you in with my crowd will take a bit of play-acting. It's the only way. As I told Kelly, if I just introduce you to everyone as a sportswriter from Atlanta, and the friend of a friend, up to write about the race, no one will give you anything other than horse and steeplechase sound bites. If they think you and I have a thing going on, then they will be intrigued, and even nosey. They will *want* to talk to you."

I still wasn't sure the charade was necessary, but if she believed it would get her friends to loosen their tongues around me, then I'd go along with it. What did Kelly say? *With Natasha, "just go with the flow."*

Natasha cocked her head and studied me.

"Kelly doesn't trust me with you, does she?" she said. "Or, is it you she doesn't trust?"

I didn't answer her.

"I love Kelly," she said, "she's one of the few female friends I have, but she holds grudges. I stole a boy in college she had a crush on, and she's never forgotten it. She takes things too seriously. He wasn't for her anyway. She was too good for him. I did her a favor."

"She probably doesn't see it that way," I said.

"I know, but I have to be me. It's one of the reasons I don't have many female friends. Kelly, as hard as it is to believe, is still one of them. I like men; I'm not ashamed to say it. If I see one I want, I go and get him. That boy *deserved* someone like me, and I don't mean that as a compliment to myself. I'm someone who's heart he couldn't break. But does that make me an awful person?"

"You're just a woman who goes after what she wants. This story actually says as much about him as you. I believe a man who is easily stolen away from his woman doesn't deserve that woman."

"Do you deserve Kelly?" she asked.

"No, I don't." I said, "Like with that guy in college, she's too good for me, too. But unlike him, if our relationship ends, she'll have to be the one to do it. Not me."

"True blue J.D. Bragg," she said.

It was the second time in twenty-four hours someone called me that.

CHAPTER EIGHT

Natasha drove us into Tryon, a picturesque little town along the north side of the North and South Carolina state line. Our destination was a restaurant named Huckleberry's, housed in a small distressed brick building with a steep red roof in a relatively new shopping center called Saint Luke's Plaza. She found a parking spot near it, and I followed her into the restaurant.

A hostess showed us to a table with a bright purple-blue tablecloth—the color of a huckleberry was my guess. The walls were a combination of stained wooden planks and the same distressed brick as the exterior, decorated in a random pattern with old tin advertising signs, various other tchotchkes, and potted plants. I wasn't quite sure what look they were going for, but it was a comfortable place, more contemporary perhaps than the antique advertising signs on the wall suggested. I noticed several diners wearing riding boots and britches. Natasha knew them, waved at them, but didn't speak. This place was obviously a horse-person hangout.

A pretty young waitress came and delivered our menus, then uncorked the bottle of wine we brought and filled two glasses for us. It tasted just as expensive as the label looked. We clinked glasses, and I studied the menu. Soups, sandwiches, paninis, and quiche dominated, but Natasha ignored the light fare and ordered the cheeseburger and fries. She was a woman after my own heart. I ordered the same thing.

"So," she said when the waitress left. "Are you going to be my boyfriend?"

I had resigned myself to the idea. "If you insist."

"Atta boy," she said, "but first we'll have to share a few personal details. Things my friends would expect us to know about each other. These people are the curious sort, they don't trust those outside our little world, and they are going to ask questions. So, we need to exchange a little history. Character traits. Even some intimate details."

"You think your friends would pry into the intimacy of our relationship?"

"It could happen. An old boyfriend and an ex-husband are still around, and you may meet them. We're still friends of a sort, but they, if for no other reason than to make a silly men's game of it, may gig you a bit by letting you know they came before you. Like dogs marking a tree. But don't let them bother you, it's just their egos."

"Okay, I said. "So, tell me something intimate about you that as a boyfriend, I would know."

She thought about it, then smiled. "I have a mole inside my upper right thigh, a crescent scar on my left buttock where a horse stepped on me after a fall, and I'm loud when I make love."

"Interesting to know, but if anybody brings up something like that to me, I will punch them in the mouth."

"How chivalrous. That would certainly shock them. This is not a 'punch you in the mouth' crowd. They might hire someone to do it, but they would rarely dirty their hands resorting to something so base. Many of them are trust-fund babies like me, and when you have several generations of wealth behind you and have never held a real job, you become different, or at least you think you are. Whether we admit it or not, many in our little community like to think of themselves as lords and ladies from another era, where palace intrigues fill our lives, and any subject is fair game for amusement since we have little else to talk about beyond our horses, hounds, charities, and leisure activities.

I couldn't tell if she was putting me on or not. "So, the old cliché 'the rich are different' is true."

"It is, in *our* minds."

"You don't seem that way."

"Thank you. I take that as a compliment, but sometimes I'm just like them. You'll see. You will be the first man I've ever gone out with who has to work for a living. Don't be surprised if my closest friends comment on that. It will be an oddity to them, and so will you, which will make some of them very curious about us. As I said, curious enough to try to get to know you, which should help you in your task."

I told her a few things about me, but none of them so intimate. If she wanted that, she could make it up. Her exes would never know. We decided I'd remain J.D. Bragg, a journalist with *SportsWord* magazine, and say we'd met in a bar on one of her shopping trips to Atlanta. I told her about my college football history, a few career-related stories, and that I'd never married. She told me about her family, I told her about mine—or the lack of them. I liked country music; she didn't. We both loved rock and roll, but she didn't like heavy metal. I was an early morning person; she was a late riser. And so on. By the time we finished, we both knew our lines well enough to take the show on the road.

"Where did your money come from, or is that a question I shouldn't ask?"

"Our money came from my great-grandfather, who was a New York financier with a seat on the stock exchange. No one has worked in my family since him, and unless we have another great depression, no one ever will."

"Must be nice."

"As Dudley Moore said in the movie *Arthur*, 'it doesn't suck.' I'm thankful for having it, but I do have something of a guilt complex, which is why I try to give back as much as I can. I'm a supporter of several charities, including a scholarship fund that helps deserving young people who can't afford it, go to college. In fact, Jamal Johnson is one of our recipients. His mother is a maid and cook for good friends of mine. I know her *and* Jamal. He is a smart, hard-working kid with good grades and high hopes. That's why I know he didn't do what they say he did, and why he wouldn't 'run away."

It was the same story Kelly got from everyone she interviewed. "But they found the rifle that killed the horse at his house," I said, to play a little devil's advocate.

"Anyone could have put it there."

"By anyone, you mean the person who actually shot the horse."

"Of course."

"Do you have anyone in mind?"

She didn't need to think about it. "Wilson Kroll," she quickly said. "The horse's owner. He's an asshole. Nobody likes him, and I wouldn't put it past him to kill his horse for the insurance money."

It was like she was reading my mind.

"Jamal worked part-time for Mr. Kroll in his stables until just a few days before the shooting. Kroll fired him on a trumped-up charge. Jamal was a good worker who had his pick of stables for summer jobs when school was out. I think Kroll planned on blaming Jamal from the beginning and set the whole thing up—the firing, the argument he claims he and Jamal had, and the rifle in the shed."

"Do you have any proof of that?" I asked.

"I don't need proof. I know Jamal didn't do it. So does everyone else who knows him."

"Except Wilson Kroll," I said.

"He's lying."

"There's a slight problem with that, you know," I said. "Wilson Kroll was out of town when his horse was shot."

"That doesn't mean anything. "He's not a stupid man. He may not have pulled the trigger, but he had it done. Getting someone else to do his dirty work would be his style."

It was all what I already believed, but it didn't hurt to hear her agree with me. "Is Kroll one of your trust-fund babies?'

"Sort of. Mr. Kroll hasn't been in the area as long as most of us, but he has one of the bigger horse farms in the area. It isn't here around Tryon. It's over in South Carolina where he could pick up a lot of land on the cheap. He tore down an old farmhouse that had been in someone's family for over a hundred years and built this monstrosity that resembles a Lichtenstein castle. He's tacky rich. His father was big in scrap iron and shipping barges on Lake Erie and left it all to him. Some call that 'new money,' and look down their noses at them."

"But not you," I said.

"I don't care about that kind of snobbery. I dislike Wilson Kroll because he's a crude man, and possibly a criminal. There are rumors he's connected to organized crime somehow, up north. He's simply an awful man."

The organized crime thing was news. "If Kroll is so rich, why would he need the insurance money?" I asked. "I mean, a couple of million bucks is a lot to me, but to a man like him, it probably doesn't mean much. Why would he risk going to jail for that?"

"A few years ago, Atlantic Magazine reported on a study done by Boston College on Wealth and Philanthropy," Natasha said. "I've never forgotten the details because it's so true. One of the things they found was that the wealthy worry about money as much as anyone. The rich are generally a dissatisfied lot. Money can create deep anxieties. Many of us still don't consider ourselves financially secure; we think there's always a need for more. If you've got fifty million, a hundred million would be better."

"Oh dear. Anxieties, how awful."

"Believe me, the pleasures of money wear off over time. Most people spoil themselves with the occasional splurge—an expensive dinner, a new dress, a day at a spa, but to the very wealthy, those things are just everyday choices. The psychological pleasure of it is lost. When special occasions happen every day, they aren't special anymore."

"Poor little trust-fund-baby," I said.

"See, just as you're proving by your snide remarks, we've lost the right to complain. If we do, you accuse us of being ungrateful. But we do have our worries. Money is both a blessing and a curse. I read somewhere that money is like fire: it will warm your feet, but it can burn your socks off."

Give me one example of how money is a curse," I said.

"Children. All wealthy parents worry that their money will ruin their children's lives. It will make them trust-fund brats if their inheritances are too large, or their children will hate them if any of their money goes to charity and not to them. They also worry that money will rob them of ambition, mess them up—give them a sense of entitlement, and prevent them from developing a strong sense of empathy and compassion."

"You don't seem to be ruined too much by your inheritance," I said.

"Three marriages?" she said. "A wasted education? Still living with my parents? Are you kidding, J.D.?"

"Well, at least you don't have children," I said. "You're spared that worry." I regretted it the second I said it.

She gave me a hurt look. "You think I should be happy about that? It isn't because I didn't try. Three marriages, two pregnancies, two miscarriages. My parents gave me their fortune. God gave me faulty plumbing."

"I'm sorry," I said. "That was cruel of me."

She waved away my apology. "Oh hell," she said. "I would probably make a terrible mother, anyway."

Somehow, I didn't believe that.

"But, great wealth *can* hurt," she said, "whether you believe it or not. "Do people love you for your money or yourself? And some non-wealthy people tend to treat the wealthy differently. You can't just be a normal person around them. It's hard for the wealthy to have non-wealthy friends. You can't share the personal problems in your life without getting: 'Yeah, wouldn't I like to have your problems.' The poor-little-rich-kid response is so obvious—and seemingly so sensible—that the rich themselves often internalize it, and as a result become uncomfortable in their interactions with the non-wealthy. Once people cross a certain financial threshold, they have the tendency to hang out with one another, to enjoy the company of people who know that money relieves some burdens but not others. Hence, this little close-knit community of horse people here.

"I'm still not feeling the sympathy here," I said. "Some wealthy people glorify their wealth and think it means they're smarter and wiser than the rest of us. And those children you say their wealthy parents are worried about? They do end up, as Warren Buffet dubbed them, 'the lucky sperm club,' displaying the stereotypical arrogance of privilege—the fast cars and excessive lifestyles. Just as many of their own parents did in their time."

"You're ignoring those who do great things with their money: supporting charities, building museums, schools, hospitals, and funding good works for people all over the world."

I know," I said. "In that respect the rich *aren't* different. There are good people and bad people, whether rich *or* poor."

"You know," Natasha said, "we're often called the 'idle rich.' But living an idle life isn't as much a personal choice as most think. It's an inevitability brought on by the curse of money. Many of the bright and intelligent attempt jobs out of college, but find themselves moving from one job or career to another. Something would always happen at each job that those who *have* to work would learn to tolerate, but the super wealthy would just say, 'I don't want to deal with this.' Eventually, they don't have a job or a career. In other cases, wealthy workers find their work viewed as a charade, so why bother if no one takes you seriously? That's what creates the 'idle rich.'"

"You'd have a hard time selling that one to the working class. Not having to work is the ultimate dream for most people."

"Without careers to dedicate their lives to, they devote their interests to other things: horses, pedigree dogs, charities, the arts, collecting expensive things. Their interests and conversations are dedicated to those obsessions. People outside their circle with different interests have a hard time joining in, and vice-versa."

Abruptly changing the subject, Natasha asked, "Where would you like to start? I'm all yours for the rest of the week. Kelly said she told you Saturday is the Annual Upcountry Steeplechase, and there will be parties all week at various clubs and people's homes, and a huge hospitality tent at the race itself where anyone who is anyone will gather. This should give you ample opportunity to talk to everyone you want."

"I'd like to start with Millie Johnson, and then perhaps talk to a couple of the boy's friends, if she can tell us who they are. I want to find out as much as I can about Jamal before meeting anyone else."

"Kelly said you knew Millie. That's certainly a coincidence."

"I went to college with Jamal's older brother Taylor."

"That poor man," she said. "It's just terrible what happened to him. I've never met him, but Mrs. Johnson once showed me a picture of him. He was handsome. I thought he looked a lot like Denzel Washington. And now this. Mrs. Johnson must be going out of her mind."

CHAPTER NINE

Millie Johnson lived in the middle of the Dark Corner in South Carolina's Greenville County. Her house was just a few miles south of Tryon and west of the town of Landrum in Spartanburg County. I remembered the house. Small, with white clapboard siding, blue trim and a wide front porch with a couple of rocking chairs on it. It was well-kept and homey, and had changed little.

Flowers grew around the house in flower beds, and pots of them hung from the porch—all of them full of wildly colored, blooming spring flowers. A large oak shaded the front yard, providing a cool and comfortable space for the wrought iron bench beneath it.

The storage shed where they found the rifle sat behind the house, with a lean-to stall for a cow or a horse attached to it. There was no livestock in it at present.

Beside the building, a fenced-in garden grew with verdant rows of what looked like young corn, tomatoes, pole beans, and other vegetables, all looking healthy and well-tended.

There were two cars parked near the house; an older Ford sedan, tan in color, and a gleaming new black Jaguar XF with Illinois plates.

"Nice car," I said, looking at the Jag.

"The tan one is Millie's," Natasha said. "I don't recognize the other one. She must have company."

As we got out of the car, several chickens, loose in the yard, ran around a corner of the house and disappeared in back. Natasha had called and told Mrs. Johnson we were coming, and she met us at the door. She was a short, plump woman, a little grayer than I remembered her, and normally with a pleasant face.

It was now spoiled slightly by eyes as red as the comb of the rooster I'd just seen in the yard. She had done some heavy crying, and from the wounded expression she wore as she looked at me, she wasn't finished.

"J.D., it's so good to see you," she said. "I didn't know you were friends with Miss Natasha. God certainly works in mysterious ways."

I marveled at her because she never seemed to hold me responsible for Taylor's injury. I think she knew I carried enough guilt, without needing to add to it.

She and Natasha hugged, and there was a genuine warmth in their embrace.

"Taylor told me you were coming," she said. "Are you gonna' help find my boy?"

"I'm going to try, Mrs. Johnson."

She stood and looked at me for a long probing moment as if she was trying to read the sincerity of my words in my eyes. The grief on her face was intense.

"He didn't do this J.D.," she said, "and *nobody* is trying to find out the truth of it. They've done got him convicted, and they aren't even looking for him anymore."

She led us into her living room, and Natasha and I took a seat on a sofa with doilies on the arms. The room was modestly furnished, but neat and comfortable. Framed photographs lined the mantle of a small fireplace, and on several side tables around the room. There was no sign of who owned the Jag out front.

Mrs. Johnson took a picture off the mantle and handed it to me. "That's Jamal last December when he won an award on his high school debate team," she said.

Jamal was holding up a small trophy and grinning like he'd just won the Super Bowl. "He grew into a handsome young man," I said, handing the photo back to Mrs. Johnson.

"I think something bad has happened to him," she said. "I pray it isn't so, but I just can't help thinking it. Why else would he not let me know where he is?"

Natasha hugged her again. They stood in that embrace for a while; then Mrs. Johnson seemed to regain her control and stepped away, placing the photo back on the mantle, and wiping her eyes with a tissue she took from a pocket.

"Where are my manners?" she said. "I've got coffee made, and I baked some of those peanut butter cookies you used to like so much, J.D. You remember them?"

"How could I forget, Mrs. Johnson. They're the best cookies I have ever eaten."

You all just sit right there, and I'll get us some," she said.

We followed her orders and sat while she served us the cookies and coffee. She sat down in an overstuffed chair across from the sofa and joined us. The coffee was excellent, and the cookies were everything I remembered. Even after the hamburger from lunch, I couldn't help eating three of them. I didn't know her employers, whom Natasha said were friends, but if Millie Johnson cooked everything this good for them, they must value her enormously.

A man suddenly entered the room from the back of the house and took a chair against the wall. He was possibly the scariest looking man I'd ever seen, and I had stared into the eyes of the meanest of men; NFL-sized defensive tackles whom I was sure were insane, and who wanted nothing more than to kill me on the next blitz.

He wasn't an ugly man, quite the contrary. What made him scary was his eyes, which he had focused on us with a menacing glower. The pupils were dark as midnight, the whites so bright against his black skin they seemed lit with a powerful light from within. It was like you could physically feel his gaze when he settled it on you, and even if you couldn't describe the feeling, it left you with a vague uneasiness. He telegraphed a primordial warning most males would recognize. His look said, "Fuck with me at your own peril."

He was dressed in black from head to toe, with short hair and a large diamond stud in an earlobe—which if real—was at least a couple of carats. He looked several years older than me, almost as tall, and muscled like a gym rat.

Mrs. Johnson introduced him to us.

"This is my nephew, Alvin Brown, my late middle sister's boy," she said, smiling warmly at him. "He came down from Chicago last night to keep me company and help out for a few days. He lived with us when he was little, and he's like my third son. Alvin, this is Natasha Ladd, my friend, and another friend, J.D. Bragg. J.D. played football with Taylor."

Alvin Brown nodded and fixed those eyes solely on me. I was incapable of returning his stare after a second or two. I wondered if the look he was giving me was his natural expression or something he affected just to frighten the shit out of people. A thin scar dissected one eyebrow giving him the impression of having two eyebrows on one side, but that only gave him character. A thin meticulously shaved goatee added a Satanic touch.

I knew who he was. Taylor spoke of him many times. He was Taylor's cousin, but more like an older brother. Taylor said Alvin and his mother lived with them as a child, but his father took them off to Chicago, and later deserted them, leaving Alvin's mother to turn to prostitution to feed the drug habit that eventually killed her. By then she had already disappeared from Alvin's life leaving him to grow up on the streets of Southside Chicago.

Taylor said Alvin had trained in martial arts and boxing and had done a bit of cage fighting in his time. The last time Taylor mentioned him was to say his cousin had started a chain of dōjōs in the Chicago area and was doing well. I guessed the Jaguar proved it, but no matter how successful he'd become, he was still someone you didn't want to mess with.

I remembered Taylor saying they called him Alvin "Big Hurt" Brown. "Big Hurt," like Frank Thomas, the White Sox homerun-hitting Hall of Famer. I didn't think Alvin's nickname came from baseball bats, unless he used them to beat people.

Mrs. Johnson went into the kitchen for more cookies and coffee, and Natasha went with her. They left "Big Hurt" and me sitting there, me avoiding staring at him.

He finally spoke.

"Taylor told me about you," he said, his voice as deep as James Earl Jones doing Darth Vader. It didn't make his presence any less intimidating.

"I hope it wasn't anything too bad," I said. "Taylor told me about you, too. The martial arts and stuff. I'd just as soon not have somebody like you pissed off at me."

I'd tried for a smile from him but didn't get it.

"He asked me to help you find Jamal," he said.

I wanted to tell him that if I needed somebody maimed or killed, I'd call him, but thought better of it.

The top button of his shirt was open, revealing a tattoo against his dark skin.

It looked almost like a Star of David with crossed tridents and numbers in the middle. "Is that tattoo on your neck something to do with martial arts?" I asked.

He waited a moment to answer me.

"Gangster Disciples, Southside Chicago," he finally said. "It's a little something from my formative years."

"Oh," I said. Taylor never mentioned anything about him being a member of one of the most vicious street gangs in the country.

"I outgrew that," he said.

I'd take his word for it.

"I'll be around for a few days. You can reach me here."

The issue of my needing or wanting his help seemed settled to him.

Mrs. Johnson and Natasha came back with more coffee and cookies, and I used their arrival as an excuse not to respond. If I ever needed a bodyguard, he'd be the first person I'd call, but aside from that, he'd be waiting a long time for the phone to ring from me. I just hoped he wasn't going to be trouble. I needed a more subtle approach than he would probably bring to the table.

Alvin "Big Hurt" Brown took neither coffee nor cookies and continued to sit quietly in his chair watching us. He shared his menacing gaze between Natasha and me. I could tell it was making her nervous.

I decided to ignore the "Big Hurt," and try to get what I came for. I turned to Millie Johnson and said, "Tell me about Jamal, Mrs. Johnson. Right before he disappeared, was he acting differently, or upset about anything?"

"Not that I noticed," she said, "but I was visiting my oldest sister in Charlotte when he disappeared. She's been down with her back, and my employers were kind enough to give me a couple of days off to go help her look after her kids. She's got a house full of them."

"When was the last time you saw Jamal?" I asked.

"That Friday morning," she said. "I sat him down and had a talk with him before he caught the school bus. I wanted to make sure one more time he'd be all right with me gone. He said he wouldn't be home much, anyway. He had two jobs Saturday, one doing something at somebody's stable in the morning, the other, waiting tables at a dinner party that night. He works part-time jobs when he can fit it in with school, as a waiter, dishwasher, mowing lawns, stable hand, whatever he can get. That boy is a hard worker, and he saves his money."

I'd read in Kelly's story in the *Clarion* the horse was killed sometime Friday night. Did he say what his plans were for that night?" I asked her.

"He said he was going to stay home and watch TV. He grumbled a little about not having a car. He just turned seventeen, and if I sign for him, he can get his driver's license now. Saving up for a car is the main reason he works so hard. I was surprised he wasn't planning on spending time with that girl he likes, Monique Watkins. She doesn't have a car either, but she borrows her older brother's motor scooter and sometimes comes and gets him. But there was a birthday party for Monique's younger sister Friday night, and Jamal wasn't invited. It was an all-girl party.

"Are you sure he stayed home?" I asked.

"I called him from my sister's about eight o'clock, and that's where he was. Home watching TV. After complaining he wasn't a little kid anymore and I didn't need to check up on him, he said he was going to bed. He had a long day coming up on Saturday, with those two jobs to work."

"And you believed him?"

"Jamal doesn't lie to his mama," she said, flatly.

He'd be the first kid in the history of the world who didn't, I thought.

"I had to ask," I said. "No offence meant. I was just thinking maybe this Monique Watkins popped over and gave him a ride somewhere on that motor scooter."

"Like to Mr. Wilson's stable, you mean," she said, frowning at me.

"Not at all, Mrs. Johnson. I believe Jamal is innocent. I'm just trying to learn as much as I can about his whereabouts at the time of the horse shooting. Maybe he has an alibi we don't know about."

Mrs. Johnson sighed. "I can't swear she didn't come over," she said, "but Jamal told me he wasn't going to see her and I believed him. But if he was going to Mr. Kroll's for any reason, he didn't need *her* to take him. Mr. Kroll just lives about a half-mile from here. Jamal could walk. That's one thing he liked about that job. He never needed a ride to work."

I hadn't realized Wilson Kroll lived so close. "So, how was Jamal planning to get to those two Saturday jobs?" I asked.

"He said the stable owner was picking him up for the morning job, and a boy named Willie Tee Harmon was giving him a ride to the dinner party. Jamal and the Harmon boy worked parties like that together sometimes. The police talked to Willie Tee, and Willie Tee said he gave Jamal a lift *to* the job, but not home. He told them he didn't know how Jamal got home, or what happened to him. Evidently, this Willie Tee went off with some girl who also worked the dinner, and left Jamal to find another ride or walk."

"Where's this Willie Tee live at?" Alvin asked.

He'd been listening quietly to our conversation.

"He lives in Landrum, somewhere," Mrs. Johnson said. "The police talked to this girl Willie Tee went off with, too, and she said the last time she saw Jamal, he was helping load things into the back of the caterer's van after the dinner party."

"So, she didn't know how Jamal got home, either?" I asked.

"No, she didn't," Mrs. Johnson said, "but a guest leaving about eleven-thirty saw Jamal walking down the driveway toward the road."

"At least we know he started out walking," I said.

"Someone at the dinner could have given him a ride," Millie Johnson said, more to herself than us, "but they just drove right on by him."

I heard Alvin Brown grunt from across the room.

"Do you think he would walk all the way home?" I asked her.

She sighed. "It's a long way, about five miles," she said, "but if there was no other way, he would. What choice did he have? He might have stopped in Landrum, which is about half-way home, and try to find a ride there. I know he goes to a pizza place there that's open late. Jamal is such a trusting boy. I can't stop wondering if he got in the car with somebody bad, and they did something terrible to him."

"Did the police check out the pizza place?"

"They said they did," she said. "But nobody there saw him."

"So, you don't know if he made it home," I said.

"I don't believe he did. When I got home Sunday night, his bed didn't look slept in, and he hadn't fed the chickens or the cat, which was his job. He wouldn't have neglected that. The police asked if he might have come in, packed a bag, and left again. He had several gym bags, but I couldn't tell if one was missing, or any clothes or things, like he was going somewhere. I called him all day Sunday, but never got an answer. His cell phone was dead; it went straight to voice mail."

She suddenly sobbed. "I still keep trying to call it."

I turned to Natasha "Were you at that dinner party?"

"Yes, but I left immediately after dinner. I'd been riding and working with my horse most of the day, and I was tired. Had I stayed, I feel sure Jamal would have asked me to give him a lift home and I gladly would have. I've felt guilty about that ever since."

"Oh no, Miss Natasha," Mrs. Johnson said, "It wasn't your fault. If it was anybody's, it was mine. I should have been home to look after my own child."

"It doesn't sound like either one you were at fault," I said. "I'd like to speak to a couple of Jamal's friends. Someone he was likely to talk to if he was bothered by something."

"I want to go with you when you see this Willie Tee," Alvin said. "That boy needs a lesson on keeping his word."

"Oh, shush, Alvin, Willie Tee was just being a teenager," Mrs. Johnson said.

It was startling to see someone who looked like "Big Hurt" take her reprimand and sit there like an admonished schoolboy. I thought I saw a smile flit across his lips as if her scolding raised an old, fond memory.

"If you want to talk to Jamal's friends," she said, "that wouldn't be Willie Tee, anyway." "They weren't close. Willie Tee was older by a couple of years. The one you need to talk to is Ronnie Dill. The Dills live next door, and their boy Ronnie and my Jamal have been best friends since first grade. They've been like two peas in a pod ever since."

"Do you think he might know something?" I asked her.

"I think he will tell you if he does. He's a sweet, honest boy, who has a hard life. I feel sorry for him *and* his mama," she said. Ronnie's daddy is no account. He won't work, he drinks, and I know he beats them. I've seen bruises on both of them. I don't think they get enough to eat, either. Ronnie and his mama are both skinny as rails. Ronnie's been over here at dinner time, and I try to get him to eat with us. Once in a while he will, but most of the time he just says thank you, ma'am, and says his Mama's probably got supper ready and he leaves. But the few times he has stayed for dinner he eats like a starved puppy. He wolfs his food down hardly even chewing."

I looked over at Natasha. The story of Ronnie Dill got to her, and she wore a sympathetic look. She'd probably never known a kid like that in her whole life.

"I take food over to them sometimes," Mrs. Johnson said. "I'll cook for four and take the two extra plates over to Ronnie and his mama. But, I won't do it if Mr. Dill is there. I learned my lesson on that. I thought he was gone one time because his old truck wasn't out front, but I found him sitting at the kitchen table, an almost empty whiskey bottle in front of him. He was drunk. His truck was out back where he was doing some work on it, and I hadn't seen it.

"When he saw what I brought, he got up and grabbed the plates and threw the food into the back yard. He said he wasn't taking charity from a *gosh-darned nigger*, but he didn't say *gosh darned.* I came home as fast as I could and didn't even collect my plates."

Ronnie and his family were white, I realized.

"Ronnie brought them to me the next day and apologized for his daddy. He tried to make excuses for him, saying he was just upset his truck broke down, and didn't have the money to fix it. I noticed Ronnie had a fresh bruise on his cheek, and I asked him about it. He said he stepped on a hoe and the handle flew up and hit him. That boy just breaks my heart."

"How do they live, if Mr. Dill doesn't work?" Natasha asked.

I found that question weird coming from a woman who'd never worked a day in her life, but I couldn't think of an appropriate simile for it.

"Mrs. Dill does part-time house cleaning when somebody's maid is sick," Mrs. Johnson said. "And she takes in laundry and ironing, but people don't hardly need that anymore. She also works picking peaches in season. They get food stamps, but Jamal said Mr. Dill takes them and trades them for beer somewhere. He's just an awful man, but Mrs. Dill is so beaten down she won't leave him."

I happened to look over at Alvin. Natasha wasn't the only one showing a reaction to the story of the Dills, but he didn't look sad. He looked angry. There was a fire coming from his eyes that was unnerving to see. He looked like he was about to go find Mr. Dill and beat him to a pulp. The strange thing was, I found myself liking him for it. He had a sense of righting wrongs in him that even Grandfather would have liked.

"Mr. Dill works when he needs to buy liquor and keep that old truck of his running," Millie Johnson went on. "I understand he's a fair shade-tree mechanic when he will work at it. He rebuilt an old motorbike he got somewhere and gave it to Ronnie last Christmas. I heard Ronnie tell Jamal it was the only Christmas present his daddy ever gave him. I don't know if the Christmas spirit got to the man, or he just drank too much over the holidays last year."

Mrs. Johnson turned around and looked at me.

"Oh, J.D., here I am going on and on about something you didn't come here to learn. I'm sorry, my nerves are just shot, worrying about my boy. I wouldn't be surprised if you just got up and left, to get away from this woman who runs her mouth so."

I stood up and put my arms around her. "Mrs. Johnson, with what you're going through on top of what you've been through, most people would be out of their minds by now. I can't promise I can find Jamal, but I'm going to do everything I can."

I kissed her on the top of her head and turned around to see Alvin watching me. I couldn't tell what he was thinking, but the fire was gone from his eyes.

"You said this Ronnie Dill lives next door?" I asked Mrs. Johnson.

"Well, it's the *country* kind of next door," she answered. "It's a quarter-mile down the road, but the Dills are our nearest neighbors in that direction."

I smiled at that. "I grew up in the country, too, so I'm familiar with measuring rural distances. That's probably where the term 'country mile' originates. Is there anyone else you think we need to talk to?"

"Monique Watkins," she said. "They go to school together, and she lives in Landrum and works at the Pack n' Sack at the edge of town. I've seen her there in the afternoons. Like I said, the police talked to her and said she didn't have anything of use to tell them, but you know kids. They don't always tell older people or authorities everything they know."

I wrote down Monique Watkins's name and the words 'Pack n' Sack,' along with Ronnie Dill's name, in my smartphone notebook. I included Willie Tee Harmon's name just in case I decided to try to talk to him. For Willie's sake, I'd make sure "Big Hurt" wasn't with me.

"Can I get the address of the dinner party from you?" I asked Natasha.

She spent a moment on her smartphone looking up the exact street number and sent it to my cell phone. The first chance I got I wanted to check Google maps to try to determine the most likely route Jamal would take if he were walking home from there. It was a super long-shot I'd find anything related to

Jamal, but I wanted to drive it and look it over, anyway.

I turned back to Mrs. Johnson. "So what came first? You telling the police Jamal was missing, or this man Wilson Kroll accusing Jamal of shooting his horse?"

"I called the police late Sunday after I got back from my sister's in Charlotte," she said. "An officer came out, and he was polite, but I could see that a black teenager gone missing just for a day wasn't a priority for him. Monday, that policeman came back with another one and told me about Mr. Kroll's horse getting shot and Mr. Kroll accusing Jamal of it. He'd told them Jamal had held a grudge against him for firing him, and threatened to get even. They asked if they could look around and I let them. I didn't think there was anything to hide. I just wanted them to find my boy. Then they found the rifle in the shed. I told them it wasn't his, but they didn't believe me. They tried to get me to say Jamal run off to keep from getting caught, and there wasn't anything I could say to change their minds. I finally asked them to leave. I was upset, and worried sick."

"This was Greenville County Sheriff's deputies who came out?" I asked.

"Yes," she said. "One the first time, two the second."

"Did you get their names?"

"The first one left a card. I don't remember the name of the one who came with him the second time. He didn't leave a card."

She got the card and gave it to me. It was the Deputy Waldrop I'd talked to earlier. I said I had his number and left the card with her.

"So, Jamal worked for Mr. Kroll as a stable hand, and Kroll let him go?" I asked her.

"Yes, but Jamal didn't threaten Mr. Kroll like Mr. Kroll said. That man is lying. Jamal said Mr. Kroll told him he was letting him go because he's got several full-time stable hands, and just didn't need Jamal anymore. Jamal wasn't happy about it, but he understood. He wasn't mad at Mr. Kroll, and never said anything about getting into an argument with him, or being fired for doing a bad job. In fact, he came home thinking if a part-time job ever came open again, Mr. Kroll would consider him for it. He said Mr. Kroll even told him that. So, somebody is lying, and I know in my heart it wasn't Jamal."

She began to cry again, and reached over and placed her hands on my wrists, her grip surprisingly strong. "Find my boy for me, J.D.," she said, her eyes pleading with me as tears streamed down her cheeks. "I've got to know what happened to him, even if it's something bad."

I wish I could have promised her that, but I wasn't going to lie to this woman. "I'll try my best," is all I said.

Natasha and I said our goodbyes to Mrs. Johnson, and she followed us to the door. I noticed Alvin was right behind her.

"I'll be in touch, Mrs. Johnson," I said. "If there's anything you need, just let me know."

She managed a weak smile and nodded.

Alvin followed us out on the porch, grabbed my sleeve and held me back as Natasha walked on to her car.

He leaned in and spoke into my ear in a quiet voice. "Look, Bragg, I know you don't want my help, but I made a promise to Taylor just like you did, and I'm going to keep it just like you will. I've seen that in you already. So, you can show some common sense, and let me help you, or you can be a dumb-ass and try to go it alone. But you know as well as I do we ain't looking for no missing person anymore. We're looking for Jamal's body, and the mother-fucker that killed him. I don't care how capable you think you are, I got a particular skill set you ain't got, but one you might need."

He took his arm off me and smiled. He still looked scary.

"You think about it," he said, "I'll be waiting for you to call."

He turned and went back into the house without looking back.

CHAPTER TEN

"What was that all about?" Natasha asked when I joined her in her car.

"Big Hurt and I were just getting better acquainted," I said.

"Big Hurt?" she said, her eyebrows crawling up her pretty forehead.

"That's his nickname. Alvin 'Big Hurt' Brown. Taylor Johnson told me about him."

"I keep forgetting you're Taylor's friend. What was Mr. Brown saying to you?"

"I guess he's signed on to help find Jamal, whether I like it or not. He promised Taylor he'd help, and he's going to try, with or without my say so."

"He's a tough looking man," she said.

"It's more than just a look. He's an ex-Chicago gang banger who teaches martial arts. He could probably kill us both with his index finger."

"So, what are you going to do about him?"

"Find something for him to do," I said. "There's an old saying that goes, 'it's better to have him inside the tent pissing out than outside pissing in.'"

"Who's old saying is that?" she asked.

"Another Johnson. Lyndon B."

"Why don't we get Alvin to grab Wilson Kroll and beat the truth out of him?" From the intensity in her voice, she didn't sound like she was kidding.

She turned the car around, and we sat at the end of the driveway, looking out at Belue Mill Road.

"Where to now, boyfriend?" Natasha asked.

"Let's go talk to the neighbor kid. Ronnie Dill."

"Which way?" she asked. "I heard Millie say the Dill house was a quarter of a mile away, but I didn't hear her say in which direction."

"Take a right," I said.

"How do you know? I didn't hear that."

"You aren't from the south," I said. "She said it was *down* the road. "To a southerner, unless it's actually up a hill, which it isn't because the road is pretty level along here, down means *south.*"

"Jesus," she said, "I've been here since I was a girl and I still need a special dictionary to understand you people."

As we headed *down* to see Ronnie Dill, I said, "You realize the best news might be that Jamal did shoot the horse and took off? And he's too ashamed to tell his mama?"

She gave me an inquisitive look.

"You mean if Jamal isn't on the run, then the reason for his disappearance is that something has happened to him?

"That's what his mother believes, and I suspect it's true. But, there's still a chance that the boy knew he was being set up for it and got the hell out of Dodge. I can't think of a reason why he wouldn't get in touch with his mom, but maybe there is one."

"I like that explanation better,' she said.

"But he would have had to hear about it somewhere. Were people talking about the horse shooting at the dinner party? It just happened the night before."

"If anyone was, I didn't hear them," she said. "Something like that would have spread across the dinner party like a brush fire."

"When did you find out?

"Monday, I think. But we're having lunch tomorrow with a couple of people who were at the dinner party, too. Maybe they heard something."

We came to a rusty mailbox with a faded "Dill" painted on it, which put a stop to our conversation regarding Kroll's horse shooting. Ronnie Dill's house was similar to Mrs. Johnson's in size, but shabby around the edges with peeling paint and a weedy, overgrown yard. Natasha drove in and parked.

Out back, a shirtless teenager was speedily navigating a half acre's worth of homemade dirt track through sharp turns and over big mounds in a rusted yellow, loud dirt-bike. He wore goggles, but no helmet. His long blond stringy hair flew straight out behind him like speed marks on a comic book character.

He saw us coming around the corner of the house, left the track at full speed and raced over, skidding to a stop, two feet in front of us. With his legs spread on the ground to keep his balance, he took off the mud splattered goggles, hung them on his handlebars, and gave us a suspicious look. Ronnie Dill was reed thin, his ribs prominent to the point that I could count every one of them.

"My daddy ain't here," he said. "You'll have to come back later."

"Cut the bike off, Bud," I said. "I want to talk to you a minute."

"You the law?" he asked, begrudgingly turning the ignition off.

It was suddenly peaceful and quiet, a welcome change from the loud sputtering of the bike. "That thing can't be street legal as loud as it is," I said.

"I don't ride it on the road. It ain't even got lights. You the highway patrol?"

He was trying to act tough but wasn't quite pulling it off. I was getting off on the wrong foot with this kid, and it wasn't what I wanted to do. I needed his cooperation.

"I'm not a cop. We're just trying to help find Jamal."

"Jamal?" he said. "Then who are you?"

"I'm John David Bragg, but you can call me J.D. This is Natasha Ladd. We're friends of Millie Johnson, and I'm a friend of Jamal's brother, Taylor. Mrs. Johnson told us you were Jamal's best friend. She knows we're here. We'd like to ask you some questions about him."

The kid's whole demeanor changed, and he dropped the thug act.

"All I know is he didn't kill that horse, and he didn't have no rifle. If anybody knew he had a gun, it would be me."

I had a disappointing feeling this kid didn't know anything about Jamal's disappearance. If he did, I believed he would have already told someone. But I had to ask.

"Was Jamal worried about anything, or afraid of someone before he disappeared?"

"Not that I know of. He was just being Jamal. He didn't seem scared or worried, or anything like that."

"He never said anything that made you think something was up?" I asked.

He shook his head. "No, nothing. He didn't say a word about taking off like that, either."

"Or anything about Wilson Kroll or his horse?"

He was still shaking his head. 'No," he said again. "I mean, he told me about losing his job, but he didn't seem upset about it."

"When did you see him last?" Natasha asked.

"The Friday before he went missing, on the bus coming home from school. He was clowning around like he always does and was cracking everybody up. He's the funniest guy I know," he added and smiled at the thought.

From the genuineness in the boy's face I could see just how much he liked Jamal. These guys were best friends, and Ronnie Dill couldn't hide it.

"Jamal told me his mama was going to visit her sister in Charlotte and he'd have the house to himself all weekend," Ronnie went on. "I asked him if he wanted to do something Saturday. He said maybe Sunday; he had a job at somebody's stable on Saturday morning, then he was waiting tables somewhere on Saturday night. Since he'd lost the job at Mr. Kroll's stable, he was picking up any work he could find. I asked him if they needed anybody else at either job, but he said no."

I couldn't think of any other questions to ask him. "Well if you think of something, Ronnie, will you call and tell me?"

He said yes, and took my card.

"You a sports writer from Atlanta?" he asked, staring at my card. "You know Julio Jones?"

"I've spoken to him," I said, and turned to go.

"Cool." He smiled for the first time, then just as quickly went somber again.

"Let me ask you something," he said.

I stopped and gave him my full attention. Something in his voice deserved it.

"You think Jamal is coming back?" he said as if he didn't really want to hear the answer.

This was not a kid that deserved a lie. He was searching for the truth, not some false hope or a stranger's consoling bullshit.

Ronnie Dill suddenly became the kid Mrs. Johnson told us about; a young man trapped in a hardscrabble life where there was little hope of escape or a future that was any better than the past. Looking at his thin face and sad eyes, I realized Jamal Johnson was not only his friend; he was probably the only bright spot in the boy's cheerless life.

"No," I finally said. "I don't. But I hope I'm wrong."

He nodded his head slowly, his eyes locked on an inner thought. Good news would be an unaccustomed experience for this kid, and he had resigned himself to it. He already knew Jamal wasn't coming back.

He started the bike, put on the goggles, and roared off back to his track. I watched him as he rode with a reckless abandon that gave the impression he didn't care if he lived or died. I turned and saw Natasha watching him, too. She seemed to have the same thoughts.

CHAPTER ELEVEN

"Let's go find the girlfriend," I said. We headed east toward the town of Landrum, just over the Spartanburg County line. Along the way, we passed a huge house that covered an entire wooded and pastured hilltop. The place was a faux castle, built of native granite, with a courtyard and mock turrets. All it needed was a portcullis and a moat. A vulgar example of conspicuous consumption if I ever saw one.

The stables beside it looked like they would house at least twenty horses. A small ornate sign by the long winding drive announced the place as "Hilltop Farms," with a silhouette of a jumping horse underneath.

"That's Wilson Kroll's place," Natasha said.

"Jesus," I said. "I hate the man for no other reason than he built that monstrosity."

"You wouldn't be alone. I know a couple of Kroll's neighbors who hate it, too. They call him Baron Von Kroll."

"This guy must have an ego as big as that place."

"And the taste of a carnival barker," Natasha added.

"Does he have a wife and kids?"

"A wife," she said. "Younger than him. No children by her. I think he may have an ex-wife and a daughter up north somewhere."

"I can't wait to meet this guy," I said. "Will he be at any of these parties you were telling me about?"

She thought a minute. "The one party Wilson Kroll might attend is tomorrow night at USEC, the Upcountry Steeplechase and Equestrian Club. It's open to anyone who is a member—and he is. Lots of food and an open bar.

Most of the other parties are smaller, and friends only. He may not get invited to those."

"Then let's make it to the Equestrian Center party."

"Do you have a jacket? No tie necessary."

"I actually own *two* jackets," I said.

"Stop it," she said. "I meant did you bring one?"

"I even know which side of the plate the fork and knife go on."

"Enough. By the way, the Krolls are sure to be at the race Saturday, and we'll probably run into them there, too."

"Good," I said. "It'll give me two chances to piss him off."

"You plan to piss him off?"

"The questions I plan to ask him will. He won't like them."

"You know, there's a rumor he's got connections with the Cleveland mafia, so you might want to be careful. People say his father was in with them, and so is he."

Natasha found the Pack n' Sack on the edge of the quaint little town of Landrum. Inside, two women worked the counter, and it wasn't hard to guess which one was Monique Watkins. She was young and attractive and the color of a mocha latte. The other woman was older; she was white, and had frizzy red hair and a body like a pickle barrel. An old man was buying a carton of cigarettes and a lottery ticket from the barrel lady, and she was ringing him up. The old man appeared to be the only customer in the store.

We walked over to the young girl and introduced ourselves. "We're helping Millie Johnson try to find Jamal, and we'd like to talk to you about him," I said.

"Has Mrs. Johnson heard anything from Jamal?" she asked.

"I'm afraid not, Monique, Natasha said. "You haven't heard from him either, I take it."

"No ma'am," the girl said and began to tear-up.

"Do you think you could take a short break and talk to us?" I said.

The girl looked at me.

"Who are you?" she asked. "A policeman? I've talked to the police. They didn't believe me when I told them Jamal wouldn't kill a fly, much less a horse."

"No, he's not a policeman," Natasha answered for me. "He's a special friend of mine. He's a writer with an Atlanta Magazine. He wants to write a story on what's going on up here."

"I'm going to take my break now, Louise," Monique said to the woman at the other register. The woman was still talking to the old man with the cigarettes and lottery tickets and waved a short goodbye in our direction without paying much attention to us.

We followed the girl out the door to a shady spot around the corner of the building. She leaned against the wall and looked at me.

"So, what do you want to know?" she asked.

"Everything you told the police . . . and everything you didn't," I said.

She exhaled slowly, glanced at Natasha and then back at me.

"I told the police I didn't know where Jamal was or why he went missing. I told them he'd never said anything about shooting any horse, and would *never* do that—or go off without telling anybody where he was going. He wouldn't do that to his mama, or me. But I don't think the police cared about what I said. Their minds were made up about Jamal, so I didn't try to tell them anything else."

"What else is there to tell?" I asked.

She chewed her lip and thought about it.

"Jamal knew things about the horse that got killed," she finally said. "Its name was Emperor, and Jamal was always telling me stuff about it. How it would try to go after molasses balls he kept in his pocket, or come when he called it. He loved that horse. Jamal said it couldn't 'do it' anymore, and he felt sorry for it. It was too old to race and he was afraid Mr. Kroll might put it down."

"Do it? What does that mean?" I asked.

"Emperor was supposed to be this big famous stud horse, but he was, what's the word? Impotent?"

"And Jamal knew that for a fact?" I said.

"He said he overheard Mr. Kroll talking to someone about it, and said it made sense, since he never saw Mr. Kroll and his vet collecting Emperors' semen anymore; like they did when he first went to work there."

"Did Jamal say if Mr. Kroll knew he'd overheard them?"

"He didn't say," Monique said.

"How long after that did Kroll let Jamal go?"

"Not too long, I guess. A few days."

"Jamal didn't tell you they got into an argument, or that he threatened Mr. Kroll?"

"Jamal wouldn't threaten anyone," Monique said. "That just wasn't him. The police asked me that, too, and I told them the same thing. Jamal knew he would get other stable work. He's good with horses, just natural born to it, I guess. He can talk to them, and I swear, they understand him. He says if he can't be a writer someday, he wants to be a trainer. Or maybe both, working as a trainer to pay for his writing until he becomes famous."

"He wants to be a writer? What kind of writer?" I asked.

"Novels probably," she said. "Jamal keeps a journal and is always writing things in it."

A journal. Another interesting bit of news.

"What kind of things did he write in this journal?" I asked.

"Mostly about people and ideas he has, I guess. He wouldn't let me read it. It was as private to him as a diary would be to me. But he knew things. He said that sometimes, working for these rich people he felt like he was invisible. They ignored him when he was in places where he could see and hear things he probably shouldn't have. He said he was just 'the hired help,' and sometimes they treated him like he wasn't even there. He told me once he'd heard and seen enough stuff that if he ever wrote a book about it, they'd probably run him and his mama out of the Dark Corner. He said he would call the book *Tales of The Invisible Boy.*"

"Nobody has said anything about the police finding a journal," I said. "Do you know where he kept it?"

She didn't.

"We need to ask Mrs. Johnson about it," I said to Natasha and held my fist to my ear, thumb and forefinger extended.

Natasha pulled out her cell phone, stepped a few feet away from us, and began dialing.

"Jamal would have hidden it real good," Monique said. "At least I hope so. There are probably some things in there he wouldn't want his mama to know. And neither would I."

I got the feeling Jamal and Monique may be a little closer than Mille Johnson might think. "Did you see him Friday night?"

"Mama was having a birthday party for my little sister, and I had to stay home for that."

"Do you know if Jamal stayed home, too, or went out somewhere?" I asked.

"The police asked me that. I told them what Jamal told me. He said his mama was visiting her sister in Charlotte, and he was home alone, watching TV and missing me." Monique smiled at the thought. "I was going to call him from my sister's party, but I just didn't get a chance. I had to help my mama with all the little girls. They about wore me out. After the party, I helped Mama clean up and went to bed. I was asleep almost before my head hit the pillow. I cry now when I think of him sitting at home by himself.

"So, when did you last talk to him?" I asked.

"Saturday afternoon. He was getting ready to go to work again—his second job of the day. He'd worked moving boxes from someone's house into their stable that morning. I tried to call him all day Sunday, but he didn't answer. I finally got his mama in the afternoon, and she told me he wasn't there and didn't know where he was. She sounded worried, and that's when I got worried, too."

Natasha walked back over, placing her cell phone in her pocket. "Millie knew he wrote things in a book," she said. "But she doesn't know where he keeps it. Even if she knew, she said she would never have read it. She respects Jamal's privacy. The police don't have it, and Millie said she didn't tell them about it. She said she would search for it."

When I turned back to Monique, she was standing there apparently lost in some thought.

"There *was* something . . ." she finally said, turning her focus to me. "When we talked on Saturday, he said he'd found something 'weird' where he was working that morning, but he didn't say what. I just thought of that."

"You said he was moving boxes from someone's house into their stable. Did he say who's house and stable?" I asked.

"He never said, and I never asked."

Monique looked at her watch. "I better get back in, or Louise will complain to the Manager about me."

"One last question," I said. "When you called Jamal that Saturday, did he know about the horse getting shot?"

"Oh God no," she said. "If he'd known that, it would have been the first thing out of his mouth. I told you, he loved that horse. I didn't hear about it until the police came and talked to me on Monday."

Monique probably gave me everything she had to give, but I left her one of my cards just in case she thought or learned of anything else. She was helpful, the information about Emperor's impotence was big if it proved to be true. With any luck, there might be something more in the journal about that, and maybe there was something relevant about the "weird" thing he found at the stable he worked Saturday morning. Now all I needed to do was find the journal.

As Natasha and I were driving back to her place, she looked across the seat, smiled at me and said, "You'll be heading back to the lovely Kelly now?"

I looked at her and nodded. "What time do you want me tomorrow?' I asked.

"Nothing until noon. We're having lunch with two friends who usually have their fingers on the pulse of the community and are happy to gossip about it. The main thing tomorrow, however, is the party at the Equestrian Center, a celebration for the USEC Steeplechase Saturday. Everyone will be there, and it's the perfect event to meet them. Cocktails and a buffet about six, and it will go quite late. There will be lots of people and friends from out of town, in for the race. This is a drinking crowd and tongues are bound to get loose."

"You said jacket, no tie?"

"Smart casual, as they say."

'I'll try to dress up to that," I said.

"And J.D.," she said smiling at me again. "If Kelly will let you, you can spend tomorrow night at my place. The party will go late, and you don't want to drive back at that hour, especially if you've had a few drinks." She grinned at me. "You can tell her my guest bedroom has a lock on the door, so you'll be safe."

I laughed at that, but I wasn't sure why. The look she was giving me was unsettling. Perhaps it was the devilment in her eyes. This was one feisty woman.

CHAPTER TWELVE

From Natasha's bungalow, I took Hunting Country Road west to Ridge Road, which took me into the town of Tryon. A left turn on Trade Street would put me on my route back to Pickens County, but, I pulled over at the intersection and took out the card Deputy Waldrop gave me with the address of the equine insurance investigator, Brandon Wise. The street numbers on the buildings surrounding me indicated I was close to Wise's office, so I decided to make a quick side trip before going to Kelly's. It was a little after five o'clock, but I took the chance he might still be at his office.

I found Olympic Equine Insurance in a small one-story building between a hot wing place and a barber shop, a couple of blocks north on Trade Street. The front door was open and I went in. The receptionist's desk was vacant, the desk lamp turned off, but the door to an office on the left was open, lights on inside. I walked over and peeked in.

Seated at a desk was a short, middle-aged man with thinning hair and an unusually red face that looked more like high blood pressure than sunburn. He wore a short-sleeved white shirt and necktie. He saw me and gave me a puzzled look.

"Can I help you?" he asked.

"Are you Brandon Wise?"

"Yes I am, how can I help you?"

"I'm sorry for barging in like this, Mr. Wise, but I was driving by and decided to drop in and see if you would talk to me."

"Well, I might, if I knew who you are, and why you want to talk."

"My name is J.D. Bragg, and I'd like to talk about who shot Wilson Kroll's horse."

There was a moment of silence.

"Who did you say you were?" he asked.

"J.D. Bragg. I'm a friend of Millie Johnson, the mother of Jamal Johnson, the boy accused of shooting the horse. The family doesn't believe he did it and I've agreed to look into it for them.

"Who do they think shot it?" Wise asked.

"Odds are usually on the owner, aren't they?" I said. "For the insurance money. That's what *you're* looking into, isn't it? I'd like to compare notes."

"I don't know if I can discuss that with you," he said.

"This meeting would be just between you and me," I said. "I only want to find the boy— and the truth."

He sat quietly, sizing me up, then got up and came around the desk. He motioned for me to take a seat in one of two stuffed chairs by a coffee table. He took the other one.

"You wanted to talk," he said, "so talk."

At least I'd gotten his attention. "As I said, the authorities have charged the Johnson boy for it, based on little more than the accusations of Wilson Kroll, the dead horse's owner. The family is convinced Mr. Kroll is lying, and the boy is innocent."

Wise said, "You left out the rifle they found at the boy's house, and he *is* on the lam, as they say."

"There are no fingerprints on the rifle," I said, "and the family says he has never owned a gun of any kind. They believe Mr. Kroll, or someone, placed it there to frame the boy. There were no witnesses to the shooting, nor to Kroll's claim that when he fired Jamal earlier, the boy threatened him. Jamal's account of that incident, made to family and friends is entirely different. The more I learn about this man Kroll, the more suspicious I become of him. As I see it, he's the person with the motive—the insurance money. I hear you may believe that, too."

"Maybe what you heard is just my wishful thinking," he said. "I've got a boss in Louisville, Kentucky who's not too happy about paying off a claim that large."

"I heard it *is* sizable,"

"Well, the horse was worth a lot," he said. "*Emperor*—that's the horse's name—was one of the top stud horses in this part of the country, and demanded unbelievably large fees."

"How unbelievable?" I said.

"You realize we're talking about some very rich people here?" he said.

"Of course I do."

"Well, it's a lot to *them*. Does that give you some idea?"

I got the picture. We were talking *big* money.

"Who told you about me?" Wise asked. "I haven't shared my thoughts with anyone but a Greenville County Sheriff's dep . . . Ah," he said. "Deputy Waldrop. I felt that he didn't completely buy the kid as the culprit. Am I right?"

"Maybe," I said. "He gave me your card and suggested we talk. That would indicate to me he isn't completely sold on the kid's guilt, regardless of the evidence. I think the Deputy has a gut feeling. As do I."

"Gut feelings don't help me," Wise said, "but proof would be good. Do you have any?"

"The horse was impotent," I said, and let that lay there.

I could tell from Wise's face I had surprised him.

"We don't call it impotent," he said. "We use the word *infertile*. What would make you think that?"

"Jamal Johnson told someone. They told me."

"Double hearsay," Wise said, with a disappointed look. "I can't use that."

"What if it were true and the horse was imp—*infertile*," I said, "would the amount your company pays out to Wilson Kroll change?"

"Oh, yes," Wise said. "Infertility would destroy the horse's value, and we only pay the fair market value at the time of the animal's death, regardless of the original insured amount."

"I'll bet that would make the boss-man in Louisville happy," I said.

"And Wilson Kroll unhappy," Wise said. "If he knowingly neglected to report a change in Emperor's condition to us, he would not get anywhere near the full amount of the insurance on the policy. If he shot the horse himself, he gets nothing."

Mr. Wise leaned back in his chair and looked at me.

"Unfortunately, whoever told you Emperor was infertile was wrong," he said. "Kroll's records show that the horse was fertile up to the very end."

Had Jamal misheard Kroll's conversation in the stable hall? I didn't see why the boy would make something like that up.

"And you believe these records?" I said. "From what I hear about Wilson Kroll, I don't think he's above doctoring his books if it served his purpose."

"Be that as it may," Wise said, "there's no proof."

Wise looked like he wanted to say more on the subject, but didn't.

"Who are you?" he asked, instead.

I didn't think he'd forgotten my name. "I told you," I said, "I'm a friend of the Johnson family. I played college football with the older brother, and he asked me to look into Jamal's disappearance. I gave him my word I would. Being that he's paralyzed and bedridden, he can't do it himself."

"I get it that you're a good friend, and a bit of a boy scout," Wise said. "That's not what I'm asking you. I want to know *what* you are. Are you a lawyer, a policeman, or a private investigator or something?"

"I'm an investigative journalist and writer with an Atlanta sports magazine," I said.

He sat nodding his head slowly. "That makes sense," he said. "You don't ask questions like just a family friend. Am I going to see my name in print somewhere?"

"My interest is to try to find Jamal Johnson and clear his name," I said. "If that makes a story, then I will write it. I won't lie about that. But, I won't repeat anything you say to me, or use your name as a source, unless I get your permission first."

Wise continued to study me, as if he was making up his mind about me.

"I'm going to share something with you," he finally said, "and trust you to keep your mouth shut about where you got it."

"You have my word," I said.

"I hope so, because I may be corrupting my investigation, not to mention that I could get fired for it."

He went over to a pea green metal file cabinet against a wall, took out a thick file, and brought it over.

"These are Wilson Kroll's business records," he said, and removed a small stack of letter-size papers from the top of the file and handed them to me. "I've compiled a chronological list of all of Emperor's stud service transactions for the last year. Take a quick look at them and tell me if anything unusual jumps out at you."

"Mr. Wise, I'm just an ex-jock writer. Examining business records is not—"

"Humor me," Wise said.

I removed the metal clamp that held the papers together, placed them on my knee and began to study them, one by one. Wise sat quietly and watched me.

There were a half-dozen pages filled with one-line entries; each entry numbered and dated. The date was followed by what I assumed was the name of the mare receiving Emperor's services—unless there were humans in the world with names like Lucy's Revenge or Miss Prickly Pear. Next was the owner's name, address, and stable name—if there was one. Capping off each entry were one of three words written in capital letters: FRESH, FROZEN or CHILLED, followed by the words PAID or NO-CHG.

I looked up at Mr. Wise and said, "I assume the words *fresh*, *frozen*, and *chilled* don't refer to the romantic temperament of the mare at the time of the mating."

Wise gave me a look that said he didn't appreciate my attempt at humor.

"There are three kinds of semen presentation in the mating of horses," he said, "fresh, chilled, and frozen. Each is different in quality and method."

"Sorry," I said, "I must have missed that in semen class."

"Just scan through the entries," Wise said, "and pay close attention to those three words. Then tell me what you see."

I did as he asked. It would be easier if he'd just tell me, but it was obviously something he wanted me to find by myself.

I examined the pages, and when I finished, I said, "For the first five pages, the entries are split between *fresh*, *chilled* and *frozen*, with most of them *fresh*. The last page, there are no *fresh* listings at all, only *chilled* and *frozen*, about half and half."

"Excellent, Mr. Bragg." Wise smiled for the first time since I'd met him.

"But I still don't know what any of it means."

"I will tell you," he said. "Each of the three semen presentations, fresh, chilled, and frozen, has to be weighed against the reproductive weaknesses of the mare or stallion. They each have different success rates of impregnating a mare. Fresh semen is by far the best, but collection —which refers to the ejaculation of the semen from the stallion—can't be transported and must be used immediately, with the mare and stallion at the same location simultaneously for insemination. It would be the preferred method by any mare owner willing to pay Emperor's price, and they are usually there to see and participate in the process. A fresh semen mating undergoes minimum or no processing and always has the highest fertility. It's longer-lasting once inseminated, the inseminated mare requires less frequent veterinary checks prior to conception, and it's usually the least expensive method."

"What about au naturel insemination?" I asked. "Didn't old Emperor ever get to do the dirty one-on-one with a pretty little mare?"

"Natural mating is becoming rare these days. At least in this country. Artificial insemination is actually safer than live breeding. It helps avoid harmful bacteria, bites, and injuries. Especially if you've got a rowdy stallion, as they tell me Emperor was."

"How is frozen and chilled semen any different, outside of the obvious indications of the descriptive names?"

"Frozen semen is the *least* preferred," he went on, "and is actually the most expensive process. Its only advantage is that frozen in liquid nitrogen tanks can preserve the semen for years, even long after the Stallion is dead. It can be ready and on hand whenever needed. You just ship it in special transporters, known as dry nitrogen shippers and can deliver it worldwide. The mare owners must thaw it themselves, which can often create further problems with the semen's success rate if he—or she—doesn't know what they're doing.

"So, Emperor could have become a eunuch, and Kroll could still sell his semen if he collected and froze it before the horse started shooting blanks? Don't these last records suggest that?"

"If it weren't for the *chilled* semen procedures," Wise said.

"What's the difference between chilled and frozen other than the temperature?" I asked.

"The rate of success with chilled semen isn't as high as fresh, but it's better than frozen," Wise said. "It's the chilled semen listings that prove Emperor was *not* infertile. Chilled semen must be inseminated into the mare artificially within 24 to 30 hours after collection. It's simply chilled long enough to ship it to mare owners overnight, by a carrier or post service using Styrofoam boxes or something called an Equitainer, made especially for this process. Chilled semen is closer to fresh semen than frozen, but like frozen, the mare doesn't have to be transported to Kroll's stables for the insemination. The mare's owner can handle that part in their own stable."

"So, if I'm hearing you correctly," I said, "any breeder paying top dollar for a stud like Emperor would want to go the best and most preferred route, which is fresh semen. Yet, no one in the last few months did it."

"Yes. That and the unusually large number of frozen semen procedures are what surprised me when I saw these records," Mr. Wise said.

I looked back at Wise's chronology, thumbing to the last page. The last chilled listing occurred only two days before someone shot Emperor. If these records were correct, then Emperor was firing live ammo right up to the end. Which would throw a monkey wrench into my infertility theory. But I wasn't buying Kroll's records just yet. I got the feeling that neither was Brandon Wise.

"You suspect Kroll's records are as hinky as I do," I said.

Wise didn't speak. He just looked at me and nodded.

"So, if Jamal Johnson is right and Emperor did become infertile, how do you figure it?"

He gave it some thought before answering. "Kroll may be thawing his frozen semen and shipping it as chilled, he finally said, "or he's passing off another horse's semen as Emperor's."

"Even with what little I know about the man, I wouldn't put anything past him," I said.

"What I don't know is *why* he would do it. I've checked his finances, and he's worth over a hundred million dollars. He could get sued or even go to jail for this. While Emperor's stud-fees are substantial, it's still a paltry sum compared to what Kroll's worth. Why risk it?"

"Funny you would ask that," I said. "Yesterday, I asked a very wealthy friend of mine that very question. She said the wealthy are a dissatisfied bunch. They worry about money as much as everyone else. There's always a need for more. If you've got a hundred million, a hundred and fifty million would be better."

Wise looked at me like he was trying hard to comprehend what I'd just said. Like me, he was probably struggling with the idea of anyone being unsatisfied with a hundred million dollars.

"My friend said that some college did a study on the super-rich, and that's what they found," I said.

"Kroll's veterinarian would have to be a part of any fraud," Wise said. "He would have to falsify documentation and contracts."

"Who is his vet?"

A man named Sam Squires. He works exclusively for Wilson Kroll."

"Is that common?" I asked. "A vet with one patient?"

"Well, Kroll has more than one horse, but usually it's stables a lot bigger than Kroll's that have their own personal vet," he said.

"Kroll risks lawsuits and possible jail to make a few more bucks on his stud fees on the one hand," I said, "and he pays a full-time vet on the other. Go figure.

I looked back at "Kroll's records again. "What are the entries marked 'NO-CHG?'" Were these customers who got a freebie?"

"No," he said. "Those are the matings that didn't achieve results for one reason or another. It's usually the mare's fault, and it's hard to prove, but most stud services either don't charge when that happens, refund the money, or offer a second mating."

"Have you asked Mr. Kroll about any of this?" I asked.

"Mr. Kroll is a difficult man to talk to," Wise said. "He takes umbrage at any question concerning his business. I've decided to wait until I know more before I approach him again. He merely says it's the ambiguity of the business, and that he can't control his client's preference in mating methods. The next ten matings could all be fresh ones, he says. You never know."

"Do you buy that?"

"Up to a point. But it just smells wrong. He has a horse syndicate, with investors, and if he's neglecting to push the fresh semen procedure, then he's cutting down on potential profits, which doesn't seem like a good way to keep his investor's ROI up."

"What is a horse syndicate?" I asked.

"It's an investment scheme fairly common among horse breeders and race horse owners. Kroll has built his syndicate around Emperor and its offspring. You buy into it for a percentage of ownership and share the profits. I understand his investors are friends from up north who have invested several million dollars in it."

I wondered if those friends were the Cleveland mobsters Natasha told me about. "It wouldn't be much of an investment if Emperor suddenly went infertile, would it?" I said.

"No, it would tank, and the investors would lose their money—or at least, cease to earn money on the investment," Wise said.

"I guess that wouldn't make the investors too happy, would it? Maybe Kroll feels like he has no choice but to continue selling the stud service of an infertile horse to keep the idea of a fertile Emperor alive. That is, until he could arrange to have it killed, blame it on a disgruntled employee so he could collect your insurance money, and split it with the investors to keep them placated."

Wise studied me for what seemed like an inordinate amount of time.

"You have a devious mind, Mr. Bragg," he finally said. "But it still seems like a huge risk. Why wouldn't he just give them their money back? He can afford it."

"Pride, saving face, reputation, greed, who knows? Rich people don't get richer by creating bad investments. So, what's your plan going forward?" I asked.

"I need some hard proof," he said. "Now that you've brought up the infertility issue, I want to see how many mare owners will agree to DNA tests on the foals from these latest 'chilled semen' procedures to prove it was Emperor who truly sired them. The horse is registered by ASHA, the American Saddlebred Horse Association, and I can get its DNA from them to compare to one of these new foals. That would settle the infertility thing, one way or the other. If more than one test doesn't match, Kroll will have a hard time claiming it was all just a mix-up in shipping and sending another stallion's semen was just an honest mistake."

"What about stable hands? I understand Kroll has several of them. Are they worth talking to?"

"Undocumented workers. They hear no evil, see no evil, speak no evil. In fact, they can barely speak at all, if you're expecting English. I tried, but they aren't talking," Wise said. "They're either loyal to Kroll, afraid of deportation, or afraid of him. If charges were brought, they might loosen their tongues, but until that happens, it's a waste of time talking to them."

"There's Kroll's veterinarian," I said. "What was his name? Sam Squires? I can take a run at him. Maybe he doesn't have as much reason as Wilson Kroll to keep quiet about this. Maybe if he knows we're on to them, he'll turn on

Kroll to save himself. I can probably help you get the DNA samples, too, if any of Kroll's clients these last few months were local."

"That would be great," he said, "but we need to be quick about it. I can't stall Kroll for long. He already has his lawyer calling me."

He sat and studied me.

"Do you know where this boy, Jamal Johnson, is?" he asked.

"I have a pretty good idea," I said.

"Then why not turn him up and ask him what he knows. And why he ran. If he's innocent, then he can help clear himself."

"I don't think he can do that," I said.

"Why not?"

"Because I think he's dead."

Wise couldn't hide his surprise.

"Are you suggesting Wilson Kroll has anything to do with that?" he asked.

"Perhaps," I said. "If the boy didn't shoot the horse and didn't run away, then it's the most reasonable assumption to make."

"Even if the kid's dead, it doesn't mean someone murdered him," Wise offered. "He could have had an accident. Overdosed on drugs. Skinny-dipped in the lake and drowned. Whatever."

"Could be, but I don't think so."

Wise looked at me. "Your 'gut' again?"

I nodded.

He took the pages of Kroll's business chronology from me and went out of his office. I heard a copy machine at work somewhere.

He came back in about five minutes, handed me the copies, and said, "Remember, not a word about me giving you this."

"It's our secret," I said, shook his hand, and with a promise to find out whatever I could from my end, I gave him one of my cards, and headed to Pickens County and Kelly.

CHAPTER THIRTEEN

Kelly was in the kitchen when I walked into her house. She was tossing a salad, with a colander of steaming pasta draining in the sink. Something thick and red and bubbling was in a pan on the stove, and the smell of toasting garlic bread came from the oven.

"The hunter, home from the hill," I said and gave her a long wet kiss.

"That's the first time anyone's ever greeted me with a line off a tombstone," she said.

"It's from a poem or an old song, isn't it?" I asked.

"It eventually became a song, but it's a phrase from a Robert Louis Stevenson poem, and the epitaph on his grave."

"Remind me never to play Trivia with you," I said.

"Can you take the bread out of the oven and put it on the table, and open that bottle of wine over there?"

I did as she asked, uncorked the Chianti and poured us both a glass. There was a flower arrangement on the table with candelabra lighting. She caught me smiling at her.

"*What*?" she said

"Very romantic," I said, gesturing to the table.

"I plan on seducing you."

"And I plan on letting you."

She brought over the bowl of tossed salad and another with the pasta, which I recognized as her penne with chicken and spicy vodka tomato cream sauce—one of her best recipes.

"Conversation first," she said and sat down. I sat down across from her.

"How did it go with Natasha today? she asked.

"She's everything you said she was, and she seems to have her finger on the pulse of all that's going on over there."

"But did you like her?"

"What's not to like? She's smart, has a face like a movie star, a body that would stop traffic, and more money than Lady Gaga."

"Sorry I asked," Kelly said and laughed. "Did you learn anything about Jamal Johnson?"

"Enough to get me started." Jamal Johnson would probably never be seen alive again, but Kelly probably already suspected that. I just didn't want to talk about that right now. It wouldn't serve as very good foreplay, seeing as how she was in a romantic mood.

"I talked to Jamal's mom," I said, "his best friend, his girlfriend, and the deputy who's working the case. Three and a half of them don't believe Jamal shot the horse, or ran away because of it."

"Three and a half?"

"The cop is sticking to his evidence, but I think he has doubts."

"What about the boyfriend-girlfriend charade with Natasha?" she asked. "Is that working?"

"The idea still seems silly to me," I said, "but if it gets me in with the horse and trust-fund crowd, then I'll go along with it. From what Natasha says, they're very clannish."

Kelly caught me smiling.

"What are you grinning about?" she asked.

"I was just thinking how seriously Natasha takes her part in this guise. She thought we should exchange intimate secrets, things we would know about each other if we were in a romantic relationship, just in case someone gets to prying. She says I'll probably meet an ex-husband and an old boyfriend, who might still be a bit jealous and give me a hard time. She says she wouldn't put it past them to grill me about our relationship just to see how far it's evolved."

"What kind of intimate secrets?"

"She told me she has a mole on her inner thigh, a scar on her butt, and gets loud when she makes love."

"Oh my," Kelly said. "And she thinks someone will ask you about this?"

"I know. I thought it was pretty ridiculous, too."

"What did you tell her about yourself?" she asked.

"I told her I was hung like an elephant and crowed like a rooster when I made love."

"Well, the part about the rooster is true," Kelly said, with a straight face.

"Actually, I didn't tell her anything," I said. "Since the whole damn thing is a charade and no one knows anything about me, I told her to make something up if the need arose."

"So what's next?" she asked.

"Lunch with gossipy friends, and a big steeplechase-week party tomorrow night where she says I can meet everyone I need to meet. She says the party will go late, and I shouldn't try to drive back here when it's over, especially if I've had a few drinks. She's invited me to stay the night in her guest bedroom. She even told me to tell you not to worry because the bedroom door has a good lock, so I'll be safe."

"She said to tell me that?"

"Yep. Obviously, she thinks you don't trust her."

Kelly laughed and said, "She still thinks a lot of herself, I see. She believes she's a threat. Tell her I'm not worried. I'm not that naïve little girl from college anymore. And it sounds like a good idea. Maybe even for the next couple of days. You've got work to do and you shouldn't have to spend several hours each day running back and forth over here."

"You trying to get rid of me?" I said, and laughed.

"Of course not. I'll miss you terribly, but it's the practical thing to do. You'll probably have another late night or two ahead of you."

There was that "practical" element of our relationship rearing up again. But where I would spend the next couple of nights appeared settled, and we didn't speak of it again.

We finished the meal and sat on the sofa in her living room drinking another glass of wine. We ended up necking, and surprise of surprises, ended up in her bed.

Not once during the night did I give thought to Taylor or Jamal Johnson, Natasha, or the day's events. Kelly Mayfield occupied every nook and cranny of my mind, and I tried to occupy every nook and cranny of her body. We finally fell into an exhausted, satiated sleep.

CHAPTER FOURTEEN

Wednesday at a quarter till noon, I arrived at Natasha's, pulling a carry-on bag. She was waiting for me at her house, ready for our lunch with her friends.

She saw the luggage and said, "Oh, good."

She smiled, and showed me where to put it. She had lied to me. There was no lock on the guest bedroom door.

The weather had turned cooler, and she wore pants and a sweater. I couldn't help noticing, (forgive me, Kelly), that her pants fit her shapely derrière so well they looked like they were made from a pattern shaped from an exact mold of her butt.

As we left for lunch, it began to rain, not hard, but enough to darken the soil and put a sheen on the tree leaves. We headed to Landrum, where we'd met Jamal's girlfriend Monique, but this time our destination was a restaurant in the center of town. As we drove, Natasha told me about the friends we were going to meet. For some reason, I had expected them to be female but was surprised to learn they were both men. The more I thought about it, however, the more sense it made. Natasha wasn't the type to have many female friends. She'd said so herself.

One of them was Teddy Crane, whom she said was a friend since childhood. She told me that both of Teddy's parents died in a house fire years ago. Teddy, an only child, was raised by an uncle, deceased now, too, who had lived next door to Natasha and her family. She said she and Teddy grew up like brother and sister, with romance unthinkable, too much like incest.

She also said she heard that Teddy had run through his inheritance, but she had never spoken to him about it, nor had he to her. If it were true, Teddy would face the necessity of getting a job for the first time in his life, and it would kill him, she feared. All he had ever known was the role of a renaissance man and bon vivant. She said he was a little boy who never grew up—but to her, that was part of his charm.

The second friend I would meet was Chuck Norman. Originally from up east somewhere, and bit older than us. Never married, he lived with his mother, and usually, wherever you found Teddy, you'd find Chuck. Some people thought him gay, she said, others, that he was a bit slow, but she said Chuck was just a confirmed bachelor with his own peculiar and fussy ways, shy around women, extremely polite, and with the mannerisms of someone from another era. She said Teddy often called him 'Grandma Norman,' but Chuck didn't seem to mind. "He's like a Sancho Panza to Teddy's Don Quixote," she said.

We arrived at the restaurant on Rutherford Street in Landrum called the Hare and Hound, beating her friends there. We found a table for four in a corner in the back, and no sooner sat down when two men came through the door, spotted Natasha, waved, and made their way back to us. I easily recognized who was who by Natasha's previous description. Teddy Crane was tall and dark with good looks, hair just long enough to be hip, and was sizing me up as they joined us. He looked at me with a slight snarky curl at the edges of his mouth that suggested he and I probably weren't going to get along. He was wearing an old-time ankle-length cowboy duster, an Australian flop hat with the chin strap hanging loosely around his throat, and flat-heeled boots with a buckle on the side, looking like a nineteenth-century Australian cowboy. My guess was he spent a lot of his time living in somebody else's movie.

Chuck also fit Natasha's description. He was an average looking guy, as tall and thin as Teddy, but prematurely balding, and not as handsome. The bare round spot on the crown of his head looked like he was wearing a skin Yarmulke. He dressed, I'm sure, as his father before him had dressed: a plaid, button-down short-sleeved shirt, khaki pants, and brown dock-siders—no socks. All that was missing was a Shetland 'Shaggy Dog' crewneck sweater thrown over his shoulders and tied by the sleeves around his neck. He wore black horn-rimmed glasses and was the epitome of an aging Ivy leaguer.

Natasha made the introductions and we all nodded, but no one offered to shake hands.

"So, you're Nat's latest," Teddy said right away, as he sat down, studying me like a bug in a jar.

"How did you guys meet?" he asked.

"On a shopping trip to Atlanta," Natasha answered for me. "J.D. was standing at a watch display in a Jewelry store at Lenox Mall. He was looking at a Patek Philippe. We struck up a conversation, and he asked me to dinner. How could I refuse such a gorgeous man," she added and beamed adoringly at me.

I thought we'd agreed to say we'd met in a bar, but I guess she decided to ad lib and dress up the story a bit for Teddy. I think she was annoyed by his attitude, too.

"You didn't get the Patek, I guess," Teddy said, glancing at the inexpensive Hamilton on my wrist with a look that said he wouldn't be caught dead wearing it.

Even the least expensive Patek Philippe cost more than my Jeep, and the closest I'd ever been to one was looking at it in a magazine ad.

"No," I said. "Too expensive for me."

I'd play along with the boyfriend thing, but I wasn't going to put on airs for it. I probably couldn't pull that off anyway; there was too much redneck in me.

I took a moment to look Teddy over more carefully. Most women would consider him handsome, and he obviously knew it. He wore a perpetual look of arrogance that I immediately detested. If Natasha thought he was such a great guy, she'd have to stand in line. I got the feeling nobody thought more of Teddy Crane than Teddy Crane.

Natasha told him I was a sports writer and was doing a piece on the steeplechase race and the horse community. He quickly warned me not to even think about writing a novel about it; that was reserved for himself.

"You may be the first person she's dated who works for a living," Teddy said.

"I've heard that,' I said. "Do you have horses like everyone else around here?"

"I have two," he said. "One is a jumper, and the other one is just for riding and keeping my jumper company. The jumper is something special. Great bloodlines. I've thought about getting into the breeding game, but it's such a time-consuming venture that I would have no time for my writing."

"What about you, Chuck. Are you a horse person?"

"When I was younger, but I gave it up after my father died. We have no horses now; my mother sold them."

"I'm sorry to hear about your father," I said. "When did he die?"

"When I was fourteen," he said.

"I'm not much of a horse person, myself," I said. "I'm surprised Natasha has anything to do with me."

"Nat likes only two things," Teddy said, "horses and fucking. So, you must be good at *one* of them."

Natasha didn't seem to take offense, and both she and Teddy laughed. But I didn't find it funny. Nor appropriate, being the new boyfriend, even if it was a charade. Teddy didn't know that. I was about to react but then thought otherwise. Teaching Teddy manners wasn't why I was here. But another black mark went down in my book of Teddy. I noticed Chuck didn't react one way or the other. He just looked on with a flat expression as if he was used to this kind of banter between Teddy and Natasha.

"Do you live on Hunting Country Road like Natasha?" I asked Teddy if for no other reason than to change the direction of the conversation.

"No. I live up on Hogback Mountain Road. Those big old barns on Hunting Country Road aren't my style—no offense, Natasha—but you know my personality doesn't fit there."

Now he was concerned with offending her. What a phony.

Natasha took no offense. She smiled broadly at him, and said, "Teddy lives in a restored hunting lodge on Hogback Mountain that practically hangs off a cliff," she said. "Massive timbers and quite rustic, but with all the modern conveniences. It's really cool."

"It ought to be, I've spent enough money on it," Teddy added.

"And you keep horses up there?" I asked.

"Oh no. I board them at Chuck's family's stables. My place doesn't have pastureland or room for a barn. Too steep and rocky up there."

I turned to Chuck. "How about you, Chuck, where do you live?"

"You ask a lot of questions," Teddy said.

"I'm an investigative journalist," I said. "That's how I investigate."

"I thought you were a sports writer," he said.

"Sports is my main investigative field. Right now, it's steeplechase racing. I turned back to Chuck. "So what about it Chuck, where do *you* live?"

"I live with my mother in one of those big old barns on Hunting Country Road," he said.

He'd said it so completely deadpan, without change of expression, that I took a closer look at him. There was wit in this guy I hadn't noticed.

"What do you guys think of that boy who shot the horse?" I asked. "Jamal Johnson. You think he did it? His family says he didn't."

Teddy shrugged. "I barely know him. It's not like we run in the same circles. Chuck knows him better than I do. He's done odd jobs at his place."

"He worked for my mother, not me," Chuck said.

"Yeah, but you're happy to have him do it, Chuckie boy," Teddy said. "Whatever the kid did around your place meant *you* didn't have to do it. I do more work around there than you do. Chuck and manual labor are sworn enemies," he added.

Picking on Chuck seemed to be part of the usual repertoire between the two. Chuck sat listening with a forced smile, but couldn't hide the microsecond's glint of annoyance that flickered in his eyes. If Chuck was gay like Natasha said some believed, it was probably Teddy he had a crush on.

I thought I might learn more out of Chuck if I got him alone for a few minutes. Perhaps he would even have interesting things to say about Teddy. Or was that just wishful thinking because of my growing dislike of the man.

"What about the dead horse's owner, Wilson Kroll? Do you guys know *him*?"

Teddy and Chuck glanced at each other, and neither spoke. Something passed between them, but I couldn't determine what.

"I know him to speak to, but that's about it," Teddy said. "Chuck doesn't like him, though."

Once again, Teddy had deflected the question to Chuck. Chuck was still staring at him, his expression unreadable, but something was going on between them over Wilson Kroll. Another reason to get Chuck alone.

"Why don't you like him?" I asked Chuck.

"My mother finds him quite offensive. She thinks he's rude and boorish," he said. "New money," he added as if that explained it.

It struck me as odd that he answered more on behalf of his mother than himself. I waited for him to say more but he didn't.

Our lunch came, and I spent the rest of the time tagging along with a conversation carried on mainly between Teddy and Natasha. Chuck seemed content to sit on the sidelines with me, smiling—or frowning—at the appropriate times.

I learned that some of this small clique of wealthy horse lovers, like any other social or economic demographic in America, were not opposed to taking the occasional toke off a joint or a snort of cocaine. I got the feeling I was sitting with at least two of them. I didn't get the vibe from Chuck. It made me wonder where the affluent horse crowd would get their drugs. I couldn't see them driving up to a street corner in a seedy part of Tryon or Landrum in their GMC Yukon Denali and riding breeches and asking for a dime bag. But then again, this was America, the land of opportunity. Drugs were everywhere.

After lunch, we all exited the restaurant together and stood on the sidewalk saying our goodbyes. Natasha hugged them both, and I shook their hands. Teddy tried to break my fingers, and I gave it to him right back. He'd managed to bring out the childishness in me, too, and I disliked him even more for it.

As Natasha drove us away, I saw Teddy and Chuck get into a Prius parked on the street. Chuck got in behind the wheel. "Prius," I said and grinned at Natasha. "It fits him."

She laughed. "Probably the only one in the Dark Corner. That's our Chuckie boy," she added, still smiling.

On the way back to her place, I asked, "Where do you get your drugs?"

The question threw her. "Who says I do drugs?"

"C'mon, Natasha, I'm your boyfriend. You can tell me."

She looked across the seat at me for a long moment. "What are you, a narc?" she asked and laughed.

"Just curious," I said. "You guys were talking, and I wondered how you would get it in a place—" I waved my hands around at the large country estates we were driving by on Hunting Country Road—"like this?"

"I only do it in the rare recreational moment," she said, "but I get it from Teddy."

"Teddy?" I said. I probably shouldn't have been surprised. It fit, somehow. "I know you said he'd run through his inheritance but isn't this a risky way to supplement it?"

"Oh, I think Teddy was doing this long before he ran through his money. Teddy likes to consider himself the quintessential counter-culturist."

"I can see that," I said.

"Well, just don't go telling Kelly that I've become a druggie."

"I would never say a word. Besides, been there and done that once upon a time. I was just wondering if Jamal was into to it, too."

"I don't think so," she said. "He's a good kid. A straight arrow."

"You know Jamal, I don't," I said, "but I doubt that you know everything about him."

"You're right," she said. "But if Jamal is into drugs it would come as a shock to me."

"Where would Teddy get the drugs?" I asked.

"You mean who is *his* supplier? You're sounding more and more like a narc, J.D."

"I'm just curious. Your trust fund friends are a whole new world for me."

"I know Teddy has shady friends. My last husband Ashley and I ran into him in a bar in Greenville once and saw him talking to a guy Ashley said was Eddie Smoke, a notorious local hoodlum and drug peddler. Ashley played at lawyering and hung out at the courthouse, and knew these kinds of things. Later, I tried to get Teddy to tell me what he was doing with a guy like that, and he said he was just an acquaintance of an acquaintance, and had just run into him at that bar. He said he barely knew him."

"Sounds like what Teddy said about Jamal and Wilson Kroll, too."

"What are you inferring?" Natasha asked, giving me a sharp look.

"Just wondering how much of what Teddy ever says is the truth."

"Jesus Christ, J.D.," she said. "I wish I'd never told you any of this," she said. "So, Teddy supplies a little pot to his friends. Big deal. He's my friend."

I'd touched a nerve talking about Teddy. She was overly sensitive when it came to him, with loyalty I didn't think he deserved.

"Just saying," I said, and left it at that. I needed Natasha's help and making her mad at me wasn't the way to get it. But Teddy knew things about Wilson Kroll and Jamal Johnson he wasn't telling. I'd bet my autographed Peyton Manning Super Bowl football on it, and it wasn't my instant dislike for him that made me believe it. Well, maybe that was part of it, but my gut told me Teddy was a bad actor. I just needed to keep my suspicions to myself around Natasha.

CHAPTER FIFTEEN

Natasha dropped me off at her place and told me to make myself at home while she ran some errands. The plan was to leave for the steeplechase party by five-thirty. She told me to feel free to shower or change or whatever I needed to do to be ready. She said she should be back long before then.

Five minutes after Natasha left, I was in my Jeep with the address of the dinner party Jamal worked that Friday night entered into my smartphone GPS. I wanted to drive the route he must have taken home, and since he was walking, it would most likely have been the shortest way to get there. Google maps gave it to me, and I saw that most of the route went through sparsely populated countryside except for a small strip that ran through the western edge of the town of Landrum. The dinner party where Jamal began his trek was east of Natasha's place on Hunting Country Road, among all the grand houses and horse farms, sparsely situated with heavily wooded areas and pastureland in between.

I took Hunting County Road to the South Carolina line, then turned south and did a bit of zig-zagging, and ended up on Columbus Road, which led into Landrum. The landscape was still rural, but the homes were much more modest. Small frame houses and double-wides sat along the road, separated by stretches of thick woods on either side. The chance that someone along the way saw Jamal that night was slim, but you never knew where I might find a clue to his disappearance. Looking at the GPS map, someone could have picked up Jamal anywhere between the party site and Landrum without being seen.

I drove slowly, scanning both shoulders of the road looking for I didn't know what—anything out of place, fresh tire marks, or something unusual that inspired another question to ask, or place to check out. I wondered if Deputy Waldrop drove this route, then realized he probably hadn't. This stretch of the road was in Spartanburg County, and out of his jurisdiction.

The only bit of excitement was the large dog that came out of a yard as if it wanted to chew my tires off for driving so slowly and gawking. I wondered if the dog was awake and out the night Jamal walked along here. If it chased slow moving cars, it would probably chase a pedestrian. I made a mental note to talk to the dog's owner. So far, this was my best chance to find someone who may have seen Jamal.

The road led to the outskirts of Landrum, and if Jamal made it that far, perhaps he hitched a ride home from someone he ran across. If Landrum was like most small South Carolina towns, the sidewalks would have been rolled up pretty tight by midnight, but it was another thing to check out. Maybe Jamal's girlfriend Monique could help with that.

I drove from Landrum to Jamal's house, with the rural landscape changing very little; nothing out of the ordinary got my attention. I turned around and headed back on the same route to Natasha's place to get ready for the party. The dog ran out at me again when I slowed down to look at its master's house. It was a small clapboard affair that needed painting, weeds outgrowing the grass in the yard, with a battered old pickup up on blocks near a corner of the house. There was no sign of a functioning vehicle there, so it looked like no one was home. The dog was a mixed breed with some Rottweiler or Pitbull thrown in, I suspected. Someone would need to be home to call the dog off if I came back. Otherwise, no way would I get out of the car.

I was back before Natasha returned from her errands. She came in carrying clothes from a dry-cleaner over her shoulder, and disappeared into her bedroom. I took a quick shower in the guest bathroom, put on a white shirt and chinos, knocked the dust off my loafers, and donned my navy blazer from my hanging bag. I was ready. Natasha emerged looking absolutely stunning in a little black cocktail dress, makeup for a change, and sparkly things dangling from her ears. I caught a glimpse of us in the mirror as we left. Compared to her, I would have been woefully underdressed in anything less than a tuxedo.

CHAPTER SIXTEEN

We took Natasha's SUV and drove east on Hunting Country Road to the Upcountry Steeplechase and Equestrian Club or *USEC* for short. I'd just passed by the place twice today, going to and from on Jamal's suspected walking route, but had paid little attention to it. According to Natasha, the grounds included 400 acres of forest, meadow and hiking trails, with show rings, riding trails and training facilities for the young and old for every equestrian activity imaginable. A horse lover's heaven that required a club membership for use. The property spread over both sides of Hunting Country Road, with the Equestrian Center, our destination, to the left, and steeplechase racecourse and stables, hidden mostly by trees, on the right. A beautiful and impressive place, even to a non-horse person.

We took the drive up the hill, parked and headed toward a sprawling building with dormer windows, thin white columns, and stone steps at the entry. Inside, was a large room filled with tables with white table cloths and straight-backed chairs. The place was a bit on the rustic side—with wood paneling and overhead wooden beams. A long buffet table sat against one wall laden with food—I spotted a whole smoked salmon and a large slab of roast beef with a carver in a white jacket standing behind it. A bar with a couple of bartenders stretched along another wall. We were early arrivals, but there was already a small group gathered around the food and the bar. If the attendance expectations were to match the number of tables and chairs, there would be a lot more people coming.

Natasha held my arm and escorted me toward the bar—and I happily followed, hoping they served a good single-malt scotch, perhaps even a well-aged Macallan, my one guilty extravagance—but once sampled, forever hooked.

Natasha abruptly pulled me off course and in a hushed tone, said, "That's Chuck's mother over there by the window, and she's seen me. If we don't go over and speak to her immediately, she will feel slighted and believe me, you don't want that old tyrant mad at you. Mrs. Norman considers herself the grand dame of the community, and I suppose she is. She can make life difficult in our close-knit social set if she doesn't like you. With one demeaning whisper in an ear, she could convince many here not to talk to you."

As we walked over, I noticed the old lady examining me as if I was a horse at auction. I just hoped she wouldn't try to pull open my lips and examine my teeth. She was wearing a dress from a different era, her silver hair up in a swirled heap on her head. She wore a diamond necklace that if real, which it surely was, had such large stones in it that it looked like someone had dumped the ice cubes from their drink on her ample breasts.

"I don't know why Chuck puts up with her," Natasha continued. "She's always putting him down in public like he's a backward child that can't do anything right. He must really love her because he has money enough of his own to live anywhere he wants."

"Who have we here, Natasha?" Mrs. Norman asked, in a demanding tone.

I was surprised she didn't deliver it in a faux British accent.

"Mrs. Norman, this is my special friend, J.D. Bragg," Natasha replied.

"How do you do," the old lady said, still examining me.

I fought off the insane urge to give her a sweeping bow and say, "m'lady," but I said, "Nice to meet you," instead.

"I swear, my dear girl," she said to Natasha, "I can't keep up with all of your *special friends*. Where did you find this large young man?"

Natasha dug her fingernails into my arm hard enough to draw blood, and I could only guess how hard she was fighting to stay civil to the old woman.

"He's up from Atlanta for race week, Mrs. Norman. We had lunch with Chuck today. Is he here?"

"He's probably at the bar," she said. "He won't stray too far from there. I just wish he had the sense to drink with moderation. I don't know why I let him drive me here tonight. He'll probably drink too much to take me home."

She addressed me directly for the first time.

"What do you *do*, young man?"

She'd pegged me right off as no trust-fund baby.

"I'm a sportswriter, ma'am," I said.

"He's going to write a story about our little horse community and the race this weekend, Natasha told her.

"You're not one of those disingenuous writers, are you? Asking your questions and smiling all the time, then writing an unflattering exposé that will embarrass us all? What is it they call that? Yellow journalism? I hope you're not that, young man."

"I try to write the truth, ma'am," I said. "How you interpret it is up to you."

She looked at me a moment longer, something in her eyes making chills run up my spine. I had the feeling that if she didn't like what I wrote, she would have me horse-whipped. Natasha was right. This was not a woman you wanted to cross. I pitied poor Chuck.

"Excuse me, but I see someone across the room that I *must* talk to," she said to Natasha, ignored me, and walked away from us.

"What the hell was that?" I asked. "Attila the Hun or the Wicked Witch of the West?"

"A bit of both, I'm afraid," Natasha said, "with a tad of Lucifer and Sir Richard Topcliffe, Queen Elizabeth's torturer, thrown in. She's always verbally abusing poor old Chuck. I remember being at their house once when Chuck sat a glass down on an old end table without using a coaster. It left no ring that I could see, and the table was nothing special, but she acted like he had destroyed a priceless antique. The tongue-lashing she gave him was unbelievable. She called him stupid, careless, and a lot worse, right in front of me. Chuck just sat there staring at the floor. I was so embarrassed for him."

We made our way to the bar for a cocktail, and the old lady was right, Chuck was standing there with an almost empty drink in his hand, looking like he was ready for another one. Having a mother like that would drive any man to drink, I thought.

"Hi Chuck," Natasha said. I nodded to him.

He was still dressed like a preppie, only the shirt was a different plaid from the one he wore at lunch, and he had put on a camel hair blazer with what looked like a family crest on the pocket. He had changed his top-siders to penny loafers—but still no socks.

I gave the bartender our drink orders. Natasha wanted an old fashioned, Chuck was drinking bourbon on the rocks, and I asked for a Macallan straight up. I was both surprised and delighted they had it. I reached for my wallet, and Natasha put her hand on my arm.

"The club membership dues cover everything," she said. "This is one of three annual parties we have here each year. The other two are Christmas and the Fourth of July, with fireworks at the track."

Free Macallan, I thought. I'll drink to that. I turned to Chuck. "I wanted to ask you something," I said. "I got the feeling at lunch you and Teddy weren't exactly on the same page when we were speaking of Wilson Kroll. Was there something you weren't saying about him?"

Chuck stared out the window, then turned back. "Teddy knows Mr. Kroll better than he let on," he said, "and I'm afraid for him. Teddy does things for him that could get him into big trouble. I told Teddy if he's caught, he'll get the blame, and Kroll will walk away scot-free. Wilson Kroll is a conniving, wicked man."

"I know about the drugs, Chuck. Is that it?"

Chuck glanced at Natasha irritably, as if he knew she was the one who told me. "Mr. Kroll throws parties for his friends from up north," he said. "Wild parties. Teddy supplies things for them."

I wondered what else Teddy did for the man? Kill his horse and frame an innocent boy for it? Or perhaps something even more sinister, like making Jamal Johnson disappear.

"I've said enough already," Chuck said. "Teddy is my friend, and I don't want to tell tales about him. Teddy needs the money. I can't stand to see him so desperate. It's tearing him apart. I've lent him all I can without Mother finding out. I hate to think what she would do if she knew." Chuck gave Natasha an angry look. "You're supposed to be his friend," he said. "You could help him if you wanted to."

"He hasn't asked me for anything," she said. "He knows I would help him if he'd let me."

"Maybe he's too proud to ask," Chuck said. "You know how he is."

There was an emotional edge in Chuck's voice. Maybe there *was* something to the gay rumors. Was there an unrequited love thing going on here between him and Teddy? Or was Teddy just something Chuck had few of—a friend.

Chuck turned to the bar, back to us, his shoulders slumped like someone who carried a heavy burden. With a mother like his and a friend like Teddy Crane, I could see why.

"Chuck, don't be that way," Natasha said to his back. "You know I love Teddy. We won't get him in trouble, and we won't tell him anything you say about him."

Speak for yourself, Natasha, I thought.

Chuck waved at us over his shoulder and walked away.

CHAPTER SEVENTEEN

Natasha and I moved to the buffet table. As I looked it over, she nudged me.

"Speak of the devil," she said, "that's Wilson Kroll and his wife coming in the door right now. I'm surprised. He doesn't usually come to these things."

I turned to see a middle-aged, short, stocky man walking toward us. He had hair too black not to be dyed and was accompanied by a thin, pale woman with anxious eyes. She was younger than him and with the beauty and bearing of a fashion model a couple of years past her prime. With them were two men in jackets and silk shirts, each with the top couple of buttons undone, the glint of gold chains in the bird's nest of hair on their chests visible from across the room. They looked like extras from a gangster movie.

"Introduce us," I said to Natasha.

She frowned but turned it into a smile as she stepped into their path.

"Hello Wilson, Susan," she said. "It's good to see you two here. It's been a while. How are you?"

"Natasha," Kroll said, forcing a smile. He gave me an enquiring look.

His wife said hello, and she and Natasha did the "kiss the air beside the cheeks' thing, then Susan Kroll faded into the background behind her husband as if she needed his permission to speak further.

"And you are?" Kroll said to me before Natasha could do the introductions.

"I'm J.D. Bragg," I said. "I'm with her."

She put an arm around my waist and smiled at him.

He didn't offer to shake hands or introduce his male companions. I noticed the two men examining Natasha, their eyes roaming freely up and down like they didn't care who saw it. I felt her stiffen beside me and knew they were making her uncomfortable. I stepped slightly in front of her to shield her from them.

"You're the one with the horse that got shot," I said to Wilson Kroll.

He studied me briefly before he responded.

"I've heard your name somewhere," he said. "Are you related to that newspaper publisher over in Pickens County?"

"My grandfather," I said.

"I saw you on the news. You're some kind of reporter."

"Sportswriter, actually."

He gave me a look that said he didn't see the difference.

"You writing something about the steeplechase?" he asked.

"That, and the community of horse lovers here who support it. In fact, I'd like to talk to you about your dead horse. I understand it was very valuable, and quite famous."

"What's to talk about?" Kroll said. "A nigger kid killed it out of spite, and the local yokel cops around here can't find him. I'm thinking about putting up a reward. Why don't you talk his mama into telling you where he is, and maybe you can collect it."

He studied me a moment longer, dipped his chin to me, and they moved off to the bar. One of the goons grinned at Natasha and made a barely audible kissing sound as he walked by her.

"Kroll gives me the creeps," Natasha said as we watched them walk away. "Almost as much as those two men with him."

"They do stand out a bit from your regular steeplechase crowd," I said.

"I wonder if he's throwing them one of those wild parties Chuck mentioned?" she said.

"Why don't you ask your friend, Teddy," I said. "He'll probably know."

"You really don't like Teddy, do you?" she said.

"No, and I'm trying hard to see why *you* do,"

"I know Teddy better than anyone. I'm not going to believe he's suddenly changed into this terrible person you think he is."

"When good things change, it's always before we want them to," I said. "In his defense, I don't know what it would be like to have everything I ever wanted or needed my whole life, then suddenly face losing it all. Something that traumatic could blow a fuse or two in the old operating system, I guess. Who's to say."

I showed her my cell phone with a copy of the last couple of pages of Brandon Wise's chronology of Kroll's business records. "Are any of these people here?" I asked.

She studied the list. "Where did you get this?" she asked.

"From a guy I know, who for the time being, shall remain nameless."

"You can tell me. Aren't I part of the team?"

"I gave my word to keep him out of it. I keep my word."

"You're no fun at all," she said, but grinned at me. "At least tell me why you want to talk to them."

"They're mare owners who did business with Wilson Kroll's stud service. I'd like to talk to them about those experiences. Monique told us Jamal said Kroll's top stud was infertile. I want to know what they can add to that."

"This one is here," she said, pointing to one of the names, "I saw him earlier. "There, she said, nodding at an elderly couple at a table across the room. "McCauley and Edith Kennedy. I know them. They're nice people, and I'm sure they will talk to you."

I looked at the list. Mr. Kennedy had bred a mare named Edie's Girl with Emperor, a year and a half ago—a fresh mating marked as PAID, so it was apparently successful. Then several months ago, Kennedy used Emperor twice again with the same mare, Edie's Girl, both fresh procedures. The first was marked NOCHG, the second PAID. Which inferred that the first time didn't work, Kennedy got a do-over, and that one bore fruit. What interested me about these two was they were the last *fresh* matings with Emperor before they all went to *frozen or chilled.*

CHAPTER EIGHTEEN

I followed Natasha over to the Kennedys table, and she introduced me, telling them I was a sportswriter, writing a story about the community and the Upcountry Steeplechase. She asked if they would mind sharing some of their experience raising and training thoroughbred horses with me.

Natasha said, "Mr. Kennedy has raised several steeplechase champions."

"Impressive," I said. I hope we're not intruding."

"Not at all. We'd be happy to help if we can," Mr. Kennedy said. "Do you write for some horse or steeplechase publication?"

"I'm with *SportsWord* magazine," I said.

"I know that magazine," he said, "but I didn't know it covered equine sports."

"We cover the results of most major flat track races, but I don't do that. I'm a feature writer, and this is as much a human-interest piece, as it is about the race this weekend."

They invited us to sit with them.

Mr. Kennedy was a distinguished looking man with a thick head of the whitest hair I'd ever seen and bright cerulean blue eyes. He wore a brown corduroy jacket and a beige necktie with tiny prints of horses on it, looking every bit the horse breeder. His wife was pleasant looking and probably considered "cute" when she was young.

"What would you like to know?" Mr. Kennedy asked.

What I wanted to know was if Wilson Kroll's prize horse was infertile and he had it killed it for the insurance money, but I couldn't begin with that.

"How long have you been breeding and raising horses?" I asked.

"Since I was a child," he said, smiling. "My father raised horses in Maryland and I helped him with them from a young age. Her father raised horses, too," he added, looking at his wife. Their place was right next to ours, so you could say we grew up in the business together."

"We were childhood sweethearts," she smiled and said, "and we shared such a love for horses that after we were married and set out on our own, we bought land down here and built the house we still live in."

"Do you breed your mares to your own stallions, or do you use stud services?" I asked, already knowing the answer to half of that question.

"Both," Mr. Kennedy said. "There are always better stallions elsewhere that can sire more valuable foals. You can't afford to own them all. Lineage and breeding, that's the name of the game."

I know absolutely nothing about horse breeding," I said, "Maybe you can tell me how you do it."

Mr. Kennedy took me through the whole process with a detailed description so vivid that anyone outside of horse breeding, myself included, would probably find uncomfortable, especially in mixed company. The part about jacking off a stallion and then sticking a hand and arm up to the elbow in a mare's vagina to insert the semen was particularly X-rated. Edith Kennedy and Natasha listened in as if we were discussing pie baking. I tried to avoid their eyes and couldn't help looking at the buffet table and hoping that these horse people all washed their hands before coming here tonight.

When he'd finished, I said, "I was just talking to another breeder, Wilson Kroll. Do you know him?"

"Yes, I know him," Kennedy said, and looked like he'd just bitten into something sour.

"It's a shame about this horse of his getting shot," I said. "What was its name, Emperor? I understand he was a very valuable stallion. Did you ever breed any of your mares to him?"

"Three times," he said and gave me an evasive look. It was apparently a subject he wasn't comfortable talking about.

"How did it go?" I asked. "Were the matings successful?"

Again, I got the sour expression.

"The first time was, the second two weren't." he said.

Kroll's records showed the first of the second two was marked NOCHG, but the next one, the one I assumed was a do-over, was marked PAID, and was therefore successful. What was going on here?

"Do you have to pay for the service if a mating is unsuccessful?" I asked.

"Not usually, with a *reputable* breeder," he said.

Ah, I thought. The first shot fired at Wilson Kroll.

"So, what went on with these last two matings? Why didn't they work?"

"It depends on who you talk to," he said. "Mr. Kroll and I have differing opinions. He blamed it on my mare, I blame it on his stallion."

"So, did you end up paying, even though no foal was produced?" I asked.

"Yes, I did," he said, and there was an underlying tone to his voice that said he was still angry about it. "But there's no use talking about it now," he added. "What's done is done."

"I'd still like to hear about it," I said.

"Nothing was wrong with my mare," he said, his face darkening. "My vet checked her out thoroughly. She was ovulating both times. She is a foaling machine. She is presently carrying a foal from a different stud service."

"So what was the problem?"

"I questioned the quality of Emperor's semen, and so did my vet. Kroll took offense. He produced a document that showed Emperor was registered and in good standing with the appropriate horse associations, his semen tested for fertility, viability, and freedom from disease, and approved for breeding. It was signed by Kroll's veterinarian, Samuel Squires. My vet expressed his doubts about that report, and Mr. Kroll didn't take that well. We got into it, words were said, and Kroll hung up on me. He sent a bill, and I got a lawyer. It wasn't a matter of money anymore, it was a matter of principle."

"What happened then?"

"My lawyer wanted Kroll to get a third-party veterinarian do another semen evaluation on Emperor. When Wilson heard that, he got madder than hell and said that just the suggestion of that amounted to slander, and he threatened to sue me."

"What did you do?"

"I sat down and thought about it long and hard. The stud fee for a horse like Emperor was substantial, but the legal fees would top that if I went to trial and lost. My lawyer advised me to drop the case. He said we couldn't win it. Even if we got a judge to sign an order to test the horse, the new test wouldn't supersede Kroll's vet's test, which was done—supposedly—at the time of the mating. I knew I was in the right, and Wilson Kroll was wrong, but I realized it's impossible to win a battle over principle if you're fighting someone with no principles. So, I paid his bill to be done with it."

"I take it you and Wilson Kroll don't do business anymore," I said.

"Of course not," Kennedy snapped. "This is the first time in a long time I've even been in the same room with the man."

He had obviously seen Kroll.

"What would you think if I told you Mr. Kroll stopped selling Emperor's fresh semen presentations right after the failed attempts with your mare, and for the last few months has sold only chilled and frozen semen?"

Kennedy stared at me a little too long, a crease forming between his eyebrows.

"I don't believe I told you the dates of my trouble with Kroll," he said. "You seem to know more about this than you let on, Mr. Bragg."

He and his wife were both frowning at me.

"What is this your story of yours really about?" he asked.

"It's what I said it was. But there may be a subplot. I don't think the kid, Jamal Johnson, shot Wilson Kroll's horse. I think Emperor became infertile some time back and Kroll had it killed before anyone could learn of it. I hope to prove that."

Kennedy was slowly shaking his head. "Mr. Bragg, you seem like a nice fellow, but you don't know who you're dealing with. There's a part of my story I didn't tell you. Two days after Kroll heard we were going to ask for the semen evaluation, a couple of men caught my lawyer in a restaurant parking lot in Greenville and damn near killed him. They beat him senseless. He has a wife and two young kids. They never found out who did it, nor why. I have my ideas, of course, but I've got no way to prove it."

"When did your lawyer advise you to drop the case," I asked.

"When I went to visit him in the hospital the next day."

"Who did he say beat him up?"

"Muggers. They took his wallet and watch. It was dark, they hit him from behind, and he couldn't describe them. Or at least that's what he said. I think he was afraid to identify them. Last I heard, he was working with his father-in-law over in Alabama and studying for his Alabama law license."

"You think Wilson Kroll did it?"

It was a moment before he answered.

"Not Kroll himself, perhaps, but someone on his behalf. I hear he has mobster friends. Maybe he sent *them.*"

Kennedy stood up and pulled his wife out of her seat with him.

"Come on mother, it's time to go," he said, and turned back to me.

"Look, Mr. Bragg," he said, "Wilson Kroll is a dangerous, wealthy man who has no problem spending his money to get what he wants—or, spending it to get what he *doesn't want* to go away. My advice is to stay clear of him."

He paused long enough to make sure I understood. "Good night to you, Natasha, and good *luck* to you, Mr. Bragg."

I stood thinking as I watched the Kennedys walk away. Natasha told me the rumor about Kroll having mob connections, and I believed her. I'd seen two of them with Kroll tonight. But as to Kroll having them beat up Kennedy's lawyer, as Kennedy suspected, I didn't buy that. Mr. Wise, the insurance investigator, told me Kroll's horse syndicate had millions of dollars of his friend's money invested in it. If these mob buddies were those friends, Kroll wouldn't want them anywhere near a lawyer who was trying to prove Emperor's infertility. Any hint of that and they would suspect they were in an investment gone bad, and wouldn't be happy about it. And these guys weren't the types to take Kroll to civil court. They were more likely to take him out somewhere and put a bullet in him.

My bet for the lawyer-beating was this Eddie Smoke Natasha told me about, with Teddy Crane, the arranger, and go-between. I had Smoke down as Teddy's drug supplier, and who knows what else. It was a short leap from that to Teddy paying a couple of Smoke's knee-breakers to do an odd job for Wilson Kroll. And if Wilson Kroll would have a lawyer beaten to keep Emperor's infertility a secret, what would he do to shut Jamal's mouth?

CHAPTER NINETEEN

More people were arriving by the minute, and the place was beginning to fill up.

"Mr. Kennedy and I share the same veterinarian," Natasha said. "Dr. Whitmore. If he had doubts about Kroll's records or contracts, there were probably good reasons. Dr. Whitmore is a great vet. The best and most respected in the area."

"Do you think he's here tonight?" I asked Natasha. "I'd like to talk to him. See if he'll add anything to it, or has heard anything about Kroll's dead horse. It's bound to have been a big topic of conversation lately."

"I saw him when we came in. Let's see if we can find him."

We wandered around the room, grabbing a plate of food along the way. She introduced me to her neighbors, the Rosses, who employed Millie Johnson. They could have been as rich as King Solomon, but from their genuine friendliness to me and down to earth demeanor, they could have been anybody's next door neighbors.

I met another nice lady, a widow from a family whose name was synonymous with the tobacco industry in America, and she was as warm and friendly as your favorite aunt. The rich may be different, but to some, it's only the number of zeroes on their bank accounts.

Not everyone there were trust-fund-babies, but most *were* wealthy. I saw but didn't meet, a retired network TV news anchor whom I would have known even if I was blind. I kept hearing his familiar baritone wafting across the room. Another was an aging, but still very recognizable major league baseball player, who I think I remembered reading somewhere lived in the area and raised thoroughbred horses. I didn't get a chance to ask him if he did business with Wilson Kroll.

As we mingled, Natasha asked friends here and there if they'd seen Dr. Whitmore, her veterinarian. Some had seen him earlier; others hadn't seen him at all.

We came upon a group of men out on the front porch, drinks in hand, a few of them grabbing smokes. We caught them laughing uproariously over something, but they quieted down as we joined them. If they were laughing at something too indelicate for Natasha's ears, I couldn't imagine what that would be. She could probably swap jokes with a group of Australian sailors. Obviously, it was the stranger on her arm that put the damper on them.

Chuck Norman and Teddy Crane were on the outside perimeter of the group, Teddy in his trademark hat and cowboy duster. They didn't seem to be joining in on the joke. Both wore serious expressions as they watched us approach.

Natasha kissed Teddy on the cheek, but he was visibly cool to her. Chuck had probably told him we were talking about him and asking questions. I nodded to Teddy, but he didn't speak. He just glared at me with undisguised distaste. I guess he'd come to dislike me as much as I disliked him.

Natasha looked at him with concern. She had felt his snub, and I knew her thoughts would be antithetical to mine. She *cared* if he was mad at us.

She grabbed my arm and pulled me away to introduce the rest of group; they were the husbands of so and so, or this or that acquaintance. An ex-boyfriend and an ex-husband were in the group, which probably added to the cold-shoulder they initially gave me, but nobody asked me any personal or intimate questions. Of which I was thankful.

Teddy still watched us with a smug look that rankled me. But of course, everything he did annoyed me. I left Natasha talking to her friends and edged back over to him. I had a burning desire to wipe that smugness off his face, even if I had to tell a white lie or two to do it.

"Don't know if you heard," I quietly said, "but Jamal Johnson kept a journal—like a dairy—and I'm about to get my hands on it."

"Why would I give a fuck about that?" he snapped.

"Because I hear you're in it."

He looked at me with disbelief. "Bullshit," he said. "What could he possibly say about me? I told you, I barely knew him."

"Evidently, he knows *you*. I'll tell you more when I read the journal."

Teddy didn't respond, but his eyes revealed wheels grinding in his head as if he were trying hard to process what I'd told him.

I moved back to Natasha's side. I didn't think she'd even noticed I'd been away. She was talking and laughing, the center of attraction, which I was sure she was accustomed to in any gathering of males.

I asked the group if anyone had seen Doctor Whitmore, the vet, and for a change, got a positive answer. One of them said the doctor was down at the Steeplechase barns. Something about a sick horse.

Natasha explained to me that the Steeplechase barns were outside the narrow end of the track on the east side.

"Is that close enough to walk?" I asked.

"If you're up to it. It's five-hundred yards or so, I guess," she said, "Why?"

"I think I'll take a walk down there and try to find your vet. Want to come?"

"These Jimmy Choos I'm wearing aren't made for hiking, but *you* can go. Just tell Dr. Whitmore you're a friend of mine. He'll talk to you. I'll hang out here with the boys until you get back."

I noticed her drink was empty. "Can I get you another drink before I go?"

"If you insist." She handed me her glass.

When I got back with her drink I noticed Teddy and Chuck had left. "Where's Teddy?" I asked her.

"He's in one of his moods. Angry at the world. Chuck went to find his mother, I think."

I stayed and small-talked a bit with Natasha and her friends, then left her with them, and headed for the track.

CHAPTER TWENTY

Outside the USEC Center, I set off down the winding lane to the racetrack and the barn where I hoped to find Dr. Whitmore.

At the dead-end at Hunting Country Road, I hung a left and followed Hunting Country underneath the bridges of Interstate 26, as a steady stream of cars sped overhead on their way north to Asheville or south to Spartanburg. The highway presented a disconcerting modern sight and sound, contrasting rudely with the serene landscape of wooded hills and manicured meadows of Hunting Country Road below. I thought I heard a horse cross the road somewhere on a parallel course to me while walking under the bridges, but I realized it could have been the car tires bumping over the dividers in the concrete surface of the bridge above.

I cut through the trees off the road to the course where the Upcountry Steeplechase would take place on Saturday. The lights from the barns to my left, which must be the where I would find Dr. Whitmore, illuminated part of the track. A dense layer of grass created a surface quite different from a flat dirt track like the Kentucky Derby's Churchill Downs. The rest of the course, the infield, the other barns, and most of the four-mile track faded into the darkness beyond the barn lights.

To my right in the middle of the track was a hurdle, or jump, looking very much like a hedge grown in exactly that spot for that purpose. I knew from my homework it was constructed of a steel frame, stuffed with either plastic "brush," or fresh cut branches of evergreens, made to look like a hedge. I walked onto the track to take a closer look.

Something stopped me. I felt it a split second before I heard it as the earth shook beneath my feet. Then the sound of thundering hooves came echoing from behind the hedge. I stood frozen in place for a second, trying to figure out what was happening, then, like the quarterback I used to be, my instincts drove me toward the base of the hedge to avoid what I realized was coming. A thousand pounds of leaping muscle and bone and lethal hooves were about to come over the jump and down upon me like a crash-landing plane.

And that's what happened. The earth churned around me, dirt and grassy divots kicking up and flying into my eyes and mouth. I tried to make myself as small as I could, waiting to see if there were other horses to follow. But there was only the one, and luckily, I survived it.

The rider must have seen me crouching there, because he stopped a short way down the track, turned the horse around and rode slowly back. *What the hell was this jerk doing riding out here in the dead of night?* He could have killed me. My anger boiled over, and I wanted to drag the idiot off his horse and pound him into the ground like he almost did to me.

But something was weird here. The rider wore a mask. It was one of those creepy "Anonymous" masks the Occupy protesters wore, a stylized portrayal of a face with an oversized smile and red cheeks, a wide mustache upturned at both ends, and a thin vertical pointed chin-beard.

He carried what looked like a polo mallet in his right hand, and as he neared, he raised it and swung it at my head. I went down like a felled tree.

I regained consciousness in the back of an ambulance on the move, the siren going at full volume and a worried Natasha Ladd holding my hand. A young paramedic looked on but seemed to be paying more attention to Natasha than me. I had a terrible headache, dizziness, and no memory of why I was there.

I reached up with my free hand to find a cervical collar around my neck and a bandage on my head. The paramedic grabbed my wrist and pulled my hand down.

"Don't touch the bandage, sir," he said. "It's there to stop the bleeding, but loosely applied so as not to put pressure on the injury. If there are any bone fragments in there, we don't want them pushed down into your brain. They'll check that out at the hospital, but in the meantime, don't put your hands there."

"Thank God you're awake," Natasha said, squeezing my hand tightly. She was red-eyed from crying.

"What happened?" I asked.

"Some fool was out jumping in the dark. You were walking on the track by a hedge as he came over it, and you got hit in the head by a hoof. It was probably some kid on a dare, or with too much drink. We called the police."

Somehow that scenario was all wrong, but I didn't know why. A hundred images like pieces of a scattered jig-saw puzzle filled my head, but they were only incomplete glimpses of some bigger picture I couldn't seem to construct.

"Dr. Whitmore was the one who found you," Natasha continued. "He was in the barn examining one of Saturday's horses that has a bit of colic. He heard a horse running on the track and went to see who would be doing such a thing at night, and that's when he saw you. He sent word up to the USEC Club, and when we heard a jumper hit a man down at the track, it practically put an end to the party. I was afraid it might be you. Doctor Whitmore called the paramedics, and here we are. So, hang on, we're five minutes from the hospital."

CHAPTER TWENTY-ONE

At the hospital, my memory returned. As the doctors poked, probed, scanned, and looked deeply into my eyes and pronounced only a scalp wound and a slight concussion, my recall of the incident crystalized. The pieces of the puzzle fell together to create a bizarre scene. A horse's hoof didn't hurt me. A man on horseback, wearing an "Anonymous" mask and dressed like Teddy Crane hit me with a polo mallet.

In fact, it *was* Teddy Crane. I was sure of it. Teddy wanted me to stop asking questions about him, and so did Wilson Kroll. But while Kroll may have been behind it, It was Teddy's slim build, not short and stocky Wilson Kroll on that horse. Had Teddy made his jump a split second sooner, I would have been pummeled into the ground by his horse's hooves, and would never have seen what the rider was wearing—or what his physical characteristics were.

When they wheeled me out of ICU and into a regular room, Kelly was waiting. Once settled in bed, Kelly came over, took my hand, and squeezed it.

There's something about a near-death experience that makes you see the world in a brand new, optimistic light. Dodging such a close call was like a rebirth of the spirit. I held Kelly's hand tightly and couldn't stop looking at her. There were no words for how beautiful she looked at this moment.

"You didn't have to come," I said. "I was going to call. I'm fine."

"You may be a fine specimen of a man, but you're *far* from fine," Kelly said. "That horse could have killed you. Natasha called and said you were going to be okay, but I wanted to see with my own eyes."

Natasha came in wearing a smile, a big change from our ambulance ride. "You're looking better," she said. "A little," she added, looking at the stitches in my head.

"Look," I said, "there's something I haven't told anyone yet. You both need to listen."

Natasha walked over and stood by Kelly, apprehension on their faces.

"My brain has been too scrambled to process what happened," I said, "but it's finally clear. The horse didn't hit me. The rider did. After he jumped the hedge and missed me, he came back and hit me in the head with what looked like a polo mallet—which tells me I'm getting too close to something by asking questions, and someone wants me to stop."

"Did you see his face?" Natasha asked.

"He was wearing a mask. One of those Anonymous masks, like the Occupy Wall Street protesters on TV."

Both Kelly and Natasha were looking at me like my brain was still scrambled.

"Natasha," I said, speaking directly to her, "This guy wore a long coat with split coat-tails. They were flapping behind him off the horse's rump when he jumped over my head. It was Teddy in that cowboy duster he wears."

"That's ridiculous," she said. "You said the rider wore a mask. And Teddy isn't the only person around who wears a long coat like that."

"Name one," I said.

She couldn't.

Natasha turned to Kelly. "J.D. doesn't like my friend, Teddy Crane. He thinks he's capable of the most awful things. But he isn't. I've known him since we were kids. He's just trying to deal with some heavy personal problems, and not doing very well with it."

I would tell Kelly what I thought about Teddy later.

"You've really got it in for him, don't you?" Natasha said. "This is so not like Teddy. Doesn't it sound like some crazy teenager like the police think? Or maybe someone protesting the race or something, someone who thinks it's cruel to put horses through things like that, or that it's a sport that typifies the rich ugly American, or whatever. People are protesting everything these days, and they can get violent. Look at the tree huggers who drive iron spikes into trees to hurt loggers, or some of the 'black lives matter' bunch who burn and loot."

"Did Teddy return to that little group I left you with?" I asked.

"No, but that doesn't mean he was down at the track trying to kill you. He was angrier with me than you. He thinks I've stabbed him in the back talking about him. He's hurt. He probably went home."

"We'll just have to agree to disagree about Teddy," I said. "Time will prove who's right."

That didn't seem to mollify Natasha, and she was about to say something else when Kelly interrupted. "You shouldn't be talking about this right now, J.D. You need to rest. I'm going to spend the night with Natasha, but I'll be back early in the morning to take you home. You can stay with me and get well, and you won't be around for this crazy person, whoever he is, to try something like this again."

She gave me a quick kiss on the lips, and patted my cheek. "There's a policeman outside waiting to see you. Make it quick and as soon as he leaves, get some sleep."

"Natasha looked at me, the things she still wanted to say pooled in her eyes, but she didn't say them. She followed Kelly out, both waving goodbyes.

No sooner had they left, a stocky guy with a thin mustache wearing a dark-green uniform with a large gold badge on the shirt came in. He was carrying a campaign hat and a small notebook and a pen. He introduced himself as Deputy Howard from the Polk County Sheriff's Department, took a seat in the chair by my bed, and gave me an earnest look.

"Your lady friend said to make it brief," he said, "and I will. "I just need to know your side of things and if you recognized the rider of the horse that ran over you."

He clicked the ballpoint pen, ready to write.

"In the first place," I said, "the horse didn't run over me."

"What?" he said, surprised. "Everybody else says . . ."

"Everybody else is wrong," I said and retold the story.

When I'd finished, Officer Howard was looking around the hospital room as if he was trying to find a doctor to tell him I was still suffering the effects of the blow I took.

"Have you found the horse yet?" I asked. "Obviously, you haven't found the rider."

"We found the horse wandering loose at the north end of the track. It was taken from one of the stalls up at the barn by the USEC clubhouse—without the owner's knowledge or permission. The horse was a jumper used by the man's

12-year-old daughter, who takes lessons at the Center. And no, we haven't found who did it. Based on what everyone has said, I assumed it was someone horsing around—excuse the pun—maybe from the party up at the clubhouse."

If he was talking about Teddy, he would be right, I thought.

The cop looked at me a little longer.

"Mr. Bragg, you must know what you're saying is a little *strange*, to say the least. No one else reported the incident happening like that."

"No one else saw it," I said. "I was out of it when they found me, and a little too dazed to talk when they brought me in."

"Don't take this as an insult, but are you sure you aren't still a bit *dazed*?"

I laughed. "Believe me, it's as weird to me as it is to you, but that's how it happened."

He gave me another look and began writing things down in his notebook.

"And you have no idea why this person did this to you?" he asked. "I know you're from Atlanta, but have you made any enemies while you've been up here? Somebody who may have it in for you?"

Without more proof, I wasn't going to tell him that. "None that I know of," I lied.

Officer Howard wrote more in his notebook then stood up. "I'll make a report on this and get back to you if anything turns up. But it looks like the perpetrator, no matter what his reason for hitting you, has gotten away, and we may never find him unless something unexpected comes along. If you learn anything yourself, get in touch."

He laid his card on my bedside table and left.

CHAPTER TWENTY-TWO

I woke up Thursday morning when they brought my breakfast. It was still dark out. I was tired and groggy, and my head ached. I felt like I hadn't slept at all, which was mostly true. All night long it seemed like every few minutes a nurse would wake me up, shine a penlight in my eyes, and ask how I felt. I started answering, "pissed off that you keep waking me up," but nobody took the hint, and they kept coming.

Kelly showed up a few minutes later and finished off my terrible cup of coffee and a piece of dry toast. "You look tired," she said. "How do you feel?"

"Like I've been hit in the head with a polo mallet," I said. "But I'm okay."

"I stopped at the desk, and the nurse said you were fine," Kelly said. "They're letting you go this morning. I'll wait. I don't think you should be driving yet, so we'll leave your car at Natasha's, and I'll bring you back in a couple of days to get it. Right now, you're going home with me and into my bed until you're fit as a fiddle."

"Why are fiddles fit?" I said, "I have never understood that."

She stopped and looked at me.

"You're doing that thing you do to change the subject," she said.

"What thing?" I asked.

"Saying something silly. So, what is it? What's wrong?"

"I'm going to stay at Natasha's, at least through the race Saturday," I said. "I need to keep at this story, especially since I've got their attention. Something is rotten here, and I've got to get to the bottom of it. There's more I need to do, and I can't do it from a bed in Pickens County, even if it is the best bed in the world."

"You're hurt," she said.

"I'm okay," I said.

"I'm not going to win this argument, am I?" she said. "Will you at least promise to be careful? Not only with this creep who tried to kill you, but with that injury to your head? Aren't you aware of all the bad effects of concussions that have been surfacing lately?"

"Look," I said, "I know you're trying to do what you think is best, and I love you for it. But I'm working a story here, and you, of all people, should know I won't quit."

She sighed a great sigh and looked at me. "Okay," she finally said. "But don't go walking in the dark alone again."

"I won't," I said, grinning. "I'll take Natasha with me."

"How would you like a knot on the other side of your head?" she said. "But I'll even agree to that if her company will keep you safer."

"Come over here," I patted the corner of my bed.

She did, and I took her hand. "That guy Natasha stole from you back in college? He must have been a complete idiot. Natasha Ladd can't hold a candle to you."

She gave me a kiss on the lips.

"I'll call you every day," I said. "And keep you posted on things."

"Just take care of yourself, that's all I want."

"I promise. So, let's get me out of here."

Kelly went to speed up my checkout and I lay thinking maybe I *could* use some help. Somebody to watch my back. I was a threat to someone, and would only become more threatening the longer I poked my nose into things. I thought of Alvin 'Big Hurt' Brown, Mrs. Johnson's scary nephew. He wanted to help, so why not let him?

After Kelly dropped me off at Natasha's and headed home to the *Clarion,* I called Millie Johnson's house. Alvin Brown was still there, and she handed the phone off to him.

"Somebody tried to kill me last night," I said. "Can you meet me somewhere?"

"Name the place," Alvin said.

I gave him the name of the 'Hare and Hound,' the restaurant where Natasha and I had lunch with Teddy Crane and Chuck Norman.

"I can be there in fifteen minutes," I said.

"Give me thirty," Alvin said. "I just finished my morning workout. I need to shower."

"See you there," I said. "It's on Main Street in Landrum. You can't miss it."

I was seated at a table in back when Big Hurt showed up. The restaurant was half-full with the lunch crowd, and still filling. It might have been my imagination, but an audible hush fell over them as Alvin came through the door. He stood for a second or two looking things over, his gaze like a laser slicing a path through the room, assessing everything and everyone in it. I thought I saw a couple of people flinch as his look passed over them. It was as if he approached all things with his defensive antenna up. He was dressed in all black again, wearing a black t-shirt with a large logo for "Chi-town Marshal Arts" on the front. It fit him like a second skin, and emphasized his chiseled biceps, pecs, and broad shoulders. Although I couldn't see his abs through the shirt, I knew they would resemble a washboard. He spotted me and came over.

"With a name like Hare and Hound," he said as he sat down, "I'm guessing this ain't no soul-food restaurant."

I caught him looking at the stitches in my head.

"I think I just figured out why you need me," he said.

"I guess I do need somebody to watch my back," I said. "I don't seem to be making too many friends up here. There are also two guys that need watching. I can't cover them both."

I brought him up to date on things as quickly as I could: Wilson Kroll and my ever-growing suspicion he killed his prize stud horse and blamed it on Jamal; that Jamal may have known things Kroll didn't want known—like the horse's infertility—and the insurance making it worth more dead than alive. I told him about Kroll's underworld friends, the parties Kroll threw them, and the drugs Teddy Crane supplied, and how Teddy might be doing other dirty work for Kroll. I described the mask-wearing mallet-wielding guy who tried to kill me, coattails flapping, and how Teddy often wore a cowboy duster, an affectation of trying to look cool. I told him about Eddie Smoke, and how he was probably

Teddy's drug connection. Alvin was staring at me when I'd finished. "You surely have popped the top off a whole can of shit, haven't you?" he said. So, what do we do?"

"We need to gather some real evidence. Most of what I've got is supposition."

"You're thinking this Wilson Kroll and Teddy Crane are responsible for Jamal's disappearance?" he asked. He'd stopped grinning.

I could read his thoughts. "You're not going to go all kung fu on anybody, are you? I'm in this to find out *who* did *what*—and if we find them, we turn them over to the authorities. You need to promise me that."

He sat turning the proposition over in his mind, and not looking too happy.

"I'll promise you this," he finally said. "I won't start anything, but I'm not going to take anything, either. And the cops get *one* chance to do their job."

I guess I'd have to live with that, whatever it meant. I gave a hesitant nod.

"What do I call you?" I asked. "Alvin? Al? Big Hurt? *Sir*?"

"My friends call me Alvin. 'Big Hurt' is from another life."

"Are we friends?" I asked.

"If you a friend of the Johnson's, you a friend of mine . . . until you do something to piss me off," he added, and grinned at me again.

"Alright, *Alvin*, I said. Let's get something to eat, then go for a drive. I'll give you the lay of the land."

The waiter came over and took our orders. Alvin ordered a bowl of vegetable soup and a garden salad. I ordered fish and chips.

"That fried food will kill you," he said after we ordered.

Health advice from an ex street-gang member whose hands were probably registered as lethal weapons. Could my world get any stranger?

CHAPTER TWENTY-THREE

I started out by driving Alvin west into Greenville County. When Wilson Kroll's mansion loomed into view, I pointed it out to him.

"Jesus," he said, staring at it.

"It is a little castle-like, isn't it?" I said.

"A little?" he said. "They got one like it at Disney World, only this one's bigger."

"My guess is, Kroll is going to throw one of his parties here either tonight, tomorrow, or after the race Saturday," I said. "He's already got a couple of hoods visiting, and there will probably be more. I want to see if Teddy Crane is supplying the party favors. We need to tie him and Wilson Kroll together officially."

"We try to break into that place, we gonna' need a battering ram," Alvin said.

"No breaking in," I said. "We don't do illegal. We might peek in a window, but we'll use stealth, not a battering ram."

Alvin got out his smartphone and took a photo of the place, then worked the keypad, entering something into it.

"What are you doing?" I asked him.

"Getting a picture and the GPS coordinates from the Maps APP and saving it, so I'll know where everything is, and how to get back here."

"I'm impressed," I said.

"With what? That a black street thug like me knows how to do that?" he said.

"I didn't mean that. I just . . ." I said, and turned to see a wide grin.

"I'm just playing with you, man," he said, still grinning. "You got to get a sense of humor if we're going to work together."

"You realize how much you don't look like someone with a sense of humor, don't you?"

"Looks are deceiving. I've got a great sense of humor. You know what Martin Luther King would be if he was white?" he asked.

I looked at him a second, then said, "Okay Alvin, what?"

"Alive," he said and broke himself up. "Sense of humor," he said. "You ain't got one, you might as well be dead." He went solemn again. "But I got a serious side, too," he added, staring out the window. "I try real hard to keep a lid on that one."

"Hence the nickname 'Big Hurt?" I asked.

He gave me a menacing look. "Hence," he answered.

We drove west to the intersection with Oak Grove Road and did a U-turn, went past Kroll's castle again, and then back to Landrum, where Alvin picked up his Jaguar. From there he followed me up the route I had decided was Jamal's way home from the dinner party. The same dog ran out again, first at me, then at Alvin behind me. We crossed back into North Carolina and onto Hunting Country Road.

I'd called Natasha from the car and asked her to show us the way to Teddy Crane's house. Alvin's job would be keeping an eye on him, while I watched Wilson Kroll. Hopefully one, or both of them would lead us to something interesting.

Alvin followed me into Natasha's driveway and we parked in front of her bungalow. He walked up and joined me as I got out of the Jeep. I saw him looking at the big house next door.

"That belongs to her parents," I said. "Natasha lives in the bungalow here."

"Some neighborhood," he said.

He was taking pictures when Natasha came out.

She nodded to me, and turned to Alvin.

"How are you Mr. Brown?" she said with her most charming smile. "I'm happy you've agreed to help," she added.

"Call me Alvin," he said, looking at her.

I noticed the fearsomeness in his eyes had faded.

"Your parents kick you out? he said, nodding to the big house. "Or did you run away from home? If you did, you didn't get far."

Natasha was taken back at first, then laughed. "A little bit of both," she said.

Alvin laughed, too. We were becoming an odd assortment of friends.

Natasha got into the Jeep with me, and we headed out, Alvin followed. He and Natasha stayed in constant contact on their cell phones as she led us to Teddy's house on Hog Back Mountain Road. Once there, Alvin would find a hidden spot nearby and stay to spy on him, while I would come back and stake out Castle Kroll.

"I don't know what you think you'll catch Teddy doing," Natasha said to me. "You've got the wrong idea about him, you'll see."

"Yes we will," I said. "That's the whole point of this."

She just shook her head and looked out the window. We went west out of Tryon, found Hogback Mountain Road, and followed its winding route up the back side of the mountain. At some point, we passed back into South Carolina and into the Dark Corner, then made our way toward the TV tower looming above on the pinnacle of the mountain.

As we neared the top, Natasha announced that Teddy's place was coming up on the right. It was the rustic mountain cabin Natasha said it was, but bigger than I had envisioned. There was obviously a lot of remodeling done to it over the years, but it was still essentially a log cabin, with a wraparound porch, a second story, native rock front steps, and a stacked-stone chimney at one end. It perched at the edge of a box-car-sized chunk of granite with a cliff's-eye view of the trees and hills and steep valleys to the north. There was little sign of human habitation in any direction.

Parked out front was the obligatory horse-country Suburban, dark green and several years old, with a few dents and scrapes on it. It looked almost as bad as my old Jeep. A candy-apple-red Harley Davidson chopper sat in an open garage to the side of the house. Natasha said those were Teddy's only vehicles, so he was probably home.

Natasha and I both scrunched down in our seats and looked away as we drove by the house. Teddy didn't know Alvin, so there was no reason to have him do it. In my rear-view window, I saw him taking pictures again. Natasha spoke to him on the phone and told him we'd go past the house a short distance and turn around. That way, if Teddy saw us go up, he would see us go back down again, and hopefully, take us as rubbernecking tourists out for a drive.

"I feel horrible about this," Natasha said. "I'm betraying Teddy. A friend wouldn't help you spy on him."

"I'll never tell him you helped."

We turned around and Alvin took the lead. After we passed Teddy's house again, he found a narrow dirt road leading off into the trees, stopped and backed up it far enough to hide the Jag from the road.

I drove past him and took the phone from Natasha. Alvin was still on the open line.

"You all set?" I asked.

"Who is this guy, Grizzly fuckin' Adams?" Alvin said. "We in the fucking wilderness here. I was hoping we'd be closer to civilization. I'm going to need some food."

"We'll bring you something," I said. "What do you want?"

"Sushi would be great, but my guess is the only thing they do with raw fish around here is roll it in cornmeal and deep fry it."

"Sushi?" I said to Natasha. "Alvin's getting hungry."

"There's a place about fifteen minutes east of Tryon just past Columbus in Mill Spring," she said. "It's pretty good."

"Surprise," I said. "We got your sushi. It's not far."

"Do I need to be worried about food poisoning?" he said.

"Natasha said it was actually a good place."

"Then get me an assortment of *nigiri* and a couple of bottles of water. And tell her my life be in her hands. I'll stock up for tomorrow when I leave tonight—after our boy turns in."

"Take me home," Natasha said, "and I'll go get it for him. You can then go see what Wilson Kroll is up to."

"Natasha will bring your food," I said to Alvin.

"For a rich white girl, she's alright," Alvin said. "Underneath the thousand-dollar-an-ounce perfume and silk blouses and shit, she's more like us than she realizes. She's a hunter, not a gatherer."

"Is that what you think we are?" I said. "Hunters? I'm not sure I see it that way."

"Skin color and upbringing aside, Bragg, I think you and me are much the same. We both got predatory demons inside us we turn loose on the unrighteous like the avenging hand of God. I've seen it in you. We don't rest until we track them down and bring justice to their sorry asses. You're afraid to admit it because you want to be socially acceptable. That's one place we differ. I don't give a damn."

"Jesus Christ, that got deep all of a sudden," I said, but I couldn't help thinking there was some truth in there somewhere.

It was almost dark when I got to Wilson Kroll's Castle, and I arrived just in time to see a small car with a lighted pizza sign on top go through the gate. I pulled over by the fence, doused my headlights and took my old pair of Weiss binoculars from the glove compartment. A Ford sedan with Ohio license plates sat in the circular drive in front of the house—probably belonging to Kroll's two buddies from the USEC party. The pizza driver parked beside it and got out of the car bearing a couple of pizza boxes, walked up to the front door and rang the bell.

Mrs. Kroll came to the door wearing a gray sweatshirt, and matching sweatpants. Lounging-around-the-house wear, I guessed. She paid the delivery guy and took the pizzas. I watched until the door shut behind her and the delivery man left.

I called Alvin and told him it looked like Kroll and company were in for the night, with no plans to party, and if so, I would most likely cash in early.

"I probably won't be here much longer, either," Alvin said. "I walked up and looked into Teddy's window. He was on the couch in gym shorts and a t-shirt nodding off to an old black and white movie on TV. Leftovers of a TV dinner and a couple of empty beer bottles were on the coffee table in front of him. When he turns in, I'm going into Tryon and get me a motel room. I don't want my coming and going at all hours to bother aunt Millie. She needs her rest, and I doubt we wrap things up this early the next couple of nights."

"I hope you're right," I said. "I'll be terribly disappointed if we don't catch Teddy and Wilson Kroll in some nefarious activity together."

"*Nefarious activity*, Alvin said and chuckled. "Running around with you is bound to improve my vocabulary," he added, and chuckled again.

"Are you making fun of me?" I asked.

"Just ain't used to hanging with such erudite white folks."

"*Erudite*?" I said. "Who's putting on whom here?"

"*Whom* indeed," Alvin said, chuckled again and hung up.

The guy still scared the shit out of me, but I was beginning to like him. I sat and watched Kroll's castle for a while longer, long enough to convince myself they were indeed staying in tonight. I called Natasha. She said she was a half-mile from Alvin with his sushi delivery.

I told her what Alvin had just said about Teddy, and that Kroll seemed to be having a quiet night at home, too, with the little lady and his wise-guy friends.

"How about you meet me for a bite to eat somewhere after you drop off Alvin's sushi?" I said. "I'm getting a little peckish myself. Pizza, maybe. For some reason, I've got a craving for a slice or two."

"Side Street Pizza on South Trade Street in Tryon," she said. "They have pasta, too, and serve beer and cocktails. How does that sound?"

"Then that's the place," I said. "I'll meet you there."

CHAPTER TWENTY-FOUR

The façade of Side Street Pizza looked like an old farmhouse, with a cozy little front porch, but I couldn't tell if it was authentically old, or just made to look that way. I went inside and found Natasha already sitting at a booth just inside the door. From the size of the crowd the food was probably good.

I joined her, and she handed me a menu.

"So, no wild party tonight at Kroll's Castle," she said.

"And your boy Teddy is in for the night."

"Tomorrow night would be my guess for Kroll to throw one of his parties," Natasha said. "It could be after the race Saturday, I suppose, that's the *big* party night. There will be after-race parties going on everywhere, with lots of people out and about, party-hopping from one to the other. But after-race celebrations are traditionally open to everyone, and I would think that after a day of drinking, some bold party-goer might see all the lights on at Kroll's house and the cars out front, and decide to party-crash to check out the Kroll castle. Kroll would probably want to avoid that and keep *his* party off anyone's radar. Tomorrow night would do that."

"We'll see," I said. I must have been wearing a hangdog look, because I caught Natasha studying me.

"You've got something on your mind?" she said. "What is it?"

"I was just thinking how much Kelly would enjoy the race this weekend."

"Then have her come over."

"Not unless we drop this boyfriend-girlfriend charade we've been carrying on. It's accomplished what it was meant to accomplish anyway. And what would Kelly do? Go as Alvin's date to keep up the ruse? Nothing against Alvin, but I don't see the need for that—and if she looks unattached, Teddy would end up hitting on her, and I'd have to punch him out."

"As Alvin's date, *nobody* would hit on her," she said laughing.

"Alvin wouldn't just punch him out," I said, "he'd kill him. This charade is getting too complicated. It's time to end it."

"Are you breaking up with me?" She said and faked a pouty face. "You're such a party pooper," she added, sighed dramatically, and began studying the menu.

"I was thinking," she said after a moment. "If Wilson Kroll *is* going to throw one of his infamous parties, he wouldn't invite his wife, unless they're even kinkier than I think they are. If she goes away somewhere tomorrow, it will be a good sign something is up."

"I agree," I said. "I'll stake out the place earlier than I'd planned, and watch for that."

"Not without me, you won't," she said. "I'm having fun."

"Fun? Have you ever been on a stakeout? We'll just be watching Kroll's place, hour after hour, all day long. It'll bore you to death."

"I'll bring a book. But you're not keeping me away."

"What if I gave you something else to do?"

She shot me a suspicious look.

"Like what?"

"Go to Mrs. Johnson's house and search for Jamal's journal. Get her to help you. Go through everything. Check for loose floorboards or baseboards. Look in the attic. Underneath the house. She'd likely feel more comfortable letting you pry through their stuff than me."

She sat and thought about it for a minute.

"I can do that," she said. "If you promise to call me if anything exciting happens."

"Deal," I said, reluctantly.

She leaned over the table toward me, looking over my shoulder and said, "Doctor Whitmore, my vet, and his wife are sitting in the back."

I turned to see a distinguished looking gentleman with gray hair and a woman who looked enough like him to be his sister, rather than his wife.

"If you want to talk to him, you'd better hurry," Natasha said, "It looks like they're leaving."

She was right; the waitress was handing the Doctor the check as we spoke.

I got up from our table and made my way back to theirs.

"Dr. Whitmore?" I said, "I'm J.D. Bragg, and I wanted to thank you for your help at the race track last night."

He looked up at me with surprise. His eyes went from my face to the stitches in my head, which I'd tried to hide with an unsuccessful comb-over.

"My goodness, young man, I didn't expect to see you up and around today, I'm glad you are, but maybe you shouldn't be. A horse's hoof is a whole lot harder than your noggin, and you took quite a knock."

The fact that it wasn't a horse's hoof was a whole other conversation I didn't need to have with him right now.

"I see you're about to leave, but I wonder if I could impose on you for a couple of minutes before you go. I have some questions I'd like to ask you."

Natasha appeared at my side and greeted them both. "Dr. Whitmore, I apologize for this intrusion, but J.D.'s writing a story on our steeplechase week, and I've promised him you would talk to him. He was looking for you at the track when he was hurt."

The Doctor and his wife both were looking at us with puzzled expressions.

"It would probably be a lot quieter outside," Natasha added. "I'll keep Margaret company while you're gone, if she doesn't mind staying a little longer."

"Well, I'm not sure what I can add to your story, but I'd be happy to try," Dr. Whitmore said and stood, pulling a pipe and a pouch of tobacco from his coat pocket.

"Margaret won't let me smoke in the car, so I'll take this opportunity to have my after-dinner pipe outside."

I followed him out the front entrance to the sidewalk and waited until he packed his pipe and lit it.

"I wanted to talk to you about Wilson Kroll's champion stud-horse, Emperor. The one that was shot," I said.

He looked surprised. "I'm not sure that I can tell you anything about that. Perhaps you should talk to Mr. Kroll or *his* vet."

"I don't think I can get the answers I want from them," I said. "You may know Kroll claims a kid named Jamal Johnson killed the horse because of a grudge the boy held against him. I don't believe that."

"All I know is what I read in the papers," Whitmore said.

"You've been a vet around here for years, Dr. Whitmore, and I'd bet you hear things, even about horses you don't treat. I think Kroll's horse was infertile, and he had it shot before anyone found out, and framed the kid to collect the insurance. I also believe Kroll has been fraudulently selling another horse's sperm and passing it off as Emperor's. If you know anything about that, please tell me. I won't say where I got it."

"You want me to gossip," he said. "I don't want to do that."

"Help me clear the name of an innocent boy, Doctor Whitmore."

The Doctor chewed on his pipe looking at me.

"I may have heard something in that respect," he said, "but it's just suppositions, and I won't repeat them."

He stood up, tapped his pipe empty on the side of the building, and put it back in his pocket. "However charming I know Ms. Ladd to be, I'm sure Margaret is ready to go home. She's an early to bed, early to rise woman, and has been for the fifty years of our marriage."

He seemed a bit hesitant to leave as if he was deciding something.

"Talk to Wilson Kroll's vet, Sam Squires," he finally said. "We've known each other for a long time. I hate to think this, but if Kroll is up to any fraudulent shenanigans, then Sam would have to know. There's no other way. What you've said takes a licensed veterinarian's stamp of approval."

It was what Brandon Wise, the insurance investigator, said, too.

Doctor Whitmore looked at me with genuine sadness. "Sam Squires was once a good man, and I would hate to think he's stooped to something like this, but he's not the man I used to know. He's suffered some bad times over the past few years, and it's changed him. He lost his only son in Iraq, and his wife went into severe depression. She eventually killed herself with an overdose of sleeping pills. Sam went downhill fast after that. He started drinking heavily and lost what business he had. I got most of it."

"Then how did he become Wilson Kroll's vet?" I asked.

"It surprised me when Kroll hired him, which made me look at Kroll for the first time as a benevolent and kind-hearted man. He gave Sam a steady job, helped him settle his debts, and get off the booze. Sam straightened out for a while—went to AA and all that—but recently he's started drinking again, not as much as before, but steady. He paces himself like veteran alcoholics do, so you don't notice he's snockered twenty-four hours a day. He has become a distressed man again.

"The last few times I saw him he seemed to be carrying around a heavy burden, and I don't think it has anything to do with the loss of his son or his wife. Something is troubling him again. I believe Sam is a man with a conscience, and I think he wants to talk about it, tell somebody, but can't, or won't. It could have something to do with Kroll, I don't know. Maybe if you told Sam what you believe, he would unburden himself."

"It's worth a try," I said. "If Squires came clean with Mr. Wise at the insurance company, maybe Wise can make it easier on him. I want to talk to Dr. Squires."

Whitmore looked at his watch. "Well, if you want to do it tonight, you can find him where he is every day about this time, sitting at the bar at McGourty's pub, just up the street."

"Thank you, Dr. Whitmore," I said.

He nodded at me, and I followed him back inside.

Natasha and Mrs. Whitmore looked up as we came in.

"Did you order for us?" I asked Natasha.

"I didn't know how long you'd be out there, so I didn't want the food to get cold. Did I do wrong?"

"No, that's perfect. Let's go someplace else to eat. McGourty's Pub. Know where it is?"

"Of course," Natasha said. "It's near Huckleberry's, where we had lunch the day we met. Why are we going there?"

"I need to see a man about a horse there. Tell you about it on the way."

She shrugged her shoulders and smiled. "You're the boss, big man."

I thanked Dr. Whitmore and shook his hand before leaving.

CHAPTER TWENTY-FIVE

We left our cars parked at Side Street Pizza and walked north on Trade Street to McGourty's Pub. It took less than five minutes. As we walked, I filled Natasha in on who we were going to see, and everything I knew about him.

"I know who Sam Squires is," she said. "It's terrible about his son and his wife, but if he's had anything to do with Jamal's disappearance I'm not going to feel sorry for him."

"That may be the leverage we use to get him to talk," I said. "Even if Squires shot the horse, as long as he doesn't have anything to do with Jamal's disappearance, and I can convince him Kroll does, then maybe he will fess-up to the Emperor scam to distance himself from anything more criminal. If I can get him to tell Mr. Wise at the Olympic Equine Insurance Company about it, then we've got Kroll by the ba—well, let's just say we've got him nailed."

"J.D, you can say *balls* around me," Natasha said. "I've seen them. I've even held—"

"Stop it," I said.

"Why J.D., that's the first time in years I've seen a grown man blush."

I tried to ignore her.

We entered McGourty's Pub. There were people there, but it wasn't crowded. "Look for the most depressed guy in the place," I said.

"I told you I know who he is. That's him at the far end of the bar, sitting alone. The tall, thin guy in the checked shirt and the long face. You're right. He does look depressed."

There were two open stools next to him, and we took them—me, the closer one to him. The bartender came over, and I ordered a beer and two menus.

Natasha checked out their wines and settled on a glass of house Merlot. The menus came, and we both ordered cheeseburgers medium, hers with fries and mine with pimento cheese and onion rings. When we placed our orders, I looked at Sam Squires and said, "Excuse me, aren't you Doctor Squires?"

He turned to look at me, his movements slow, his expression showing his thoughts were coming back from someplace far away.

"*Horse* Doctor Squires," he said. His speech was as slow as his movements. "Do I know you?" he asked.

"I don't think so," I said. "But I know you." I decided his long face and droopy eyes didn't help his down-in-the-mouth look. It was a face that would probably look depressed even if he weren't. But maybe I was judging him too harshly. He'd been through enough with the tragedies of his son and wife to pull down anybody's face, I guessed.

He looked around me at Natasha, and his eyes seemed to register a sharper focus, like he recognized her. He reached for a pack of cigarettes on the bar, took one out and lit it.

"I need to ask you a couple of questions," I said.

He caught the bartender's eye and pointed to his glass. The bartender nodded and began to make him a fresh drink. Squires turned back to me.

"What kind of questions? he said, eyeing me suspiciously.

"I want to know if you're willing to go down with Wilson Kroll when the cops get him, which they will inevitably do," I said. I gave him my most serious glare, but I probably just looked tired. I saw him, like Dr. Whitmore, glance up to my head and the stitches. Even horse doctors seemed keen on noticing fresh wounds.

"Who are you, and what are you talking about?"

I spoke to Natasha over my shoulder, "Why don't you go get us a table. I believe Sam would rather talk to me one-on-one."

Natasha got up and took her wine to a table without saying a word.

He watched her go and gave me a nervous look.

"I'm going to tell you something," I said, "and I want you to listen carefully. It may keep you from spending too much time in prison. Come clean about what you and Wilson Kroll have been up to. Get out ahead of it before it's too late."

"I don't know what you're talking about," he said. He was a terrible liar. He swallowed hard and looked at me as if he'd been expecting this moment.

"I'm talking about criminal fraud. Things like selling sperm from an infertile horse. That's a neat trick. How does one manage that? But you know how, don't you, because you're a part of it. Then the horse—good old Emperor—gets shot for the insurance money before anyone finds out he's infertile. But here's where the trouble is. Somebody did find out. An innocent black kid who Kroll then accused of being the shooter. Only he didn't do it. Who knows, maybe you did."

"I don't know what the hell you're talking about," he said, angrily, but there was a noticeable fear behind the anger.

I decided to heap it on. Here's the real kicker," I said. "I'm sure you're aware the kid in question, Jamal Johnson, has disappeared. Now let me ask you this. If the boy didn't shoot the horse and believe me, he didn't, why would he run away? I think they'll eventually find his body somewhere, and this thing you're into with Kroll won't be just fraud, there will be a murder charge added to it. They will at least charge you as a co-conspirator."

Sam Squires was visibly shaken and sat staring at me as if he was having difficulty processing what I'd just said.

"I didn't have anything to do with that boy. I would never . . . I don't know anything about him. If something has happened to him, it was Wilson's doing, not mine."

I had him. I placed a hand on his shoulder. "Sam, I know about your boy and your wife. I don't know how anybody could get through something like that. People say you were a good man before all the tragedy befell you. I think you still are. And I believe this is your chance to prove it. Wilson Kroll is a bad man. He took advantage of your situation, and before you knew it, you were in too deep into his criminality to get out. Now's your chance."

"Are you a cop?" he asked.

"I'm just a guy who knows what you and Kroll have been up to," I said. "And if I found out so easily, you've got to know the police will, too. It's just a matter of time until everything comes crashing down. Don't get caught up in things you didn't do."

I took the business card of Mr. Wise, the insurance investigator, out of my pocket and placed it on the bar in front of him.

"Talk to this man before it's too late," I said. "He'll take it from here. I'm sure if you cooperate, he'll try to make it easier on you. Nailing Kroll is worth several million dollars to him and his company."

"I know who he is," Sam said, looking at the card. "He's already been out asking questions. Do you work with him?"

"Let's just say we're working together with similar purposes," I said.

He looked as if he was going to push himself away from the bar, but didn't. His hands were trembling, and I couldn't help feeling sorry for the guy. Steve-the-bartender looked at us and started to come down the bar, but thought better of it and began laboriously shining beer glasses. I figured I'd done my best with Sam Squires and to say more might be too much. The guy seemed shattered.

I tapped a finger on the card in front of him. "Call this guy, Sam. Tell him everything. I don't want to see you go down with a scumbag like Wilson Kroll. Believe me, that's coming, and a lot sooner than he thinks."

I picked up my beer and joined Natasha at a table by the window.

"Well?" was all she said.

I watched Sam Squires pay his tab and stand up. He stared at Wise's card a moment, then picked it up and left through the back door.

I grinned at Natasha. "I think we just nailed Wilson Kroll's sorry ass to the wall."

"You're kidding," Natasha said. "How?"

"I think Sam Squires is going to rat him out."

"So, why don't you seem happy?"

"Oh, I am. It's just that the worst part of this—the question of Jamal Johnson's innocence and disappearance—remains unanswered."

Natasha was nibbling on the last of her French fries. My cheeseburger and onion rings were almost cold, but I ate them anyway, and we headed back to Natasha's place.

I called Kelly and brought her up on the day's events. I didn't tell her I was exhausted, my stitches itched, and my head ached. I said I was doing great. I asked her to come to the race with us on Saturday, reassured her I would drop the silly boyfriend-girlfriend charade Natasha and I had been playing. It had served its purpose. She, not Natasha, would be my date and that would make me tremendously happy. Kelly enthusiastically agreed to come. Five minutes after we hung up, I was sound asleep in Natasha's guest bedroom.

CHAPTER TWENTY-SIX

Friday I awoke rested and feeling better. It would take more than a polo mallet to the head to take me out of the game. Or so I would like to think. I still had a mild headache, but I would grin and bear it, hoping it would eventually go away. I popped some aspirin to help it on its way.

Natasha and I agreed that while I watched the Kroll Castle and Alvin stayed with Teddy, she would go to Millie Johnson's to search for Jamal's journal. I called Alvin, who was already on the job. He said there was no movement at Crane's cabin. Teddy must be sleeping late.

I was at my usual spot near Wilson Kroll's place by nine o'clock, drinking a take-out coffee I'd bought along the way. There were a couple more cars in Kroll's drive now, parked next to the one with Ohio plates I'd assumed belonged to the two goons I'd met with Kroll at the USEC Center party Wednesday night.

I pulled the binoculars out and studied the two new vehicles. They were both late model Lincolns, one dark blue, the other black, both with rental-car company decals and Greenville-Spartanburg airport stickers on the back bumpers. Whoever came in them flew in and drove from the airport since last night. They were here, I assumed, for the race, and hopefully, for a party Wilson Kroll would throw for them tonight.

Around lunchtime, one of the several garage doors on Kroll's castle rolled up. Kroll's wife came out pulling an overnight bag on wheels. She put it in the back seat of a Lexus, got in, and drove away. Whatever was going on, she wouldn't be there for it.

Not long after that, ten men came out of Kroll's castle, one of them Kroll. They split up and got into the two Lincolns. They were laughing and talking so loud I could hear their voices from where I was sitting, but couldn't make out the words. They were all dressed in loudly-colored golf shirts and wildly-patterned slacks. Several wore golf hats or visors. If I opened the trunks of the two cars, I would expect to find golf clubs. Kroll got behind the wheel of one of the airport rentals with a fit-looking silver-haired gentlemen riding passenger. Three other men took the back seat. The other five took the Lincoln, the two goons from the USEC party among them. They all drove away.

I ducked down in my seat as they went by, and then followed. They drove out Oak Grove Road to Highway Eleven, turned right, went a couple of miles west, and into the gated community of the Cliffs at Glassy, a swank housing development and golf club on Glassy Mountain. The golf course, I'd heard, was carved out of the top of the mountain. Glassy was the western half of the same ridge that formed Hogback Mountain, but unlike Hogback, which was mostly uninhabited, impressive houses with spectacular cliff-side views covered Glassy. From below, the mountain resembled a contemporary, expensive version of a cliff dwelling.

The gate and guardhouse stopped me. They required credentials to enter. You had to live there, be a member of the golf club, or a guest of someone who was, or you couldn't get in. It didn't matter. I knew where they were going and what they were going to do. I didn't think anyone would wear those colors if they were up to no good. I've never understood golf attire. They looked like circus clowns.

I called Natasha, and she said she and Millie Johnson had turned the Johnson house upside down and found no sign of a journal. She didn't think it was there and wondered if someone already found it—or if Jamal gave it to someone.

"By the way," I said, "Kroll and his buddies are playing golf right now at the Cliffs at Glassy, and I've got some time on my hands. Want to have lunch?"

"Sure," she responded. "How about that Pizza place we didn't get to eat at last night?"

"Okay," I'll meet you there. I'll call Alvin in the meantime and see if he wants us to bring him something."

My pizza was good, and Natasha had pasta, which also looked tasty. I ordered a to-go turkey sub on wheat, no mayo, and a large unsweetened iced tea for Alvin.

Surely that would be on his diet. There was nothing fried on it. I called him and told him about it, and he said Teddy was still there, and hadn't left his cabin all morning.

Natasha was staring at me when I put the phone away.

"Do you really think it's necessary to watch Teddy?" she said.

"We've been over this," I said. "You're the one who told me Teddy sells drugs. Chuck said he supplied drugs to Kroll's parties. Teddy says he doesn't know Kroll—obviously not true. I'd like to prove it."

"Why don't I just ask him?" she said. "He would probably tell me."

"Let's do it my way," I said. "If it doesn't work, I'll let you ask him. But until then promise me you won't tell him what we're doing."

"Oh, all right," she said, sighing. "But Teddy doesn't have anything to do with Kroll's dead horse, and certainly not with Jamal's disappearance. You'll see."

"So, no luck finding Jamal's journal," I said, to change the subject.

"Unless he has a super-secret hiding place. Millie and I did a thorough search and came up with nothing. We even knocked on walls and closet floors for hollow spaces," she said. "I've been thinking. If someone put the rifle in the shed out back, maybe the same someone went into the house and found the diary."

"Possible, I said. "But before we give up, why don't you go back and talk to the girlfriend again. Make double sure he didn't give the journal to her, or she can't guess where he hid it. Maybe she'll tell you something she wouldn't say in front of me. I'll try that red-headed kid again—Jamal's buddy, Ronnie Dill. We didn't ask him about the journal, since we didn't know about it at the time we talked to him."

I told her it looked like Kroll was planning a party for his friends tonight, and not to wait up for me. She wanted to come along on the stakeout, but I talked her out of it again, saying that Alvin and I might do a bit of party crashing and she didn't want to be there for that. She reluctantly agreed.

"I called Kelly and invited her to tomorrow's race," I said. "I informed her we'd dropped the charade and you and I are going to the race as what we are. Friends. And Alvin? Well, let's let Alvin be who he is, a scary *new* friend."

"We are friends, J.D., no matter how hard you've resisted me trying to make you more than that. It's just my nature. But if we change our story now, what about those people I've told we're more than just friends? They're going to think I'm a liar."

"You've never struck me as someone who cares very much about what other people think of you. And I mean that as a compliment."

"You're right," she said and laughed. "My reputation was shot a long time ago, so why not add liar to it."

"Anyway," I said, "your scheme enabled me to enter the community to meet the people I needed to talk to, and I thank you for that."

"Okay," she said. "You're welcome." She seemed to resign herself to the new plan.

"Could you call Kelly and tell her the particulars?" I asked.

"Of Course," she said, "and I'll get our tickets and passes from USEC."

Natasha left, and I took Alvin's lunch to him.

"Still no sign of Teddy?" I said after I'd parked the jeep and got into the Jag with him. I didn't think Kroll and crew would be finished golfing yet, so I decided I could keep Alvin company for a little while.

"Holed up like a hibernating bear," Alvin said, unwrapping his sub sandwich.

"I wish I knew if he had an 'Anonymous' mask and a polo mallet stuck in a closet."

"When he leaves, I could look," Alvin said.

I gave that some thought. "No, stay on him. If he's bringing drugs for a Kroll party,

maybe we'll catch him in the act. I wouldn't want to miss that. Proof of the deal would give us leverage on him, which we could use to try to get him to open up about what else he does for Kroll. Like shoot his horse and help frame Jamal for it."

I told Alvin about Wilson Kroll's crowd of new house guests, his wife leaving with a packed bag, and we both agreed a party was on. I left Alvin to eat his sandwich and headed to Ronnie Dill's house.

CHAPTER TWENTY-SEVEN

There was a beaten up old Chevy pickup parked in Ronnie Dill's front yard when I arrived. It looked like *daddy* was home. I figured Ronnie would be home from school by now, too, so I got out and walked up to the front door and rapped my knuckles on it. A heavy-set balding man in a dirty wife-beater and a three-day-old beard opened the door. He took one look at me, glanced at my Jeep in the yard, and said, "We ain't buying any," and shut the door on me.

I knocked on the door again, a little louder this time. The man I assumed was Mr. Dill, opened it again.

"Are you fuckin' deef? I told you we didn't want any of whatever it is you're selling. Now git off my porch."

"I'm not selling anything, and I'm not going away. This is about Jamal Johnson, a missing boy, and I'm here to talk to your son Ronnie about him." I lied and said, "Now you either get him to the door, or in about fifteen minutes you'll have to deal with a yard full of Sheriff deputies. Now, go get him."

He stood and looked at me for a couple of seconds, probably trying to decide if I was on the level or not. Then he turned around and yelled, "Ronnie, get your ass out here."

I guess my bluff worked.

He gave me one last scowl and disappeared inside.

Ronnie appeared, and I said, "Come outside and let's talk."

He gave a nervous glance behind him, then came out, closing the door behind him. He followed me out into the yard and stood waiting for my question, wearing an expression like he was expecting bad news. This poor kid, I thought. He was like a beaten puppy, cowering at every human encounter.

Over his shoulder, I saw the curtains in the window move. I kept my voice quiet, mostly out of spite, just so Ronnie's old man couldn't hear.

"I wanted to ask you about Jamal's journal."

He gave me a blank look, which was disheartening. He didn't know anything about it.

Then a thought seemed to pop in his head, and he said, "Do you mean that *notebook* he was always writing in?"

"Yes, that's it," I said, relieved. "Do you know where he kept it?"

"No," he said. "Jamal wouldn't let anybody read it, not even Monique. I asked him one time what he was writing in there, and he just said, 'personal stuff.' I figured it was like a diary, you know—like girls keep. I kidded him about that, but he just said it was for the book he was going to write someday. I believed him. Jamal is killer smart."

"So, you have no idea where he would have kept it?" I asked, trying not to sound too disappointed.

"Somewhere in his house, I guess. Miss Millie don't know? Ain't much gets by her."

"Not this time, I said. She doesn't know where it is, and we've looked. I was hoping there may be something in that journal to help explain why Jamal went missing. Give it some thought. If you think of some secret place he would keep things, call me."

As I started to walk off, he asked. "Is there any word on him?"

I shook my head.

He stood slump-shouldered and watched as I drove away.

I'd no sooner made it back to my stake-out spot at Kroll's when Natasha called. She said she'd talked to Jamal's girlfriend Monique again, and had nothing new to add.

At about five-thirty, the two cars with Kroll and his guests came back. They all disappeared into the house, and seemed in high spirits.

Later, a van arrived with the name of a caterer on the side. A man and a woman dressed in white chef's jackets made several trips into the house, unloading dishes in elaborately covered silver salvers, along with folded white table cloths and a large arrangement of flowers. I guess even *made-guys* like a bit of floral adornment.

Moments later, another van arrived and delivered what looked like a couple of cases of champagne, and a box of booze.

My phone rang. It was Alvin.

CHAPTER TWENTY-EIGHT

"Our boy is on the move," Alvin said. "Teddy's just past Landrum gassing-up on Highway 14 south. Meet me at the intersection of Belue Mill Road and Highway 14. Google maps show it's a four-minute drive from where you are, and you should be able to beat him there if you hurry. Pick a spot on the shoulder to park that heap you drive, and watch for his dark green Suburban. But don't let him see you. I'll be right behind him, and I'll swing over and pick you up. Be ready to jump in, so we don't lose him. And stay on the phone in case he goes in a different direction. Worst case scenario is we follow him in both cars with me guiding the way."

"I'm already rolling," I said, with Google Maps on my cell phone, showing me the way.

The intersection of Belue Mill Road and Highway 14 was heavily wooded on all sides, but someone had cleared a narrow strip of ground along the shoulder just before the two roads crossed. I pulled off the road onto it, parked, and pulled the sun visor down so Teddy couldn't see me when he came by. I didn't have to wait long—a green Suburban came flashing by headed south on 14, Teddy Crane at the wheel. I jumped out, locked the Jeep, and spotted Alvin's Jaguar approaching from the north. By the time he pulled over and stopped, I was at the edge of the highway, ready to jump in. Alvin's Jag barely came to a stop before we were off and running again. NASCAR Pit crews would have been proud of how synchronously we pulled it off. Teddy's SUV was still in sight ahead on Highway 14, but probably too distant to recognize me in his rearview mirror.

"The small town of Greer is also this way," I said, "but I think he's heading to Greenville."

"My money's on Greenville, too," Alvin said. "If he's going for drugs, I'm sure the drug of choice for Kroll and his guests would be high-grade flake, and I doubt something like that is part of any stash Teddy keeps on hand. So, the city is most likely where he'll find enough for a party."

I agreed with Alvin. I couldn't see the Cleveland guys stooping to crack cocaine or meth, and money would be no object. They'd go for the purest nose candy the highlands of Colombia could offer—and this required a dealer with heavy chops. Like Teddy's friend Eddie Smoke, I thought.

We followed Teddy at an inconspicuous distance, eventually coming onto Wade Hampton Blvd, where he hung a right, which would take him into Greenville proper. We'd guessed that one right, too.

Teddy led us through the city to the west side of town, the real estate becoming cheaper and shabbier as we drove. Teddy finally pulled into an apartment complex that looked more like a cheap motel than a building of permanent abodes. He parked at one end; we parked at the other. Alvin's shiny new Jaguar would look out of place here, I first thought, until I noticed a couple of Cadillac Esplanades and a tricked-out Harley at the other end.

There was a large dumpster bin between Teddy and us. Alvin nodded at it. "We'd get a better look at them from behind that," he said.

We got out and stealthily made our way over to it, each of us taking a side to peer around.

Teddy was out of his car and knocking on the door of a ground-floor apartment. He was wearing his slouch hat and cowboy duster. So far, I hadn't seen him dressed any other way. When the guy chose a role, he stuck with it.

The door opened, and he went inside. A minute later, six young women came out and got into his Suburban. Four more girls followed them out and got into an older Buick sedan parked across the lot—with one of them taking the wheel. They wore clothes that left no doubt as to their profession: skimpy outfits that showed a lot of leg and cleavage. A hooker for everyone, including Kroll, if my math was correct. The wife was away, but was she too dumb to suspect what went on at her husband's parties? They certainly had an interesting marriage.

"Our boy Teddy is supplying more than just drugs," I said to Alvin. "He's not only a pusher; he's a pimp." I wondered what Natasha would say.

Teddy came out with another man, middle-aged, dark-haired, and built like a cement block with arms and legs. I figured this was my first look at Eddie Smoke. He fit Natasha's description to a T.

Teddy was carrying a small package, which I guessed were drugs, and stuffed it into the pocket of his duster.

Another man came out and said something in Eddie Smoke's ear. I couldn't swear to it, but Smoke seemed to glance in our direction before turning back to Teddy and saying something. Teddy got into the SUV with the girls and drove away, the Buick following.

I heard the scuff of a footstep behind us and turned around. Alvin must have heard it too, because he turned with me.

Three guys with serious attitudes were giving us a hard look. One was taller than me, and a little heavier, the other two were smaller, but no less unfriendly looking. The tall one wore jeans, a sweatshirt chopped at the shoulders, and shit-kicker motorcycle boots. He had more tattoos showing than unadorned skin. We'd let Smoke's thugs sneak up on us.

"Who the fuck are you?" the tall one asked.

"City of Greenville Dumpster Inspectors," I said. "We're making sure this dumpster isn't rusted out." The two short ones glanced at each like they might even buy that, but the tall one wasn't as dumb.

"Bullshit," he said. "You got about three seconds before you find yourself in that fuckin' dumpster with your asses kicked."

"What if I said we were vice cops?"

"You'd be a lying sack of shit. I know all the vice cops."

"DEA?" I tried.

He turned to his two sidekicks. "He thinks he's funny," he said. "You guys think he's funny?"

I thought for a second one of them was going to answer yes, until the look the tall one was giving him changed his mind.

"He ain't funny at all," the sidekick said, as the other one nodded in agreement like a bobblehead doll.

I looked over my shoulder and saw Eddie Smoke and the man he was with making their way toward us. They were halfway here, and we were already outnumbered. It was about to get out of hand. I turned to Alvin, who had yet to say a word.

"I think it's time to go," I said to Alvin, nodding toward Smoke and the other guy who were closing in on us.

I took a step toward the car, and the tall guy put his hand on my chest and shoved me backward.

"You ain't going nowhere, dickhead," he said, opened his mouth to say something else, and Alvin chopped him in the nose with the side of his hand, and the guy went down like he'd been poleaxed. I heard Alvin yell "*Contact,*" right before he hit him. I had no idea what he meant by that.

One of the other hoods made a quick step up when the big fellow went down, and not to be left out, I gave him my best right hook to the chin. He dodged at the last second, and I caught him in the throat. He went to his knees hawking like he'd swallowed a chicken bone. The sound of running feet closed in on us from behind, Eddie Smoke, if that's who he was, was pulling a gun from his belt. Alvin grabbed my arm, and we ran for it. We made it to the car, got it started, and peeled away before Eddie Smoke, and what was left standing of his gang, could catch up.

We were a block away before I asked Alvin what the hell he meant by yelling "contact" when he hit that guy. He sounded like a World War I aviator starting a biplane.

"The dude made the first contact," Alvin said. "He pushed you, and that started it. At that point, we were within our legal rights to defend ourselves. So, I did."

"You actually thought that through before you hit him?"

"Didn't have to think," Alvin said. "It's one of the things I teach."

"I was too scared to think," I said. "I just hit the guy to keep him from hitting me."

"But you didn't have to hit him in the throat," Alvin said. "A blow to his hyoid bone could've killed him. We just needed to discourage them enough to escape. Never use more force on an opponent than is required. That's another thing I teach."

"I was aiming for his chin," I said. "But I missed."

Alvin turned to me, his face serious. "You need to be more careful next time," he said. "Only kill the people you desire to kill."

Next time? Desire to kill? I just stared back at him. There were so many things wrong on so many levels with what he said I didn't know how to respond.

"It would probably be best to keep your Jag hidden for the rest of the time you're here," I said. "So that there isn't a *next time.*"

"I don't do hiding to well," he said. "There will either be a next time with these guys or not. It's up to them."

"I guess you're right. So, what do we do?"

Alvin looked over at me again and grinned. "We say 'fuck it' and get on with things. We got Teddy Crane by the short hairs. He's a pimp and a drug peddler. What's he gonna' do? And when Eddie Smoke sees we ain't coming back at him, he'll lose interest in us. Teddy Crane is the one Smoke needs to worry about. Crane will probably sing like Whitney Houston if he's ever arrested."

"Can't argue with raw logic," I said.

CHAPTER TWENTY-NINE

We went back and picked up my car, parked Alvin's Jag behind a little church off a side road near Kroll's place, and Alvin and I took up my regular place behind the trees outside the castle. There was no sign of Teddy's SUV, so he either had come and gone, or we were way off in where we thought he was bringing the drugs and call girls. But I didn't think so. The sun was already down over Hogback Mountain, and Kroll's place was ablaze with lights. A shindig was definitely going on.

I turned to Alvin. "Think we should go take a closer look, just to satisfy ourselves Teddy delivered the merchandise?"

Alvin nodded. "Probably best to wait until it gets a bit darker."

"There's bound to be security," I said. "We'll need a plan."

"Get in quick, stick to the shadows, and run faster than them if they chase us," he said.

"That's your plan?"

"You got a better one?"

"What if there are cameras?"

"Who they gonna' show the pictures to? What they gonna say, 'look here officer, some guys been looking through my windows at us snorting coke and fucking prostitutes?'"

"They'll know who we are."

"They already know who we are."

Obviously, Alvin took this sort of thing more casually than I did.

We sat and watched the house as an occasional shadow moved across the curtains on the downstairs windows. The three cars from before still sat in the circle drive out front. No other guests had joined them unless they were dropped off while we were tangling with Eddie Smoke's people. I didn't think anyone else was coming. That would unbalance the boy-girl ratio, and someone would have to take seconds. Kroll's class of guests probably wouldn't go for that.

The front gates between the stone pillars were closed, and it was a safe bet the place was locked-up tight, so probably no outside security guards. Everyone there was in on the fun. We'd have to make our way onto the property near where we were parked, where the fence was easier to cross over, and there was a good cover of trees skirting the pasture and leading to the side of the house.

Finally, it was as dark as it was going to get. I turned off the dome light in the Jeep, and we got out and walked around the car and crawled over the rail fence that fronted the pasture. So much for Wilson Kroll's security gate. There were no horses out, as far as I could see. Kroll, I'm sure, had them stabled for the night. When we got to the house, we split up, me coming in from the side to try to get a peek through a front window, Alvin circling the house to check out the back and the other side.

I edged up to the window where I saw the shadows on the curtains and looked through a split in them. Music came from the room, and several couples were slow dancing. The female half of one couple was a young redhead in yellow leather hot-pants that I'd seen get into Teddy's SUV earlier. Another female I recognized was leaning over a coffee table snorting lines of coke with the silver-haired man who rode to the golf course with Wilson Kroll. So, Mission accomplished. Teddy was Kroll's procurer of dope and girls—at the least.

I took a step closer to get a better look, and all hell broke loose. Bright spotlights on the eves of the castle glared on, and an alarm went off. Evidently, there were motion sensors near the house. If there were cameras, I didn't see them. Alvin came around the corner in a dead run straight at the tree line. I turned and ran, too.

The alarm went off as fast as it came on. I guessed Kroll didn't want to attract too much attention or call out the security service that probably monitored the system. Men poured out of the front door like an offensive line coming out of the tunnel before kickoff. I didn't think they saw us because they split up and headed in different directions around the house. The hookers streamed out behind them holding drinks and laughing and giggling like this was all part of the festivities. Wilson Kroll turned them around and herded them back into the house like a muster of colorful peahens.

Alvin and I made it back to the car, did a hasty U-turn and went back out the way we came in. I kept the headlights off until we were out of sight of the house. Behind us, on the shoulder of the road a hundred yards on the other side of the house, the taillights of another car came on and sped off in the opposite direction. Someone else was parked within watching distance of Kroll's castle. Who the hell was it?

No one seemed to follow us, so maybe we'd made it without being seen. Deer, raccoons, and other roaming animals could set off a security system like that—and hopefully, that's what Kroll would think.

"I wonder if the other guy got away?" Alvin said.

"What other guy?"

"The peeping tom I saw looking in a back bedroom window when I was behind the house. He was watching a couple getting it on and took off running into the woods when the alarm went off. I was surprised he could run so fast wearing that long coat."

I realized I was looking at him with my mouth open. "Long coat?" I said.

"Yeah, and he was wearing a mask like you said the guy who hit you in the head wore. That smiley-face mustachioed mother-fucker that protestors been wearing on TV."

"The Anonymous mask," I said. "Jesus Christ, it was Teddy."

I wondered if it was his car I saw hurriedly driving away. I tried to picture the taillights, but that didn't help me identify the make of the car.

"Our Teddy boy must have felt left out of the entertainment he provided and come back to at least get a look," Alvin said, and shook his head. "Pusher, pimp, and a peeping tom. The boy is one versatile motherfucker."

"I need a drink," I said. "Follow me to Natasha's. We need to talk about all that's happened, and I know she's got an unopened bottle of good Scotch going to waste in her liquor cabinet."

"Lead on," Alvin said, and got into his Jaguar.

CHAPTER THIRTY

We both drove to Natasha's and parked out front. I could see her through the window, sitting on her sofa, watching TV with a glass of wine in her hand. I knocked on the door, and she let us in. Her hair was loose on her shoulders, she wore no visible makeup, and was barefoot. She wore jeans and a faded sweatshirt with the circular emblem of Smith College on the front. She would have been the very picture of the girl next door, were it not for her toenails, which were painted Chinese red with toe nail art of an abstract design, and the huge diamond studs in her earlobes.

"Get yourselves a glass of wine, and sit down and tell me about Wilson Kroll's party. I want to hear everything."

"I don't drink alcohol," Alvin said

"Oh, are you Muslim?" Natasha asked. "I've got orange juice and club soda."

"I'm not Muslim, I just don't put poison in my body," Alvin said without humor.

"I'll take the poison," I said.

"There's booze in the cabinet there," Natasha said. "Glasses and ice in the kitchen. I'm not much of a host, so make yourself at home Alvin, J.D. already has," she added, giving me an exaggerated wink.

She never lets up.

I went into her kitchen and brought back two glasses of ice, a bottle of scotch from the liquor cabinet, and orange juice out of the fridge for Alvin. The scotch wasn't just any scotch. It was an unopened bottle of Glenmorangie 18-year-old single malt, going price about a hundred and fifty bucks. First, free Macallan at the USEC party, and now a Glenmorangie. The Dark Corner was turning out to be single malt heaven for me. I placed the scotch and the glasses of ice and orange juice on the coffee table.

"Everything is arranged for the race tomorrow," Natasha said. "I talked to Kelly, and she's excited. She'll be here at nine, so Alvin, why don't you meet us here about that time, too. Everything starts at ten. I only have one parking pass, so we'll all go together."

Alvin gave me a puzzled look. I hadn't told him who Kelly was, so I did.

"Guess you'll be going as my date, big fellow," Natasha said to him.

"Be my pleasure, but you know what they say. Once you go black . . ."

"Yeah," Natasha said, "and I might just ruin you for all your other women. That's what they say about me."

They both laughed, so they were probably joking, 'probably' the key word here. At least Natasha was aiming her flirts at someone else for a change.

"So, don't keep me in suspense," she said. "Tell me what happened tonight."

"You aren't going to like it," I said. "We followed Teddy to Greenville where he procured ladies of the night for Kroll's party. We watched him pick them up from Eddie Smoke, along with a package that had to be drugs."

She sat for a minute staring sadly into the middle distance. "Oh Teddy," she finally said, as if speaking to him. "Are you sure about this, J.D.?"

"Positive. When we got back to the Kroll Castle, Alvin and I sneaked a look through the windows. Everyone was having a fine old time. The girls were there, and there was a lot of table-top coke snorting going on."

"Was Teddy there?" she asked, dread for the worst on her face.

Alvin and I exchanged glances. "No," I quickly said, before Alvin could speak. I couldn't imagine one good thing coming from telling Natasha we caught Teddy peeping into a window at people screwing—wearing the same mask he wore when he tried to brain me with a polo mallet. She wouldn't believe it anyway. I appreciated her loyalty to him, but she was wasting it. Teddy just didn't wake up one day and decide to be a drug dealer and a pimp. While he obviously had no experience providing for himself, with a little grit, he could have done so, and legally. My opinion of his lack of moral fortitude hadn't changed. Teddy Crane was a bad guy, even if Natasha couldn't see it.

Natasha took a bathroom break, and I caught Alvin looking at me.

"What?" I said.

"You were right not telling her about catching Teddy peepin' in that window. You need to watch it with her where he's concerned."

"What do you mean by that?"

"Rich people always stick to their own kind. When the shit hits the fan, she'll choose him over you, no matter what he's done. So, watch your back. Don't put your life in her hands."

I looked at him, then nodded. He was probably right.

When Natasha came back out, she said, "Let's talk about tomorrow. What can I do to help?" she said.

"What you've been doing. Point me to anyone else who might have done business with Kroll, or knew Jamal particularly well. Other than that, we enjoy the race and let things percolate. Kroll will probably have learned we're on to his hookers and drug parties, and I might yank his chain a bit if he's there. He seems to have a short fuse, and maybe he'll shoot his mouth off about something he shouldn't."

"Oh, he'll be there," Natasha volunteered. "He's got a couple of horses in the race."

"Then he'll be surrounded by his friends from the party. If they're investors in Kroll's syndicate like I think, they'll have a stake in those horses, too. So Alvin, be somewhere close when I talk to him. I wouldn't like it if some wise-guy-type got into my face."

"Leave them to me," Alvin said. "You'd probably hit him in the neck."

Natasha gave us both an inquisitive look but didn't say anything. Neither did we.

"Then there's Kroll's veterinarian, Sam Squires. He's had time to contact Brandon Wise, the insurance investor, and come clean—if he's going to do it."

"Or he's halfway to Alaska by now," Natasha said.

"I don't think so. I think Squires will do the right thing."

"You'll trust him, but not Teddy, whom I've known all my life," Natasha said, an edge to her voice.

I stole a look at Alvin, who shot me a glance that said, "See?"

Alvin went to his motel room in Tryon, Natasha went to bed, and I made myself a cheese sandwich, poured myself another scotch, and called Kelly.

I filled her in on the day and night's events and told her I had Alvin "Big

Hurt" Brown watching my back now. I kept my description of Alvin to a minimum. Meeting Alvin in person would do far more to lessen her worries for me than a description ever could.

CHAPTER THIRTY-ONE

I was up before Natasha on Saturday morning, showered, shaved, and dressed. I made coffee, found a box of pop tarts in the back of Natasha's pantry, and stuck a couple of them into the toaster. When that was ready, I took a cup of coffee and the tarts out to the living and room and turned on the TV to a local station.

There was breaking news of another murder by the Carolina Stalker serial killer, this time in nearby Greenville. A prostitute like all the others. The overly-coiffed female announcer said the woman had arrived home around four A.M., and her attacker followed the 23-year-old into her apartment, strangled her, then post-mortem, mutilated her mouth and lips. That Modus Operandi matched all the other serial killings, including the two-gallon clear plastic zip bag over her head, which the killer used to avoid blood splatter.

Agent Mosley R. Smith of the FBI, who was shown at the scene, but not interviewed, was said to lead the investigation, in cooperation with the Greenville Police Homicide Division, SLED, the South Carolina Law Enforcement Division, and members of the Greenville Sheriff's Department. Every available police officer seemed to be hard at work on the case, making it easy for me to believe no one was looking too hard for Jamal.

Natasha came out in her pajamas and fetched a cup of coffee of her own. "What's this?" she said, nodding to the TV and sitting down on the sofa next to me, pulling her bare feet underneath her.

"Another Carolina Stalker serial murder. In Greenville," I said.

Natasha looked at me with widened eyes.

"Oh my God," she said. "Greenville. Could it be one of the girls from Wilson Kroll's party?"

"I was wondering that, myself," I said. "If it was, they'll probably find out."

"And learn Teddy's part in it," she said.

Her first sympathetic thought was for Teddy, not the murdered girl.

"They'll find out about Wilson Kroll's sex and drug parties, too," I said. "And it won't be good for either one of them."

"And you'd like that, wouldn't you?" she said.

"It doesn't matter what I'd like. This is out of my hands."

I could feel her watching me.

"Well," she said, "What are you going to do?"

"I honestly don't know," I said, looking at her. "There are more hookers in Greenville than the ones who attended Kroll's party. But if it turns out to be one of the girls from there . . ."

"I know. You'll have to tell the police about Teddy."

I didn't answer.

She got up and went into her bedroom and closed the door. A couple of minutes later, I heard her shower running.

Natasha came out forty-five minutes later in a summer dress with prints of colorful flowers. She carried a big wide-brimmed peach-colored hat with a dark red ribbon, a hat like ladies wear at the Kentucky Derby.

She stood for a minute looking at it, then sailed it like a frisbee into a chair in the corner. "I was going to be in the hat contest, but I'm not in the mood for it today."

"Did I do that?" I asked. "Put you in a bad mood talking about Teddy?"

"No, J.D. I put myself in a bad mood *thinking* about Teddy. It makes me sad how he's wasted all his family's money and is screwing up his life. You don't know him, but he could have been anything if he'd just tried. It breaks my heart."

She regained her composure and forced a smile.

"Don't say anything else," she said. "I didn't work this hard on my mascara to have it run down my face. So, let's change the subject before I cry. It's race-day, and supposed to be fun."

I heard a car pull up out front, and I could see out the window it was Kelly.

"Here comes your *official* girlfriend," Natasha said and leaned over and kissed me hard on the cheek. "I enjoyed the relationship, even though it was in name only."

Kelly knocked at the door, and let her in. "I'm glad you came," I said, and we hugged and kissed. Her hair smelled like strawberries, and it felt wonderful to have my arms around her.

She stepped back to look at me. "Is that lipstick on your face?"

I shot a glance at Natasha, and she grinned at me. The kiss was for Kelly, not me.

"Hi, Kelly," Natasha said and came over and hugged her, too. "Don't worry. The lipstick isn't J.D.'s fault. I just said good morning to him with a little old kiss on the cheek."

I couldn't read the look Kelly gave her, but a game of some kind was on.

"Alvin Brown, Mrs. Johnson's nephew, will be coming with us," I said. "Don't let his looks scare you. Underneath, he's a teddy bear."

"More like a grizzly bear," Natasha said, laughing. With what happened at the track the other night, you should be glad J.D. has a bodyguard like him."

"Bodyguard sounds good to me," Kelly said, giving me an inquisitive look.

I'd told her about meeting Alvin at Mrs. Johnson's, but not much else.

Another car pulled up outside. It was Alvin. Natasha let him in and introduced him to Kelly.

"Nice to meet you Alvin," Kelly said, and gave him a kiss on the cheek. "Thanks for looking out for J.D." She stood back and looked him over. "I won't worry about him anymore."

Natasha took Alvin's arm and we headed to her car. We were off to the races.

CHAPTER THIRTY-TWO

The crowds were beginning to arrive at the track for the 70th annual running of the Upcountry Steeplechase. Natasha said twenty thousand spectators were expected.

Several cops were directing traffic along Hunting Country Road, as people were parking their cars in vacant lots temporarily designated for that purpose. I noticed no one parked on the shoulders of the road, which must have been forbidden by USEC. After all, USEC and the track was situated in the middle of a private neighborhood. Other cars were streaming into the track area itself, to park on the sloping hillside across from the stands at the finish line. These were the tailgaters Natasha said tried to outdo each other with their lavish spreads. She said it wasn't unusual to see champagne and caviar, roast duck and filet mignon served on white linens spread out on the grass.

We all came in Natasha's SUV, and she parked in a reserved parking area right at the track. We made our way into the infield and toward the largest of the sponsor and hospitality tents. Admission to our tent was by special pass only, which was above and beyond the cost of the tickets for the race. Natasha footed the bill for everything. I had no idea what it cost her. Probably more than my weekly salary.

The tent was filled with chairs and tables with white tablecloths and flower arrangements, and a long bar with several white-shirted bartenders behind it. This was a fancy affair. A table covered with food ran the distance of one side of the tent, a guy in a chef's jacket and hat stood by a huge slab of roast beef, carving knife at the ready. I almost laughed at the sight. It was only a little after ten in the morning, but I guessed roast beef was okay for breakfast, too. The bar along the other side was already doing business. This was a drinking crowd.

Natasha told us that when the races started the best place to be was along the track by the viewing stands just outside the tent, which meant we could easily come back inside for food and drinks whenever we wanted.

People were streaming in, the women wearing colorful dresses and decorative hats—with Natasha and Kelly looking as good or better than most of them, sans the hats. The men dressed as country squires, some even wearing trilby hats and neckties. I started to feel underdressed in my navy blazer, chinos, and ankle high Duck Boots, even though Natasha said I was perfectly attired, especially with the waterproof Duck Boots. Natasha had suggested that both Alvin and I buy the boots for the event. There was a heavy dew that morning, and the grass would be wet, especially if we went out on the track.

I had no desire to go out on the track again. I'd been there, done that, and still had the stitches in my head to show for it. Alvin was dressed in Alvin clothes: a long gray cardigan, unbuttoned, a white silk mock-neck shirt underneath, black jeans, creased, silver belt buckle and matching silver watch, the customary diamond studs in each ear, with his sculpted physique underneath it all the finishing touch. His Duck boots were black on black. Alvin managed to look amazingly street, chic, and horse-race appropriate at the same time. I noticed people looking at him, and moving aside as we walked among them.

We made our way to the bar, and ordered Bloody Mary's—all except Alvin, who had a club soda with lime, sticking to his vow of alcohol abstinence.

I saw Teddy Crane enter the tent. He wasn't wearing his trademark Australian flop hat and long cowboy duster today, but he *was* in cowboy attire. He wore a western shirt with pearl snap-buttons, jeans, alligator cowboy boots and a lacquered-straw cowboy hat. He had on a belt with a buckle shaped like a horseshoe, almost as large as the real thing. He saw us and made an immediate turn toward the far end of the bar.

Natasha saw him, and said, "He's still mad at us, I see."

"What a shame," I said.

"Well, I don't want him mad at me," she said, and headed over to him.

The rest of us took our drinks and found a table.

A few minutes later, Natasha came back and joined us.

"I've never seen him this angry," she said. "He called me a deserter, and said you were out to get him."

"I guess he's heard we followed him when he went to get Kroll's dope and women," I said.

"Yes," she said, "and he said to tell you to keep your effing nose out of his business."

"Did you tell him I was just getting started?"

"I'm not going to make this worse than it already is," she said. "He's working the barns and paddocks today and I doubt if we'll see him again."

Natasha turned to Kelly and said, "the Hat Contest is about to begin and you'll enjoy that." She turned to me and added, "There will be a lot of pretty ladies competing in it, so there's something for you and Alvin, too . . . if Kelly will let you look at them."

Will she ever let up? I wondered.

We grabbed our drinks and went back out the front entrance of the tent and made our way to the Hat Contest. The contestants were already making a circle around the judges who walked about in the middle examining each woman's wildly colored and fancy chapeau.

The whole thing lasted about thirty minutes, and Kelly enjoyed it, more than Alvin and I did, despite the lovely contestants, but we didn't say that to her. The winner of the contest, wearing a hat with a live parakeet in a small cage on top, had many supporters, and got a resounding ovation. Kelly was having a good time and it made me happy to see her happy.

I still hadn't told her every detail of what I was doing, but this wasn't the time and place. I hoped she understood. I knew the newspaper woman inside her was dying for information, but for the moment, I wanted her to enjoy the races and our time together. We didn't get enough of these times, and we could both stand a few hours off the job.

We went back inside the tent and sat at a table munching on small roast beef sandwiches with horse radish and sweet pickles, and potato salad. I spotted Chuck Norman and his mother at a table on the other side of the tent.

Natasha nodded hello toward them, and so did I. They nodded back.

Mrs. Norman was drinking something that looked like Port or Sherry and Chuck had a cocktail. I'd never seen anyone look as bored and miserable as Chuck Norman.

"Is Teddy still mad at Chuck, too?" I asked Natasha.

"I think he is. Look at poor Chuck. He looks like he's at a funeral. Races are supposed to be fun. Think we should ask him to join us?"

"Sure," I said. I wanted to talk to him more about Teddy, anyway. "I'll go ask him."

"What are you, Mr. Bragg," Mrs. Norman said, as I approached, "some kind of Lothario? I was under the impression when we first met that you and Natasha Ladd were in a relationship. Now, I see you today with another young woman, and you two look very chummy. Have you and Ms. Ladd parted ways, or are you just fooling around on her?"

"Neither," I said. "You must have misunderstood my relationship with Natasha. We're just friends. The lady I'm with today is the one I have a relationship with. My girlfriend and Natasha are old college friends."

"And who is that disturbing looking black man?" she asked. Mrs. Norman and Chuck turned to look at Alvin.

"He's a friend, too," I said. "He's the cousin of the Johnson boy who went missing."

"You and Natasha fooled me, too." Chuck examined me over his glass. "I thought you two were together."

"I apologize for the misconception," I said.

"You and Charles seem to be on opposite ends of the romantic relationship scale," Mrs. Norman said. "You have too many, and he has none. I've been trying for years to get him to find a woman and produce grandchildren for me, but with no luck. There he sits, as celibate as the Archbishop."

Chuck sat quietly, a blank look on his face. If he was bothered by what his mother said he didn't show it. "You haven't seen Teddy, have you?" he asked. "I was looking for him."

"He's here,' I said. "Natasha said he's working the barns and paddock area today, not that I know what that entails."

"Oh, I forgot." Chuck said.

I got the feeling he didn't know anything about that. Perhaps he and Teddy really were on the outs. Maybe if I got him away from his mother, and got a few more beers in him, he'd open up some more about Teddy.

"Chuck, why don't you join us? We're going out to the track in a minute."

He shot a look at his mother.

"He needs to stay here with me," Mrs. Norman said.

Chuck did as she said but didn't look happy about it.

A part of me felt sorry for him, but another part thought, *Man up, Chuck.*

I said my goodbyes and went back to our table. We got another drink and headed out to the track.

Alvin seemed to be having a good time. Steeplechases and the type of people who attend them were probably a foreign experience, but I didn't notice him acting like he felt out of place. I figured that no matter where Alvin Brown found himself, he was always comfortable. I think he naturally expected everyone and everything to adapt to him, not the other way around.

CHAPTER THIRTY-THREE

We stood by the rail with our drinks, watching the unfolding pre-race events taking place out on the track. A parade of miniature horses went by, followed by a line of small, ornate buggies and wagons, some filled with kids. Later, horses and riders dressed for a fox hunt came along, hounds out front barking and yipping. A prayer was said by someone at a microphone in front of the stands, quieting the crowd for a minute or two, and afterward, there was the releasing of the doves, whatever that represented. Then a woman out in front of the stands sang the National Anthem, acapella. There was applause, which turned to cheers, and someone with a bugle played "Go To The Post." Race day had officially started.

I looked at my watch, it was already one-thirty, and the race schedule I'd picked up showed that the first race was about to begin. There would be six races, one every half hour, and the purses were quite substantial. There was betting, I noticed earlier, with wagers taken by a gentleman near the stands wearing a snap-brim hat and holding a fistful of bills and a small notebook. I wasn't sure what the gambling laws were in North Carolina, but whatever they were, no one seemed too bothered by them.

None of us were interested in placing bets. Alvin, Kelly and I were ignorant of the horse stats and chances, and Natasha said she didn't gamble. She said she took her risks on husbands, not horses.

"Natasha," I said. "You're the expert here. Why don't you give us a Steeplechase 101, so we'll know what we're watching."

"I'd be happy to," she said. "Gather round, students. There are six races, all two and three-eight's miles. They are limited to ten horses each, but there are usually not that many—maybe six or eight on average.

"They jump over the same obstacles used up and down the East Coast, where most steeplechase races are held. The fences consist of a steel or wood frame stuffed with plastic "brush," with a foam-rubber roll covered with green canvas on the takeoff side. Horses jump the fence in stride, much like humans in track and field events. The fences are provided by the National Steeplechase Association, and are shipped to racetracks by truck and set up in advance of the races."

"They look like real hedges from this side, don't they?" Kelly said.

"Yeah, I got a close up look the other night," I said.

"Steeplechase races don't start from a gate like flat-track races," Natasha continued. "Instead, horses are lined up in post-position order and start from a standstill or a walk. Post positions are drawn in the presence of those making entries for the race. The horses are started by the Starter when he drops the flag."

She went on to say the horses were all thoroughbreds, and many were flat track racers first, but probably would never have been Kentucky Derby winners. Steeplechase horses were usually older than flat-trackers, and had the jumping skills, heart and stamina to run the longer steeplechase races.

"A steeplechase horse hates the starting gate and loves the turf," she said. "They really don't get excited about running any distance shorter than 2 miles. Their brain engages and their bodies go to work when asked to jump a 4-foot fence every eighth of a mile or so. I read once that there are few athletes like a thoroughbred steeplechase racehorse—they race at great speed, fly over fences, and will eat a carrot out of your hand afterward."

It was clear Natasha loved everything about the sport. She was a devoted steeplechaser.

She went on to tell us that most of the jockeys were professionals—with a few amateurs—and were both men and women, many from England or Ireland. All jockeys are small, but steeplechase jockeys weigh a little more than flat-track jockeys—roughly 140 pounds compared to 110 pounds. Height was not an issue; qualifying was based purely on weight. She said that the purses at the Upcountry had grown every year and were becoming quite significant for the National Steeplechase Association circuit.

She stopped talking and looked up the track. "Lesson over," she said. "Here come the horses. Let's watch."

We all stepped closer to the rail and watched as the horses came thundering down the track from around the bend.

Their hooves were a drumbeat beneath my feet that I felt all the way to my stomach. I had already experienced that sensation the night the masked rider came over the jump and down on me, and that was only one horse. Here there were eight of them; horses and riders, flowing over fences without indecision or falter as smoothly as trout over a rock in a stream bottom. I had to admit; a steeplechase held a vigor and beauty flat track racing couldn't touch.

The race ended as the winner flashed across the finish line to the roar of the crowd of thousands. In the trees at the top of the hill behind the tailgaters, a large flock of birds took flight, set to wing by the crowd's ovation. Only then did the realization fully register that we were in the middle of a usually peaceful country landscape.

As the horses were called to post for the second race, I spotted Wilson Kroll down the rail with his gang of guests. He caught me looking at him and stared back. The old saying, "if looks could kill," crossed my mind.

I turned to Alvin, caught his eye and nodded at Kroll's direction. Alvin leaned back to see around the line of people standing along the rail between us.

"Wilson Kroll?" he asked.

"And his Cleveland guests," I said.

Alvin stared at them. "Interesting bunch," he said. "They stand out from this crowd as much as I do."

"Let's go have a chat with them," I said to Alvin and excused us to the ladies. Kelly shot me an inquisitive glance.

"We'll just be a minute," I said.

Natasha had seen them by now and leaned over to explain to Kelly who they were. Kelly's interested look slowly turned to one of concern, as she listened.

Alvin followed me over to them.

"Enjoying the races, fellows?" I said as we reached them. "Anybody got a hangover?" Alvin took a position behind me, legs spread, arms crossed, and gave them his "Big Hurt" stare.

None of them spoke, but their eyes went back and forth between Alvin and me.

Finally, Wilson Kroll spoke. "I heard you've been sticking your nose into my business, Mr. writer man," he said.

Teddy probably told him, I thought. I was hoping it wasn't his veterinarian, Sam Squires. I was counting on him going to Brandon Wise and telling all to him—without Kroll's knowledge.

"Just working on my story about the wonderful world of steeplechase and those who support it," I said.

"Bullshit," he said, scowling at me.

Several bystanders at the rail turned and gave him a severe look. He didn't seem to care.

"You're just a muck-raking asshole," he said. "Up here to uncover whatever dirt you can find on us rich folks. I know your type. You're suspicious of anybody with money and a lifestyle you'll never attain."

"For me to muck-rake," I said, "there has to be some muck there to rake. If there is, then it's called journalism. And that's what I do."

One wise guy leaned in and said, "Where we come from, some mutt sticks his nose in somebody's business, they find his nose in a landfill—with the rest of him still attached to it."

They all laughed.

"Must be Cleveland humor," I said to Alvin. He snorted, and they all looked at him, then at me, as if they were wondering how I knew where they were from, and what else I knew about them. Alvin didn't move, he just stood and returned their looks, his expression unchanged.

"Who's this guy?" Kroll asked, nodding at him but looking at me.

"He's with me," I said, and left it at that.

He kept looking from me to Alvin, and evidently decided this wasn't the time or place to continue this. "If you don't mind, Mr. Bragg," he said, "I'm here with my guests to enjoy the races. Now leave us the fuck alone." He turned to his guests and said, "C'mon guys, let's go get our bets down. I'll pick us another winner."

"Enjoy it while you can, Mr. Kroll," I said, smiling at him. "I have a feeling your luck is about to change." Alvin and I turned and went back to Kelly and Natasha. I could feel Kroll's eyes on my back as I walked way.

CHAPTER THIRTY-FOUR

Between races, Natasha said, "The sun is getting to me. I'm going in for a cool drink."

That sounded great to us all, and we followed her in.

On the way, Kelly took my arm and spoke quietly in my ear. "We need to do things like this more often. I'm enjoying this, especially since no one's been hurt, like the last steeplechase I attended. We spend too much time at home."

"Are you saying you don't like being at home alone with me?" I asked.

"You know better than that," she said. "But we can't 'do it' twenty-four hours a day."

"Who says?" I asked.

We were standing at the bar when I saw Brandon Wise, the insurance investigator, come into the tent. He spotted me and hurried over as if I were the sole reason he was there. I told the others to get me a beer and grab a table, and I met him half way. He motioned me over to a corner where we would be out of earshot of the nearest table.

"I'm glad you're here, Mr. Bragg," Wise said. "I found an envelope pushed through the mail slot in my office door this morning. It's from Sam Squires, Mr. Kroll's vet. He's confessed to a list of fraudulent business activities that he and Wilson Kroll have committed. He verifies that Emperor had indeed become infertile, but Wilson Kroll continued to sell the horse's services by substituting semen from another of their stallions and passing it off as Emperor's. He also says Kroll had the horse killed. It's everything we talked about, all signed and sealed—Wilson Kroll on a platter. He won't get a dime from us, and may even go to jail."

Wise paused and studied me. “Would I be right to guess this was your doing?”

“Any part I may have played in this is irrelevant,” I said. “I am but a seeker of the truth, and when found, that truth is my only reward.”

“What baloney,” Wise said. “But I’ll keep you out of it if that’s what you want.”

“It is,” I said.

“Squires says the fraud was to keep the news of Emperor’s infertility a secret from his syndicate investors long enough to arrange for the horse to be put down in a way that wouldn’t implicate him. So, he blamed it on the kid. He planned to split the insurance money with his investors to make up for their lost investment, just like you said.”

“Is there anything else in there about Jamal Johnson?”

“Just that Squires claims *he* didn’t shoot the horse, or frame the Johnson kid for it. He says we might want to talk to someone named Teddy Crane about that.”

"Gotcha!" I said, not realizing I'd spoken it aloud until I saw Wise staring at me.

“You know this guy?” he asked.

“I do,” I said. “Crane is a local man who does things for Kroll. I’d like to hear what more Squires can tell us about him.”

“I’d like to talk to Doctor Squires, too,” Wise said. Have you seen him here? I’ve been trying to call him all morning, but he isn’t answering. I could make my case against Kroll even stronger if Squires will testify in person, in front of witnesses. That would not only help *me* but all those people who are going to want their stud fees back. This will most likely end up in both civil *and* criminal court.”

“If Doctor Squires is here, I haven’t seen him,” I said.

“I heard Wilson Kroll is here,” Mr. Wise said. “I want to talk to him, too.”

“I don’t mean to tell you your business, Mr. Wise,” I said, “but I strongly advise against that. Trust me when I say, it’s not a good time to confront him one-on-one. It could even be dangerous. He has some old friends from up north down here right now, and they’re the kind of people who could easily make Kroll’s problems go away—like disappear—so they’ll never be found again.

Don't become a problem to him just yet. Take these papers to the police, or at least to your company lawyers, and let them confront Wilson Kroll."

"Jesus," he said. "You think he's that dangerous?"

"I do," I said. "And so are his friends."

He stared at me for a long moment. "Okay," he finally said. "Maybe I'll do it that way."

"Let me know how it goes," I said. "Just don't broadcast my interest."

"Of course," he said, and left to look for Sam Squires.

I walked back to the table and sat down. Kelly, Natasha, and Alvin were looking expectantly at me.

"That was Brandon Wise," I said. "He's the insurance guy investigating Kroll's claim for his dead horse. He and I have struck up a partnership of sorts. It seems that Wilson Kroll's vet, Sam Squires, has had an attack of conscience and confessed to a long list of fraudulent activities he and Kroll committed in Kroll's stud service business. He also admitted that Kroll was responsible for his horse's death, and blamed it on Jamal to collect the insurance money. The reason he killed the horse was that it had become infertile, and if that got out, it would not only have destroyed the horse's value, but the value of an investment syndicate Kroll had created around it—leaving his investors with huge financial losses. The insurance money was Kroll's way of placating these investors without suffering an out-of-pocket loss himself. Squires gave Mr. Wise a signed confession to all this."

"Oh my God, J.D.," Natasha said. "Does that mean we've busted Wilson Kroll?"

"That's the way it looks," I said, and turned back to Alvin. "This clears Jamal's name. He's innocent."

"Did Squires say anything about what happened to Jamal?" Alvin asked.

I frowned at Alvin and tilted my head ever so slightly toward Natasha, cutting my eyes at her and quickly back at him. She wasn't paying attention and didn't see me, but Alvin got it and gave me a slow nod. What I had to say, I didn't want her hearing. Sam Squires suggested we talk to Teddy Crane. I didn't want Natasha to get upset and run to Teddy. I wanted to spring this on him myself, to see how he reacted—with Alvin along. It was time Teddy fessed up, and a little Alvin-type persuasion might just help.

Alvin stood up and pulled out his phone. "I'm going somewhere quiet and call Aunt Millie. At least clearing the boy's name will be of some comfort to her."

"And I need to go to the little girl's room," Natasha said. "Want to join me, Kelly?"

She didn't, and after Natasha had left I found her looking at me.

"What are all these little eye signals back and forth with Alvin?" she said.

"You don't miss anything, do you?" I said.

"We're supposed to be working together. So tell me what's going on, or you're getting more stitches in your head."

"Brandon Wise told me things I didn't want Natasha to know. Sam Squire's confession indicates her friend Teddy Crane in the horse shooting, and maybe in what happened to Jamal. Natasha has a blind side when it comes to Teddy, and she would run to tell him. I want to confront him first."

"So, you think Teddy Crane shot the horse and is responsible for Jamal's disappearance?" Kelly said.

"Here's how I see it. Wilson Kroll was looking for a way to get rid of his high-priced horse, which had become infertile, and he needed to still be able to collect on the insurance. Sam Squires' confession proves that. Then Kroll learns that Jamal, his stable boy, overheard a conversation about the horse's infertility. Kroll can't allow that to get out, so everything comes to a head. Then Kroll has a big idea. He'll make Jamal a scapegoat, then get rid of him before he can talk. Kroll fires Jamal with the plan to fabricate a reason for Jamal to hold a grudge. Then Kroll pays Teddy Crane—who desperately needs money—to kill the horse, set Jamal up with the rifle in his mother's shed, and do away with Jamal. All the while Kroll is off somewhere with an iron clad alibi. What's the murder of one black kid when it comes to several million bucks?"

"Poor Jamal," Kelly said. "He didn't deserve this. I feel so sorry for his mother and brother."

"It's not much of a consolation, but Sam Squires confession now proves Jamal didn't kill Kroll's horse. At least that clears Jamal's name."

"The rest of it's going to be hard to prove, though, isn't it?" Kelly said.

"Doctor Squires' confession nails Wilson Kroll for the fraud and for having his horse killed. So he's toast. But the part Teddy Crane played in it, Squires left a little vague. He obviously knows Teddy was involved, but it doesn't look like he has provable details. I think Kroll kept him in the dark about that. There's not enough in Squires' confession to convince the police, either. That's why I need to find Squires and talk to him."

"But the police will know now that Jamal didn't shoot the horse," Kelly said, "so why would they still believe he ran away?"

"They'll probably say Jamal knew Kroll was going to blame him and was afraid the police wouldn't believe him over Kroll. But when Jamal disappeared, I don't think he even knew about the horse shooting, let alone that Kroll was going to blame him. Besides, I think Jamal would've told his mother if he'd decided to take off somewhere—whatever the reason. I believe he's lying at the bottom of a lake or in a shallow grave somewhere. And unfortunately, finding the body might be the only way to prove that to the cops."

Kelly absorbed everything I said. In the wrinkle in her brow, I could almost see her newspaper mind outlining the story for the next edition of the Clarion. She was wearing her professional face. It had been a while since I'd seen it, and it was easy to forget that underneath all the beauty and sexiness was a serious, intelligent, newsperson. It was in her genes, just like my grandfather, and I had to admit, mine, too.

CHAPTER THIRTY-FIVE

Alvin and Natasha came back just as the next race was about to start. I asked Alvin how it went with Millie and Taylor Johnson.

"It is what it is," he said. "They're glad to get Jamal's good name back, but it's a long way from getting the boy himself back."

I told Kelly and Natasha that Alvin and I were about raced out, and were going to look for Brandon Wise, the insurance investigator, to see if he'd located Sam Squires. As I'd told Kelly, I wanted to talk to Squires myself, to see if he could add anything to Teddy's involvement in Jamal's disappearance.

Kelly looked at me like she wanted to go with us, but seemed to realize we didn't want Natasha along, so she stayed to keep her company.

When we were out of earshot, I told Alvin what Squires wrote about Teddy in his confession, and told him that while we'd keep an eye out for Wise and Squires, we were going somewhere else first. "Teddy's working at the infield barns and paddock area," I said, "and it's time we had a little heart to heart with him."

"Bout' time," Alvin said, wearing that face I was hoping would scare the bejesus out of Teddy.

We found Teddy easily; he was leading a horse from the barns to the paddock area through a crowd of onlookers. He saw us coming, and for a second it appeared he wanted to run. His eyes darted from us to the barn then back again. He must have chosen fight over flight because he stayed with the horse and fixed us with an angry glare as we approached.

"We need to talk to you," I said.

"I'm busy," he said, as he continued to lead the horse. "I can't talk right now."

Alvin took a step toward him. "You ain't got a choice." Teddy looked at Alvin, who was glaring back at him. Teddy blinked first.

Teddy turned to an older man coming from the barns behind him, leading another horse.

"Larry," Teddy held out the reins to the approaching man. "Take Song Girl for me; I need to take a break."

Larry took Teddy's horse, along with the horse he was already leading, and moved off into the paddock area.

Teddy turned and headed toward the barn. We followed him.

Just inside, away from the crowds, he faced us. "So, what's so goddamned important you've got to talk to me right now?"

"You know Sam Squires?" I asked. "Wilson Kroll's veterinarian?"

"What if I do?"

"He just ratted out Wilson Kroll for a fraudulent scheme with Kroll's stud-service. Signed a confession to it, and turned it over to the insurance investigator working Kroll's insurance claim."

Teddy's eyes widened, but he didn't speak.

"Kroll is done," I continued, and then stretched the truth a bit. "Squires also said Kroll had you shoot the horse, and you helped frame Jamal Johnson for it. That's conspiracy to commit insurance fraud, my friend, and maybe a lot more—if Jamal turns up dead. Which I think he will."

His complexion went a shade lighter.

"Jamal Johnson ran the fuck away. I didn't do anything to him."

I noticed he didn't deny shooting the horse, or framing the boy.

"We both know he didn't run," I said. "He's lying dead somewhere, and either Wilson Kroll killed him, or had you do it. The boy knew Kroll's prize horse was infertile, and Squires' confession proves it. Kroll had to shut the kid up."

Teddy's eyes went back and forth from me to Alvin. I wondered if he were weighing the flight or fight response again. Alvin must have too, because he moved over to the doorway, blocking it.

"You've got to be dumber than I think you are," I said, "if you don't know that Kroll will lay the horse shooting, framing Jamal, and maybe even Jamal's disappearance on you the second they corner him. You're a sitting duck. Why don't you come clean now, and get ahead of it before it's too late?"

"This is bullshit!" Teddy shouted, spittle flying from his lips. "I haven't killed anybody."

"You tried to kill me, Teddy," I said.

"What the fuck are you talking about?" he said. "Are you crazy?"

"It was you at the track that night. Hiding behind that 'Anonymous' mask. I recognized the duster and the Aussie slouch hat. You're quite the horseman, but you need to work on your nighttime polo. You didn't hit me hard enough."

"Anonymous mask?" He said.

"Yeah. The one you were wearing when we saw you peeping into to a bedroom window at Kroll's place, watching his Cleveland guests fuck the whores you brought to their party."

Teddy stared at me, his eyes crazed like a wild animal caught in a trap.

"Leave me alone. Just leave me alone," Teddy said and made for the door.

Alvin stepped in his way. "Is it time now to beat the truth out of him?" Alvin asked.

"Let him go," I said. Teddy Crane's world was about to come crashing down on him harder than any beating Alvin could give him. It would become a game of who could rat out the other one first, and my money was on Wilson Kroll.

We watched him go. He was heading in the direction of the parking lot.

"I guess Teddy's race day is over, I said.

"So what's next, Kemosabe?" Alvin asked.

"We watch what happens," I said. "And listen. I think there's about to be a falling out among thieves, and maybe the answers we're looking for will come tumbling out. I don't think our Teddy boy is going to confess like Sam Squires, so it may be the only way we'll ever find out what happened to Jamal."

CHAPTER THIRTY-SIX

After the races were over, our foursome, led by Natasha, went to a party in Tryon at the Melrose Inn. It was a historic place, and already crowded when we got there. There was a cash bar and live music with a scraggly looking bunch occupying a bandstand. I quickly learned they could go from country to rock and roll without missing a beat; they played a lot better than they looked.

Natasha soon got ahead of us on the drinks and was in a weird mood. One minute she was the life of the party, the next, in the depths of the doldrums. The sun and the drinks from the day were getting to us all, I guess, except for Alvin, who didn't drink. He stuck to club soda and was automatically the designated driver for the night.

I danced with Kelly most of the time but gave Natasha the occasional spin. So did several of her friends in the crowd. Natasha was rarely without a dance partner, I noticed. Or a drink. Alvin alternately danced with both women as the night went on. I noticed he had smooth moves, even though he pretended not to enjoy the music coming from what he called "a hillbilly band."

They played an old familiar slow number, and Kelly and I danced to it, exchanging a long kiss and probably making a spectacle of ourselves. An elderly couple next to us on the dance floor, stared at us with disapproval. I recognized them as people Natasha had introduced me to at the USEC party on Wednesday, but I couldn't remember their names.

The woman continued to stare at me. "We thought you were Natasha Ladd's friend, young man," she said, haughtily. "I guess we were mistaken."

"Oh, she won't mind," I said, "this is my sister."

Their looks went from disapproval to disgust.

"Well, I never." I heard the woman say, as we spun away from them.

"John David, you're awful," Kelly said, laughing.

Much later, I came out of the men's room to find Natasha waiting for me. She locked her arms around my neck and gave me a big sloppy kiss. Before I could disengage, I looked up and saw Kelly standing there watching us.

Natasha saw her, and let me go. "Oops," she said and giggled.

"She's drunk, Kelly," I said. "This is not my doing."

Kelly did an about-face and walked away.

She was sitting at the table waiting for me. She didn't look happy.

"You're angry," I said. "I understand, but it wasn't my fault."

"I'm a number of things," she said, "and that's just one of them. All I know is that I'm not having fun anymore."

"Natasha is shitfaced," I said. "Before she molested me, she kissed a couple members of the band. One of them female."

At that moment, Natasha came up, flopped down in a seat, and put her head in her hands, oblivious to us.

Alvin sat without emotion, watching the unfolding drama.

"Let's get out of here," I said. "Except for Alvin, we've all had enough to drink today. We'll let him drive us back to Natasha's."

"I don't think I can spend the night under the same roof with her," Kelly said. "I might strangle her in her sleep."

She laughed, and so did I. "I won't let you murder anyone," I said. "I'll keep you occupied. All night, if I have to."

"Tempting, but I would know she's in the next room. Besides, you rarely hear me say this, but I'm just not in the mood. So, I'm going to say no. I'm tired and need a good night's sleep. It was for times just like this that God invented motel rooms. I'll get one where Alvin is staying. He can drive us to Natasha's, we'll get our cars, and I'll follow him to the motel."

"You shouldn't be driving anywhere," I said.

"You may not have noticed, but I stopped drinking back at the race track. I've had club soda's with Alvin since we've been here and I'm capable of driving all the way home. But it's late, and I'm not going to."

Natasha raised her head three inches off her arms and moaned, "I'm going to be sick."

Alvin held her head while she puked on a curb in the parking lot, and then drove us all back to Natasha's place. Natasha didn't say a word the whole way, either asleep or to put it less politely, passed out. I tried all the way to get Kelly to forget about the motel but failed. I'd learned long ago that once she made up her mind, it was hard to change. But at least she was talking to me, her anger targeted at Natasha. Their friendship had taken a serious hit.

When we arrived, Natasha awoke suddenly and was the first one out of the car. She stumbled drunkenly into the house like she was about to be sick again. Alvin, Kelly and I got out and stood looking at each other, no one making an attempt to follow her in. Kelly kissed me on the cheek and said, "Good luck. I'll see you in the morning." Then she went with Alvin to their cars. Natasha had evidently become my problem by default.

In the house, I found Natasha draped over her toilet, passed out again. I picked her up and put her to her bed, still in her clothes. Then I went out to look at what I'd seen as I'd entered her bungalow.

The living room was a mess. Desk drawers in the little cove Natasha called her study were standing open, papers from them and books from bookshelves strewn on the floor. I also noticed my laptop was missing from the desktop where I'd been using it to begin my story.

Natasha had left her front door unlocked, as usual, so you couldn't accurately call it a break-in, but someone had robbed her—or us. I went back into her bedroom and looked at her dresser. Those drawers were open too. I didn't expect to find anything of value left in them, but I was wrong. There was a jewelry box in one of them crammed to the lid with watches, rings, earrings, and bracelets, each one probably more valuable than ten laptops. Either it was one dumb thief, or he came just for my computer and notes. I suddenly thought of Jamal's journal. Maybe that's what the thief was looking to find. Teddy knew about it because I told him at the USEC party. *Was this his work?*

I took Natasha's shoes off, pulled the covers over her, and turned out the lights. She was dead to the world. I went to lock her front door, reminded of that old saw about closing the barn door after the horse is gone—when I heard a car pull up out front. I looked through the glass side panels of the door to see

Eddie Smoke and a couple of his thugs get out of a black BMW. One of them was the guy Alvin punched out. As they walked under the porch light, I could see gauze stuffed up his nostrils. Alvin must have broken his nose.

Were they here for payback? I started to lock the door before they could get to it but decided if they wanted me bad enough, they'd just break it down. My Glock nine was in the Jeep's glove compartment, where I usually kept it, so I was unarmed. My best bet was to try to talk my way out of whatever they had in store for me. I didn't think I'd done anything to them severe enough to die for, but with guys like this, you never knew.

I opened the door for them. Eddie Smoke and I looked at each other. I wondered if they were the ones who stole my laptop and were back for the journal. A favor to Teddy, perhaps.

"This him?" Smoke said to the tall guy with the gauze in his nose.

"He's the one hit Randall," gauze-nose said.

"Is the other one here?" Smoke asked me. "The black dude?"

Eddie Smoke was even more wide-bodied up close. He was built like a stump.

"What do you want?" I said, not answering his question.

"So, you're Bragg," Smoke said. "We didn't actually meet the other day. I'm Eddie Smoke." He didn't offer to shake hands; he kept them in his pockets.

I wondered what he had in there. A knife? A gun? He didn't strike me as a guy who would go anywhere unarmed.

"Why are you here?" I asked.

"I have two problems I hope you can help me with," he said. "The second one depends on the first."

He seemed to be working very hard on his speech patterns as if he were trying not to sound like a redneck street thug, but his eyes contradicted it. They were solid black and held the all the compassion of a barracuda. I let him talk.

"We have a mutual acquaintance I occasionally do business with," he said. "My first problem is what to do about that acquaintance if he talks too much to you about that business."

"What's the second problem?" I asked.

He studied my face for a long moment, then said, "You. I'm wondering how much of that business you're going to put in that story I hear you're planning to write."

I motioned at the papers scattered on the floor and the desk with the drawers that stood open. "This isn't your first visit tonight, is it? I asked.

He looked around at the open desk drawers and the scattered papers on the floor, then got what I meant.

"You think I tossed this place? Fuck you. Whatever this is, I didn't have a thing to do with it, and anybody says I did, I'll put a cap in their ass."

His thug side had shown up, but, unless he had Oscar-winning acting talent, he was telling the truth. He'd been genuinely surprised and angered when I accused him of it. When he calmed down, he asked, "So, what's it gonna be? You helping me out here or not?"

"What if I said *not*?"

He gave me the full effect of his emotionally void eyes for a second.

"Believe me," he finally said, "That's not the right answer."

"Have you heard about this kid Jamal Johnson who went missing up here?" I asked him.

He looked at me as if I'd completely missed the point of the conversation.

"The kid who shot the horse?" he said. "Yeah, I read about it in the papers. So, what?"

"He didn't shoot it," I said.

"I'll say it again, so fucking what?"

"Since the boy didn't kill the horse, he wouldn't have run away. But, he's still missing, and I'm trying to find him. I'm not interested in your business. I couldn't care less. I'm only interested in finding out what happened to the boy, and who was responsible for his disappearance. If it turns out it's this acquaintance of ours—let's call him Teddy—had nothing to do with the boy's disappearance, then I'm not interested in him, either. But if he did, I'm going to do everything I can to bring him down. What happens between you two is up to you."

"So, you wasn't watching me?"

"We were watching Teddy."

He stared into my eyes a long time, his face emotionless as if he were trying to read my compass as a man. Could he trust me to keep my word? I knew that was the thought running through his head.

"Okay," he finally said. "We've got a deal."

"What deal?" I said. "I told you what I was going to do. How is that a deal?"

Eddie Smoke grinned at me for the first time.

"Let me explain it to you," he said. "You stay out of my business, and don't mention my name anywhere, anytime, and I won't blow your fucking head off. How about that as a deal?" He looked at me a moment longer, then turned around and went to his car. Gauze-nose and the other guy, who'd yet to speak a single word, followed him out. They got into the BMW and drove away.

Eddie Smoke wasn't even out of sight before I called Alvin to ask about Kelly. He said he'd rented her a room two doors down from his and gave me her room number. He advised me to leave her alone tonight, and give her time to get over it. He said she was bummed out, and angry she'd let Natasha get to her. But she brightened up, he said, when he told her to put her room on Natasha's tab. Natasha had insisted on paying for Alvin's room, and had left him an open tab.

I laughed at Kelly's reaction. Maybe Alvin was right, and by morning we would all be laughing at tonight's episode. I hoped so. I might not know where my relationship with Kelly was eventually going, but I knew I didn't want it harmed by something as silly as this.

I gave Alvin a condensed version of the break-in, my missing laptop, and Eddie Smoke's visit. He got a kick out the tall guy's broken nose. He, like me, believed it was Teddy who had tossed the place, looking for Jamal's journal, and stealing my computer to see if I was writing about him.

Alvin said he'd bring breakfast in the morning and hopefully deliver Kelly along with it. That was good because I doubted Natasha would be able to handle cooking breakfast or even eating it. My guess was she'd be suffering a world-class hangover, which would serve her right for causing the crap between Kelly and me.

I took Alvin's advice and didn't call Kelly. I went to bed.

CHAPTER THIRTY-SEVEN

Daybreak was barely glowing through the bedroom window curtains when I awoke to someone snoring softly beside me, an arm and a hand with red painted nails draped over my shoulder. I turned to find Natasha sound asleep, and as naked as the day she was born. Sometime during the night, still inebriated, she must have undressed and slipped into bed with me.

I sensed a shape in the doorway and looked up to see Kelly standing there staring at us, slowly shaking her head in disbelief.

"The front door was open . . ." she said. "I'll be out on the sofa. As Desi Arnaz says to Lucy on their old TV show reruns, 'you got some 'splainin' to do.'"

This time, the unlocked front door was on me. I forgot to lock it after Eddie Smoke left. I pushed Natasha's arm off my shoulder, untangled the sheets from around me, pulled on my pants and went after Kelly. She was sitting on the sofa, calmly waiting.

"This isn't what it looks like," I said. "You've got to believe me. I just woke up two seconds before you came in and discovered Natasha in my bed. Absolutely nothing happened. I found her sick again after you guys left and passed out on the toilet. I put her in her bed—fully clothed. She must have awoken in the night, still drunk, and took off her clothes and climbed into my bed. I swear to God I never touched her."

She looked at me for a long moment, then smiled and placed a palm on my cheek. "I believe you," she said. "This sounds too much like Natasha not to be true. You're also a terrible liar, and I can tell when you're telling the truth. Lying just isn't in your tenet. You have your grandfather to thank for that. Principles, code of honor, and all that. But it doesn't mean I have to like it. So, I'm going home before Natasha comes out and I have to listen to her embarrassing explanation—or lack thereof. I don't think we're friends anymore."

"You are a wise and understanding woman," I said. "A goddess among mortals and I'm the luckiest guy on the earth to have your trust."

"Don't push it," she said, grinning. "And if you know what's good for you, you'll pack your bag and come home. Tonight." She gave me a quick kiss, a last look, and left.

Ten minutes later, Natasha came out of the bedroom with a sheet wrapped around her. "What was I doing naked in your bed, J.D.?" she asked, with a bewildered look.

"Nothing," I said. "You must have come visiting during the night. I didn't even know you were there until I woke up."

"So we didn't . . ."

"No," I said. "We didn't."

"I guess you noticed I can't hold my liquor," she said, somewhat sheepishly.

"Everybody noticed," I said. "Especially Kelly, when she came in and saw us in bed together a little while ago."

"Oh, God, she saw us?" Natasha said.

"She saw all of you. I still had my underwear on."

"What did she do?"

"She forgave me. But I can't say the same for you. You two will have to work that one out. She's gone home."

"I'm so, so, embarrassed. I can't remember anything that happened last night. I'll make this right with Kelly somehow," she said. "But not now. Now I have to go back to bed." She went to her bedroom holding her head and walking like she was stepping on broken glass.

I went in and got dressed. When I came out, Alvin was at the kitchen table laying out several kinds of fresh fruit, some granola bars, and a bag of Hardee's sausage biscuits.

"The sausage biscuits are for you," he said.

"Kelly was here earlier," I said.

"She checked out early this morning before I woke up. She go home?"

"Yes," I said. "After she saw Natasha in bed with me, naked."

That stopped him. He looked at me like he was waiting for the punchline. Finally, he realized I was serious.

"Damn," he said. "You surprise me, brother. I don't know whether to think less of you or envy you."

"Nothing happened, Alvin," I said, and told him how Natasha got there.

I talked while he made coffee. When the coffee was ready, he brought me a cup.

"You must be so fucked," he said. "I mean, you didn't *get* fucked, but you *are* fucked. Know what I'm sayin'?"

"I would have thought that, too," I said. "But Kelly believed me. She trusts me. She's angry at Natasha, not me. She wants me home tonight."

Alvin stood with a cup of coffee in his hand and stared at me. "A trusting and forgiving woman," he said with amazement. "Now, I *do* envy you. Where can I find me one of them?"

"Sorry, bud. Kelly's one of a kind."

We sat and ate. Alvin ate a banana, an apple, and a granola bar; I wolfed down a couple of sausage biscuits. I talked to Natasha through her bedroom door and told her we had food. A weak voice announced she didn't feel like eating anything and she just needed to go back to bed. She said for Alvin and me to make ourselves at home.

"What now?" Alvin asked.

"I want to talk to Sam Squires to see what else he can tell us. After that, I'm out of ideas. Like I said yesterday, we'll just have to wait and see what transpires."

I sipped another cup of coffee and thought about Kelly. She *was* one of a kind, as I'd said to Alvin, and trusted me completely. I don't know if I could ever trust *anyone* that much. I brought that baggage to every relationship I'd ever had.

It wasn't like she'd never been hurt. She had. She told me that before she came to work for my grandfather, she'd lived in Charlotte and worked at the Charlotte Observer. She'd fallen in love with her boss, a married man whom she thought was separated from his wife and headed for divorce. But that turned out to be a lie. She found out that he and his wife were trying to have another child, and the whole newspaper staff knew that before she did. It broke her heart.

The experience should have left her with trust issues, but it didn't. She got over it. She didn't let it cripple her and become a disabled veteran of relationships like I was. Why were the two women in my life, my sister Eloise, and Kelly, more emotionally secure than me?

Until Kelly, I was someone who never allowed a relationship to go too far. A shrink I once dated said I had abandonment issues, caused by my parents dying before their time. In the mind of a kid, she said that was taken as abandonment, and I'd built a wall around me to keep that from ever happening again. It was the reason, she said, I jumped ship when any relationship started to get too heavy. I broke it off before they could do it to me. That was probably just so much psycho-babble, but all I knew right now, at this moment, was that I didn't want to lose Kelly. And that was a first.

CHAPTER THIRTY-EIGHT

My cell phone rang, and I answered quickly, thinking it might be Kelly. It wasn't. It was Brandon Wise, the insurance investigator.

"Mr. Bragg, I have terrible news. I went to Sam Squires house last night and found him dead. He killed himself. He didn't answer his door when I knocked, so I went around and peeked into the little windows in his garage door to see if his car was there. That's when I saw him, hanging from a rafter by one of those orange heavy-duty extension cords. I called the police right away. They said he'd done it about eight o'clock last night."

He paused a moment, then said, "I wanted to tell you I may not be able to keep you out of this. I showed the police the document Squires slipped through my mail slot. They grilled me about it last night, and want to talk to me again today. I'm on my way there now. If they ask who else knows about his confession, I won't lie to them, Mr. Bragg. You must understand that."

"Do what you have to do, Mr. Wise," I said.

"The man had to be terribly despondent to do a thing like this," he said.

He was right, and I felt partly to blame. I saw what an emotional state Squires was in when I approached him at the bar. I knew about him losing his wife and his son, and I took advantage of his despair to get him to confess.

Then my suspicious side flared up.

"Are the police positive it was a suicide?" I asked. Squires could have told Kroll he was going to rat him out. And I told Teddy Crane about Squires' confession yesterday mid-afternoon, plenty of time for him to pass it along to Wilson Kroll—or go to Squires' house himself and confront him about it. It wouldn't be the first time I'd come across a murder made to look like a suicide.

It happened just a year ago over in Pickens County.

"The Police are convinced," Wise was saying. "He left a suicide note. I don't know what he wrote exactly, but they said it was in his handwriting. They authenticated that. All they told me was that it was an apology for what he'd become. Why, do you think someone may have murdered him and made it look like a suicide?"

Was I just trying to blame everything bad that happens on Wilson Kroll and Teddy Crane? Probably. I couldn't deny my prejudices when it came to them. But I didn't know where to go with it unless the police found proof—or Kroll or Crane confessed—which wasn't likely.

"I guess not," I said to Wise. "If the suicide note is legit."

"Everything indicates that," he said.

Alvin was watching me with questioning eyes when I hung up, having heard my end of the conversation.

"Sam Squires hanged himself," I said.

I contemplated where Squires' death left us. Alvin seemed to be doing the same thing. Squires swore he didn't shoot Kroll's horse and said we should talk to Teddy Crane. I'd wanted to know why Squires said that, but now, that opportunity was dead. Literally.

"Let's go look for Jamal," I finally said. "I've got a hunch I want to check out."

CHAPTER THIRTY-NINE

We took my Jeep, and I drove the route again that I thought Jamal Johnson would have most likely taken if he walked home the night he disappeared. When I came to the house with the dog, I pulled in and parked near the front door. This time a slightly newer pickup that looked like it might be drivable sat next to the older one on blocks. Someone was home.

The dog came out from under the porch barking and snarling like he was going to chew my tires off the rims. I honked the horn, and we sat until a man came out, glared at us, and ordered the dog back under the porch. The dog begrudgingly slinked away and lay down in a space hollowed out in the dirt, keeping his eyes on us.

The man wore a stained white wife beater, jeans, and combat boots with the laces untied. He was either growing a beard or hadn't gotten around to shaving for a few days. It made me wonder who was rougher looking, the dog or the man.

He came down the steps, and Alvin and I got out of the car. The dog growled from under the porch but stayed put.

“Can I help you?" The man asked in an unfriendly tone, his eyes shifting back and forth between us.

“That dog run out at everybody like that?” I said.

“What's it to you?” the man said.

“Do you remember if he happened to bark at a kid walking down the road about midnight, a couple of weeks ago?”

The man took his time as if thinking about it, but more likely he was deciding whether to tell us or not.

"Yeah, a nig . . . black boy,” he said, glancing at Alvin. “It woke me up.”

"Did you respond to the dog's barking in any way?"

"I got my twelve gauge and went outside. Then I called Merle off."

"Merle?" I said.

"Named him after Merle Haggard."

"Perfect," Alvin said.

"Did you speak to the boy?" I asked the man.

"No, I didn't speak to him. But I stayed out in the yard and kept my eyes on him until he went around the bend. Anybody coming down the road at that time of night is probably looking to steal something."

"Especially if he's black," Alvin said.

The man looked at Alvin but didn't comment.

"He's gone missing," I said. "A lot of people have been looking for him."

He stared at my old jeep. "You're not the law. Who are you?"

"A friend of the family, I said. "And this is the boy's cousin," I added and nodded over my shoulder at Alvin.

"Maybe he went off with the people in the car," the man said.

"What car?" I asked, and Alvin and I exchanged glances.

"The one that come along right behind him," the man answered. "They must of stopped for him because I heard them racing their engine after they went around the bend. It was a still night and sound carries out here."

"Do you remember the make of the car?"

"One of them big SUVs. They all look alike to me. It was a dark color. That's all I seen."

"It didn't come back this way?"

"Naw, I guess it went on into Landrum. What was that colored boy doing out here at that time of night, anyway? He could of gotten himself shot."

"Walking home," I said.

I looked at the man a moment longer and we got back in the car, backed out of his driveway, and headed down the road. The dog bolted out from underneath the porch and saw us on our way.

Around the bend, the road was a desolate stretch. There were no houses along it, no traffic, and thick stands of trees bordered both sides. I parked along the shoulder and turned to Alvin. "It's a long shot," I said, "but let's take a walk. Maybe we'll find something."

Alvin nodded and got out of the car. "I'll take one side, you take the other," he said and walked across the road.

I started down the right side, looking for anything: refuse, trampled grass, weeds, tire tracks on the shoulder, broken glass—whatever looked suspicious or out of place.

We went about fifty yards without talking, or seeing anything out of the ordinary, or noticing anything that suggested Jamal passed this way. I began to pick up a foul odor ahead as I walked, and it got stronger with every step.

I looked at Alvin across the road. "You smell that?" I asked.

He did. "What is it?" he said, wrinkling up his nose. "Roadkill?"

"If it is, then somebody's hit an elephant," I said. It was stronger and more repugnant than any dead animal I'd ever encountered. The odor was stifling and seemed to come from somewhere back in the trees to the right. I stepped across a shallow roadside ditch and walked into the woods through a thick undergrowth of weeds. Alvin walked across the road and followed me in.

A buzzard took flight from back in the bushes somewhere and startled us both. I took another step and stopped abruptly. Alvin almost walked up my back. He looked around me at the putrefying body that lay half-buried in a shallow ditch, ravaged by carrion birds and woodland animals. Just enough was left of the face and arms to see the black skin of a young man. We'd found Jamal Johnson.

I turned and looked at Alvin and watched his face go from shock to grief to the most intense anger I've ever seen. No words could have more clearly conveyed what he would do if he found the person who did this to Jamal.

I pulled out my phone and called nine-one-one.

CHAPTER FORTY

Alvin and I waited by the side of the road until the police came. It was two Spartanburg County Sheriff's cruisers, one deputy in each car. They got out of their cars and approached us apprehensively. One introduced himself as Deputy Brownell, the other Deputy Lewis. I told them who we were, pointed to where they would find the body, and told them who I thought it was. Lewis stayed with us like he thought we were going to flee the scene, as Brownell went into the bushes.

Deputy Brownell came back out a minute later looking a little green around the gills. I knew the feeling. I was still on the verge of tossing the sausage biscuits from breakfast.

"Young black guy," Brownell said to Deputy Lewis. "Probably the missing kid we've been looking for. It looks like murder to me, somebody trying to bury the body like that. I've called it in, and there's talk of getting the Greenville County Sheriff's office involved, too. It's our jurisdiction, but it may be their case."

Brownell looked at us. "I need to see some I.D."

We got out our wallets and gave him our drivers licenses. He spoke to someone into the microphone clipped to his shoulder, reading out our names and driver's license numbers.

Alvin had yet to say a word. I noticed they were eyeing him with more interest than me. Something told me he was accustomed to that experience.

When Deputy Brownell got off the phone, he asked me how we found the body.

"You got homicide detectives coming?" I asked.

"Yes, sir. Probably from both Spartanburg and Greenville Counties, along with a CSI team."

"I'll wait and talk to the detectives," I said.

He didn't seem too happy about that; I guessed he thought I was disrespecting him.

"What about you?" he said to Alvin.

"I'll wait," he said.

"Okay, if that's your wish," Brownell said, rather gruffly, "but I'm going to have to place both of you in our cars until they get here."

He took my arm and led me to his car, had me put my hands on the roof and spread my legs. He frisked me, taking away my cell phone. Then he placed me in the back seat, shut the door and walked away. They did the same thing to Alvin, putting him in the back seat of the other car. I guess they didn't want us talking together.

At least the air smelled better in the car. The motor was running, and the air conditioning on. I watched as the two deputies talked to each other, and to others on their radios. Deputy Lewis then went into the bushes to see Jamal for himself. He came back out quickly, looking like he was sorry he did it. Deputy Brownell was getting orange traffic cones out of the cruiser's trunk and placing them ahead and behind us on the road.

When he'd finished, he came over and opened my door.

"Whose Jeep is that parked up the road there?"

"Mine," I said.

"Is there anyone in it?" he asked.

"No," I said.

"Do I have your permission to look inside?" he said.

"No problem," I said, and watched him as he walked up the road toward my car. He went into the front seat, and I could see him searching through the Jeep's console and glove compartment. I suddenly realized that my Glock nine was in there. While I had a concealed carry permit for Georgia, South Carolina was one of the few states that didn't share a reciprocal agreement. I didn't know how that would affect having a gun in my car. I could see him looking in the back seat, and then he got out, opened the hatchback, looked in it briefly, closed it, and came walking back. He had my Glock in his hand.

He walked up and opened my door. "You got a permit for this gun?"

"Concealed carry, but for Georgia," I said. "Is that a problem here?"

"You're to keep the weapon in your glove compartment," he said. "Don't go carrying it around on your person up here. South Carolina doesn't honor a Georgia CC."

"I'm going to hang on to it," he added. If it turns out the victim was shot, we'll want make sure this wasn't the gun that did it. We'll return it to you as soon as we can if it clears."

"It will clear," I said.

He chewed his lip for a second, looking at me, then said, "You said you were trying to help the family find this kid. I guess you did that, didn't you?"

"Yeah, I'm sorry to say."

"The other guy the kid's family?" he asked.

"A cousin," I said, and looked at Alvin in the back seat of the other squad car. Alvin didn't look happy, but for him, looking unhappy wasn't anything out of the ordinary.

"He has an interesting background," Deputy Brownell said.

I didn't comment. He'd obviously run a check on Alvin too.

Another Sheriff's cruiser pulled in and parked on the opposite shoulder. This one bore the insignia of Greenville County, and Deputy Waldrop, whom I'd talked to the other morning, got out and came over. Deputy Brownell closed the door on me again and met him halfway. They talked for a minute, but I couldn't hear what they were saying.

Finally, they came over and opened my door and peered in. I nodded at Deputy Waldrop, and he nodded back.

"Deputy Waldrop says he knows you," Brownell said. "You want to talk to him, or do you still want to wait for the homicide detectives?"

"I meant no disrespect, Deputy Brownell," I said. "I was just trying to keep from having to tell my story twice. Deputy Waldrop already knows how I feel. Too many people say too many good things about Jamal Johnson for him to be guilty of shooting any horse. He was a good kid. And that guy that accused him? I don't believe him. He's an asshole and a crook."

"A man named Wilson Kroll," Deputy Waldrop said to Brownell. "I took his statement when his horse was shot. We first thought he might be the shooter, especially after we heard how much insurance he had on the animal. But Mr. Kroll had a solid alibi, and the evidence did point to the kid—Kroll said the boy held a grudge against him and had threatened him. And we found the rifle used to shoot the horse at the kid's house."

"Do you still believe that?" I asked Deputy Waldrop. "That the kid shot the horse?"

He looked at me like he wanted to say something.

"Something new *has* come up that has us rethinking the case," he finally said.

"The vet's confession," I offered.

"How the hell do you know about that?" Waldrop said, surprised. "I just heard about it myself."

"I've been working with Brandon Wise, the insurance investigator looking into Kroll's horse's death," I said. "You gave me his card. I also know that Sam Squires, Wilson Kroll's vet, committed suicide last night. Or at least, that's what you guys think."

"Are you saying it wasn't a suicide?" Waldrop said, another look of surprise on his face.

"I'm saying that all of this is connected, including what we've found here today. That's why I wanted to wait for the homicide detectives. To tell all of you why I think that."

"Well, you won't have to wait any longer, they're here," Waldrop said.

An unmarked, official-looking dark blue sedan had arrived and pulled up behind the deputy's unit. Two guys in short-sleeved white shirts and neckties got out. They looked like twins; both middle aged, both with expanding waistlines and square jaws. The only differences were the color and patterns of their neckties, and their hair; one had it, the other one didn't. Naturally bald or shaved, I couldn't tell.

Deputy Waldrop and Deputy Brownell went to meet them. They spoke, just out of earshot. They kept casting looks at both me and Alvin while they talked. Finally, they walked over and opened my door. They introduced themselves as Detectives Lusk and Scanlon with the Greenville County Sheriff's Department Homicide Unit.

"We'll be taking the lead on this," Detective Lusk said. "We'll have some questions for you, so sit tight until we can look at the body and get some idea of the situation."

"Where would I go?" I said, raising my eyebrows and nodding to the door of the squad car, which only opened from the outside.

"We'll be back," he said.

As he said that, a large van I assumed was the crime scene investigation unit pulled up. Lusk looked at them and said, "These guys will probably want a word with you, too, to find out how much of their crime scene you've fucked up."

I was about to say I just walked in and came right back out without touching anything, but Lusk shut my door and joined the CSI people spilling out of the van. With Deputy Brownell leading the way, they took a circuitous route to the body, evidently to avoid fouling the crime scene themselves.

CHAPTER FORTY-ONE

I sat trapped in the backseat of Deputy Brownell's car and watched one of the crime scene investigators examine the shoulder of the road, the surface of the tarmac, and the disarranged weeds that showed the path to the body. The guy stooped to look at something, too small to see from where I was sitting, then stood up and moved on to another spot and repeated the process.

Finally, the two homicide detectives along with Deputy Waldrop and Deputy Brownell came out from behind the trees. They made their way over to me and let me out of the car. Deputy Lewis went and got Alvin out of the other car and brought him over to us.

"I was beginning to think I was busted for bein' black at the scene of a crime," Alvin said.

"Sorry," Deputy Lewis said. "Just making sure you stayed put."

"My people are used to it," Alvin said.

"It is Jamal Johnson," Lusk said. "CSI moved the body enough to get at his wallet." Neither Alvin nor I needed to hear that to know who it was. How many dead black kids were we likely to find on a Dark Corner country road? Alvin stared at the ground, slowly shaking his head.

"Take off your shoes," Lusk said. "Both of you."

The tech guy came over, took our shoes from us and placed them soles up on the pavement. He pulled a tape measure out of his bag, extended it about two feet and lined it up beside my shoes, and took a straight-on photograph of each of them. He did the same with Alvin's shoes.

"That's to eliminate any of your footprints we find at the scene," Lusk said as we watched the tech put his camera away and go back to combing the side of the road.

Alvin and I put our shoes back on.

"I hear you two have been actively trying to find the boy," Lusk said and looked at me. "Deputy Waldrop says you're a sports writer up here doing a story on yesterday's steeplechase race. Is that true?"

"Yes," I said. "I'm also an old friend of the family."

"Can I ask how you came to this little county road and went straight to the kid's body, which you can't see from the road without X-ray vision?"

"We're wondering how you knew to look here, in this exact spot," Scanlon chipped in as if I didn't understand what Lusk was asking.

It was the first words I'd heard Scanlon say since he arrived. His voice was surprisingly high for his size, and not what I'd expected. Both men stood and watched me closely, waiting for my explanation.

"Well, in the first place, we didn't see him," I said. "We smelled him. And if you guys want to talk to us further, we either need to go somewhere else, or at least get in a car and turn the air conditioning on high. Or is your olfaction on the fritz?"

"That's not a bad idea," Scanlon said, wrinkling his nose. "Let's get in the car, Bobby."

Alvin and I followed them. Scanlon got behind the wheel and started the engine and turned on the air. Lusk took the passenger seat; Alvin and I got in the backseat. Outside, the Deputies cordoned off the area with yellow police tape.

Lusk and Scanlon turned in their seats to face us, and Lusk said, "You were telling us how you found the body. Please continue."

"The night Jamal went missing, he worked at a dinner party up on Hunting Country Road waiting tables," I said, "and afterward, his ride went off and left him. Evidently, none of the guests offered him a ride, so he set out walking. I found the most likely route he would have taken home, and I checked it out. I drove it a couple of times, and both times a big ugly dog at a house around the bend ran out at me. If he chases every slow-moving car that comes along in the daylight, he's bound to chase someone walking by in the middle of the night. So, Alvin and I stopped and talked to the dog's owner. I was right. The dog ran out barking when Jamal walked by that night, and the man remembers it quite well."

"The man don't get that many African Americans walking by his house at midnight," Alvin added. "It was a memorable occasion for him. Like a Big Foot sighting."

After glancing at Alvin like they didn't know what to make of him, Lusk and Scanlon's shot each other looks like this was something the Sheriff's Department didn't think to do—or go to the trouble to do.

"The dog owner said a dark SUV came along just after the boy went around the bend," I continued, "and he heard it stop around there and race the engine."

The two shot each other looks again.

"Did the man see the driver or anyone else in the car?" Lusk asked.

"He told me he didn't, but maybe his memory will improve if you talk to him."

"Oh, we plan to do that," Scanlon said, irritated, either because I was giving him advice, or because his people had been negligent following the same path of investigation that Alvin and I took.

"It does look like a car hit the boy. Maybe this was it," Lusk said. "All of his injuries but one point to an automobile. Human hands couldn't have done this kind of damage. But according to the CSI folks, one blow to his head is raising some questions. This one came from a different angle than the others, is a sharper wound, and more to the side and back of his head. Maybe he bounced off a tree or something. What makes that important is this looks like the blow that officially killed him."

Or maybe it was a deliberate blow to the head to finish him off, I thought.

"The M.E. will be able to tell us more when we get him on the table. My guess is someone came down the road, maybe this car the guy up the road saw, didn't see the boy walking in the dark and hit him. Then he—or she—probably with a few drinks in them, panicked and tried to hide the body to avoid a DUI and a vehicular homicide charge. Maybe wanted time to repair whatever damage the accident did to the vehicle. Dumb move, but then, the driver was probably too inebriated to think straight."

"Have you seen the confession of the veterinarian for the horse Jamal Johnson was supposed to have shot?" I asked Lusk. "Deputy Waldrop has."

"Haven't read it. But Deputy Waldrop just told me about it. I understand it clears the boy of the shooting and accuses the owner. Did it for the insurance, it says."

"There's something in it that relates to this," I said, nodding toward the woods and Jamal's body. The horse's owner didn't kill the horse himself; he had someone else do it. The confession implies that a man named Teddy Crane was the shooter, and I believe he may have killed Jamal Johnson, too."

"So you aren't buying the drunk driver thing," Lusk said.

"It's possible, I suppose, but no, I'm not buying it."

"You have any proof to go along with that belief?"

"I have proof that Crane does odd jobs for the horse's owner," I said, "some of them illegal. "And I have proof he's capable of killing." I pointed to the stitches in my head. "He gave me this for sticking my nose in his business. And I know the kid had information the horse's owner didn't want him telling anyone—information that the horse had become infertile. The confession now proves it, but at the time Jamal was enough of a threat to the owner that he might have had him killed."

Lusk turned to Scanlon. "Get us a copy of this confession Al," he said. "And run a background on Teddy Crane."

"Are you going to be around for the next few days, Mr. Bragg?" he said, to me.

"I don't know. I have enough for the story I came for, so I'll be heading out soon." I fished out one of my business cards and handed it to Lusk. "But, I'd like to keep up with your progress and stay in the loop if you'll allow me."

Lusk stuck my card in his pocket, climbed out and opened the rear door for us.

"You can count on us being in touch," he said as I got out. "We'll probably want you back here at some point. Either to ask you more questions, or to testify.

The CSI people came out of the bushes carrying Jamal zipped up in a black body bag on a stretcher. Two of them hurried ahead to remove a gurney from the van and wheel it out on the tarmac. They loaded Jamal's body on it, lifted it back into the van and shut the doors.

Alvin and I stood solemnly and watched.

A hundred feet down the road a news van from a TV station stopped along the shoulder, and a blonde in a short dress with a lot of leg showing got out, followed by a bearded man in a tan safari shirt with a camera on his shoulder.

"There's one other thing I'd like to ask," I said to Lusk.

"Who's going to tell Mrs. Johnson before it makes the evening news?"

Lusk glanced at the approaching news crew, then back at me.

"We will," he said. "As soon as we leave here."

I could see in his face how much he didn't look forward to that.

The news crew was making a beeline toward us, the blonde ready with a microphone in hand and a cameraman right behind her. Lusk walked toward them, palms forward to halt their progress before they could point the camera at the crime scene.

CHAPTER FORTY-TWO

Alvin and I walked back to my Jeep. When we got in, he looked over at me and said, "Take me to my car, I got to go tell Aunt Millie about this myself. I don't want no policeman breaking it to her. Then I'll go see Taylor and tell him. Rather have them hearing it from family."

I pointed the Jeep back to Natasha's place where Alvin's car was.

"You think these peckerwoods are good enough to catch the motherfucker that did this?" Alvin asked.

"I don't know," I said. "Depends on what kind of evidence they find, I guess."

"Or somebody talks," Alvin said, with a fierce look.

"And I know you've got ideas on how to make that happen," I said.

"A few of em' downright medieval," He replied. "I'll leave you out if you want."

"How about we try some non-violent tactics first," I said.

"Like what?" Alvin said. "Kroll's vet can't do any more confessing lying in the morgue. So what's our next step, boss man, non-violently speaking?"

"It's what I said. "We let it all play out. The confession. Its effect on Kroll. What we said to Teddy. Finding Jamal's body will add to the mix. Maybe now the cops will turn up the pressure and something will break."

"My way would be quicker," he said. "Just ask those cats at Abu Ghraib."

"There's also Jamal's journal," I said. "It's got to be somewhere. A friend of Jamal's, Ronnie Dill, is looking for it, and I'll check back with him. If Jamal hid it somewhere other than in his mama's house, Ronnie Dill is our best shot to find Jamal's hiding place."

Alvin continued to show a lack of enthusiasm at my suggestions.

"We need to stay close to the cops," I said. "I want them to keep us advised on their progress. Since we represent the family, they owe us that."

"Staying close to cops is your job," Alvin said. "I got no experience in that."

I caught him looking at me.

"We still got a promise to keep," he said.

"I know, Alvin, I know. If nothing else works, we'll grab Wilson Kroll and Teddy Crane and beat the truth out of them."

Alvin grinned that scary grin.

Natasha's SUV was gone when we got to her bungalow. I hoped she'd left the door unlocked like she usually did. I needed to get my stuff.

"I'll call Natasha and tell her about Jamal," I said to Alvin. "You go take care of Millie and Taylor Johnson."

"Probably take a couple of days," Alvin said. "They gonna' need somebody to help with funeral arrangements and the like. But I'll stay in touch."

"Tell them how sorry I am," I said. "I'll come and see them when I can."

Alvin nodded, got out and went to his car.

I walked to Natasha's front door, tried it, and it opened. Natasha was a trusting soul; it was an admirable quality. I wondered how much of a dent Teddy Crane would put in it when she found out his true nature.

I called Natasha and got her voicemail. I deliberated leaving the news about Jamal, but decided it wasn't something to leave as a message. I'd keep calling until I reached her.

Then I called Kelly and I told her about finding Jamal.

"When are you coming home?" was all she asked.

"As soon as I can," I said, but I didn't tell her there was one thing I wanted to do first. I wanted to take one more run at Teddy Crane. I didn't tell Alvin, either, I wanted to try to reason with Teddy without Alvin there threatening to water-board him. Teddy must know it was over for him, and the best thing was to give himself up and cooperate before Kroll and his high priced lawyers beat him to it and concocted a story placing all the blame on him. I wasn't Teddy's enemy now; Wilson Kroll was.

CHAPTER FORTY-THREE

With my bag in the Jeep, I headed for the back side of Hogback Mountain, hoping Teddy would be home. I knew if I called first, he wouldn't be by the time I got there.

I found Natasha's SUV out front of Teddy's place. She wouldn't make my job any easier being here if she tried to stick up for Teddy. But she'd get to hear the news about Jamal along with Teddy, so if I told her what Sam Squires said in his confession, maybe she'd start taking Teddy's role in things more seriously.

Teddy's SUV and motorcycle were both parked in the open garage, so they were both here. I went over to the front of the SUV and examined the front end and bumper. There was nothing as obvious as bloodstains on it, but there were many dents, scratches, and scrapes from a dozen old altercations with objects Teddy hadn't managed to avoid. I couldn't tell if any of them was due to a collision with a seventeen-year-old boy. Maybe the cops could if I got them to look at it.

I walked up to his door and rang the bell. A chime sounded from somewhere inside. No one came, so I rang it again, and pounded the door. I was beginning to get a bad feeling.

I tried the door and found it unlocked, went in through the foyer and into a two-story great room and almost stumbled over a body on the hardwood floor. It was Natasha. She lay face down, a pool of blood spreading beneath her. A large exit wound bloodied her back, with another bullet hole in the back of her head. Her purse and car keys lay by her hand, evidence someone must have shot her as she was entering the house. They had then walked over and given her the *coup de grâce* in the head.

Across the great room, a tall window looked out on the forested slopes of Hogback Mountain. A pleasant sight—except for Teddy Crane, who lay on his side on a large Navaho rug, the back of his head blown out. I should have checked, but I somehow knew no one else was in the house. Death had come and gone swiftly, leaving the house eerily quiet.

I got my phone out and dialed nine-one-one.

For the second time in one day, I was grilled by the police. This time it began at the scene of the crime and finished in a conference room in the Greenville Sheriff's Office on McGee Street in downtown Greenville. Two County Detectives, a City Detective, a SLED agent, and a woman from the FBI's National Center for the Analysis of Violent Crime, or NCAVC—the FBI being so fond of acronyms—joined me. I'd seen none of them before.

Neither Detective Lusk or Scanlon from Jamal's murder were there, and I told these cops that they might want to give them a call as they had an interest in Teddy Crane, too. I don't know if they did. Lusk and Scanlon never showed up.

It was a gang-bang that lasted for hours. I told them everything I knew and most of what I suspected. I began by telling them who I was, what I was doing in the Dark Corner generally, and at Teddy's place in particular. Along with my usual identification, driver's license, etcetera, they examined my press credentials, something the cops at Jamal's crime scene didn't do. They asked a lot of questions about Teddy and Natasha, who they were to each other, whether they were involved romantically, and things like that. I did my best to tell them. They also asked the same things of me.

They weren't telling me much about what they thought had happened or relaying any details I hadn't already figured out the moment I arrived. They were intent on asking questions, not answering them. At first, their attitude toward me wasn't so much as a witness, I realized, but more as a suspect. I guess it was too unusual for someone to discover three murders in one day, and they had to get that out of the way first. I'd done my best to explain how my presence at both scenes was plausible, and after a while, they seemed to accept that.

They asked a lot of questions about Alvin. It seemed that they were checking into his background thoroughly. I told them that regardless of his history, whatever it was, he was with me all day and had gone straight from Jamal's murder scene to Millie Johnson's to inform her of her son's death.

I wanted to call Kelly but It took a while to get permission. I told her not to look for me anytime soon, the cops were questioning me again. I wasn't allowed to tell her about Teddy and Natasha, and a detective made sure of that by standing by the phone with a finger on the hang-up button if I tried. So, I had to let her believe they were still talking to me about Jamal's murder.

The cops finally arrived at a mutual assessment of what had happened. Someone shot Teddy Crane, execution style—one in the head, up close. Natasha came in unexpectedly and got shot for it, once in the mid-trunk, once in the head. She was at the wrong place at the wrong time.

I had them get a copy of Sam Squire's confession and go through it, telling them that my number one "person of interest" in Teddy and Natasha's murders was Wilson Kroll, who had reasons to shut Teddy up. I told them that I was at Teddy's home to get him to confess to his part before Kroll could concoct his version of a story that would lay it all on Teddy.

When they learned of Kroll's Cleveland Mob connections, they wanted to know "why not them?" I told them that if anything, Kroll would kill Teddy to *keep* the mob from learning what Teddy knew.

My second suggestion was Eddie Smoke. Teddy's drugs and call girl connection with him could be bad for Smoke if it came out. I suspected that if Kroll had Mr. Kennedy's lawyer beaten up, he'd had Teddy get Eddie Smoke and his gang of thugs to do it. Neither Smoke nor Kroll would want that to get out. The city cops seemed to know who Smoke was, and there were raised eyebrows at the mention of his name.

I grieved for Natasha throughout the entire questioning. She had helped me, hurt me, and was a pain in the ass, but I'd grown to like her. A lot. She was one of a kind. I'd told her that Teddy was bad for her, but I never realized just how bad. He got her killed.

They kept coming back at me with more questions about Teddy, and what I knew, or even suspected about him. I took them through the attack on me by the polo-mallet-wielding-masked rider at the steeplechase track and even showed them the stitches still in my scalp to prove it. I also told them how convinced I was that it was Teddy on that horse, perhaps at Kroll's behest, but they seemed only interested in how much of a grudge I might have held against Teddy. They began to lose interest—until I described the mask. Then it was like they all refocused on me like I'd just showed up and they'd never seen me before. They made me describe the mask to them again.

The County Detective turned to the FBI lady and gave her a questioning look. "Should we call Mosely Smith?" he asked her.

"I'm doing it now," she said, grabbed her smartphone and left the room. The rest of them began studying their fingernails, the table, the floor—anything it seemed, to avoid looking at me.

"Did I do something to break up the party?" I asked.

"There's someone else that we need in on this," the County Detective said.

"Who is Mosely Smith?" I asked. I'd heard that name somewhere.

The FBI lady returned before anyone could answer.

"We got lucky," she said. "Smith is still in town, and he's on his way."

"Let's all take a little break until he gets here," the County Detective said. "I could use a bathroom break and a chance to stretch my legs." He looked at me and said, "You probably could, too. But don't leave the building. Smith's going to be very interested in talking to you."

He got up and left the room along with everyone else but the FBI lady. She sat texting something on her smartphone.

"Who is Mosely Smith?" I asked her. "Why do I know that name?"

"She didn't look up, her thumbs still working hard at texting. "He's an FBI Agent."

"I would advise you to take that bathroom break, Mr. Bragg," she said. "You're probably going to be here a lot longer than you expected."

Suddenly it hit me. Agent Mosely Smith was the name of the agent-in-charge of the Carolina Stalker serial killer case. I'd seen him on TV.

But why the hell would he want to question me?

CHAPTER FORTY-FOUR

Finally, Special Agent Mosely Smith arrived. Everyone returned to the conference room, and he took over the questioning. Smith was a middle-aged man with a chocolate brown complexion who carried himself like an ex-athlete. His biceps filled the sleeves of the jacket he was wearing, and my bet was that his waistline was probably about the same size it was when he played whatever sport he played when he was much younger.

"Mr. Bragg, you said you were attacked a few nights ago by someone on horseback, wearing a mask, and he hit you with a polo mallet."

"Yes," I said.

"Describe the mask again," he said.

"It was one of those 'Guy Fawkes-Anonymous masks' that the 'Occupy Wall Street' protestors wore," I said, and described it in detail.

He sat quietly as if he was visualizing my description. "You told us that you think the man murdered today, this Teddy Crane, was your attacker. Do you stand by that?"

"I can't prove it a hundred percent, but yes. As I said, the guy was wearing a mask, and I never saw his face. But he was Teddy's size, and shape, skilled at competitive jumping like Teddy was, and he was also wearing a coat like I've seen Teddy wear. And, he was one of two people who had a reason to try to stop me from finding out what happened to Jamal Johnson."

"Who is the other one?" Smith asked.

"Wilson Kroll, the horse breeder who accused Jamal Johnson of shooting his horse, and for whom Teddy Crane occasionally worked. But Kroll doesn't fit the description of my masked attacker. Kroll is short and stocky. Crane was tall and thin. However, Kroll might have paid Teddy to do it."

"Do you have any hard proof that Crane had anything to do with the Johnson boy's death?" Agent Smith asked.

"No. What I have is all circumstantial or hearsay. Teddy supplied drugs and prostitutes to Wilson Kroll's sex parties but lied to me about even knowing him. He did other things for Kroll, too. Kroll's veterinarian implied that Teddy shot Kroll's horse and framed Jamal Johnson for it. I believe he was capable of doing other things for the man. Like killing Jamal because the kid knew things that could ruin Kroll."

"Prostitutes?" Mosely Smith said. "Tell me about that."

"Alvin Brown, Jamal's cousin, and I followed Teddy when he picked up a carload of call girls from a guy in West Greenville named Eddie Smoke. Teddy delivered them to Kroll's party Friday night. That's why I added Smoke to my list of suspects for Teddy's murder. Teddy knew a lot about Smoke's illegal activities. Now he'll never talk about them."

"We're well aware of Eddie Smoke," a detective pitched in. "A local Hood into all kinds of things. He'll eventually fuck up, and we'll get him."

Smith looked at him, then motioned for me to continue.

"At the party," I went on, "We saw a man wearing that mask peering through a bedroom window watching a guest fornicate with one of these prostitutes. It was Teddy Crane, I'm sure. He was wearing the mask my attacker wore, and the same long coat Teddy wore earlier that day when he picked up the hookers. It's Crane's trademark outfit, and he wears it often. He thinks it's cool. The coat is an old cowboy duster like they wore out west in the 1800s."

"Did he return these girls to Greenville later?"

"I assume he did, but I didn't stick around. I'd seen what I wanted to see and proved what I wanted to prove—that Teddy Crane was a drug pusher and a pimp and had an illicit business connection with Wilson Kroll. The peeping tom bit was an added insight into the character of the man."

"So, Mr. Bragg," Smith said. "Do you think Crane was capable of murder?"

"If he's the one who hit me with the polo mallet, *yes*. Look, Agent Smith," I said. "I'm trying to cooperate here, but it's time I got some answers. Why all the questions about the mask, and what does it have to do with you? I know who you are. I saw you on TV. You're the agent in charge of the Carolina Stalker serial killer case."

"More like the agent to blame," he said, "since I can't seem to catch the guy."

He sat back and studied me. "Mr. Bragg, I'm going to tell you something, but I'm going to ask you not to repeat it. You could seriously jeopardize the investigation if you do. Especially if what you've told me, and what I suspect, doesn't pan out. Can I trust you not to be the one to spill this to the press—or, since I know what you do for a living and who you're sleeping with, neither she nor you will break the story yourselves?"

"How do you know who I'm sleeping with?" I asked.

"We're the FBI, Mr. Bragg," he said, and almost grinned. "You don't want to piss us off."

"Well, when you put it that way, I promise not tell a soul. But in return, when you're ready to make it public, I'm the first reporter you call."

"I can live with that," he said.

"So, what is it with this mask?"

"We have a witness," he said. "From two murders ago. She saw the killer leaving the victim's apartment, and he was wearing the very mask you described, a cowboy hat, and a long coat down to his ankles."

I looked at Agent Smith, my mouth probably open, trying to shape what he'd just said into some semblance of understanding.

"We've been keeping this from the press. You can buy these masks on the internet, and the last thing we need is a copycat."

"Mother, Mary of God," I said. *Can Teddy Crane be a serial killer?* I leaned back in my seat, and said, "I'm blown away. I've thought some pretty bad things about him, but *never* this."

I had another thought. "Was the murdered girl from the killing in Greenville working Wilson Kroll's party?" I asked.

"According to a couple of her friends that we talked to, she could have been. They said they worked a party somewhere in North Greenville County Friday night and had just gotten back. Then they all lawyered up, and aren't saying anything else. Maybe it was this Smoke character we were just discussing who hired their lawyers."

"Well, if the murders stop now, that should be proof that Teddy was your man," I said. "But I still can't believe it. Well, I can," but it's a shock."

Smith glared at me. "I don't want to wait for that. I want proof now. I want to find that mask, or a hammer with blood on it. We know he takes pieces of their jewelry as souvenirs, I want to find it. He turned to one of the County detectives and said, "Bring our forensic people in to do a fine-tooth search of Crane's house. Your guys can help, but they need to take orders from mine."

"Fine by me," the Detective said. 'You know what you're looking for, we don't."

"Smith nodded at the FBI woman, and she grabbed her phone and left the room again. I guessed she was calling in the forensic team.

Mosely Smith looked at me as if he were trying to think of other questions to ask or things to say. He was excited about the unfolding investigation. Then he said, "I guess you can go, for now, Mr. Bragg, "but stay available."

As I stood up to leave, I said, "Can I call you tomorrow to see what you've found at Teddy's house. Obviously, I want to keep up with the investigation."

He fished out one of his cards and handed it to me. I gave him one of mine.

"I'll tell you what I can," he said.

I nodded, and left for Kelly's and hopefully, to a less insane world.

CHAPTER-FORTY-FIVE

On the drive to Kelly's, I thought about calling Alvin to tell him what had happened to Teddy and Natasha, but it was after midnight, and I figured they were all asleep—if sleep was possible after the news about Jamal. I'd call him first thing in the morning.

Kelly was waiting for me at her front door before I even got to it. We stood in the doorway for the longest time, just holding each other and not speaking. I took her in, and we sat on her sofa as I told her about Teddy and Natasha. There was nothing to say that could explain or lessen the horrific tragedy of the day's events and the pain we both felt. Kelly was almost too shocked to cry.

We talked more about Jamal Johnson's murder, too, and the incredible unfairness of it. But we said nothing about Natasha climbing into my bed, Kelly's anger at her, or anything else derogatory about her. All of that was so irrelevant now as to be disrespectful. Whatever she had done, was just Natasha being Natasha and we would both miss her.

Kelly didn't know Teddy, and we didn't talk about him much until I broke my promise to Agent Smith and told her about the witness, the mask, and the clothes—the shocking clues that pointed to Teddy Crane as the Carolina Stalker serial killer. I knew it would eat her up to have to sit on a such a blockbuster scoop, but I also knew she would do it. She said my word was her word and she would keep it.

I hadn't eaten since breakfast, and while we continued to talk, I grabbed some leftover pasta from the fridge, and I ate it with a glass of wine.

We went to bed eventually and made desperate love. I fell asleep holding her close, feeling her tears on my shoulder. All night long, tormented dreams brought a jumble of disturbing questions that circled in my semi-consciousness and never reached a conclusion. But none of them were about Jamal or Natasha or Teddy's murders—or even Teddy as the Carolina Stalker. They were all about Kelly and me. Did I decidedly want Kelly to be with me forever, or was I just afraid of what my life would be like if I lost her? I realized, even in my sleep, that this was the question of greatest importance in my life. And one I had to answer, asleep or awake.

Monday morning I awoke before Kelly, got up and dressed, made a pot of coffee, and grabbed the Greenville newspaper off her doorstep.

The headline across the top of the front page of the paper announced, "Murder in the Dark Corner," in bold type. The story about Teddy and Natasha was on one side, Jamal, on the other. I poured a cup of coffee and sat down at the kitchen table to read them.

There wasn't a lot of details in either story other than the bare bones facts and short backgrounds of the victims. There wasn't anything there I didn't already know. Thankfully, there was no mention of Alvin or me in either story. The cops appeared to be keeping everything close to the vest, which suited me just fine. I didn't want or need the press. There was no mention of the Carolina Stalker. Smith was keeping that under wraps, too.

While Kelly was in the shower, I called Alvin. He was in Taylor's room at the medical facility in Greenville.

"I was about to call you," Alvin said. "Natasha and Teddy? Damn, J.D.."

"You heard," I said.

"Well, yeah. It's all over the news."

"I found them," I said.

"Damn," he said again. "I didn't see that part. What the hell were you doing there?"

"I wanted to see if the news about Jamal would put a crack in Teddy's façade."

"Why didn't you ask me to go with you?" Alvin asked.

"I said I wanted to put a crack in his façade, not his skull."

"Then it's a damn good thing you didn't get there earlier, as Natasha did."

"You got that right," I said.

"They said somebody shot Teddy 'execution style,' but don't name no suspects or reasons why. What's your take?"

"Wilson Kroll or Eddie Smoke, pick one," I said. "Teddy had too much on both of them, and they all know this whole thing is about to blow up. I think Natasha went to see Teddy at the absolute worst time she could, and walked into the middle of it."

"Damn," Alvin said for the third time. "You think we caused this?" he said, his voice taking on a hushed tone, probably to hide what he was saying from Mrs. Johnson and Taylor.

"Perhaps we sped it up a bit, but Teddy was bound to end up with something bad happening to him. But Natasha getting caught up in it . . ."

"That's the motherfucker," Alvin said, completing my thought.

"How are Mrs. Johnson and Taylor doing?" I asked.

"They want to talk you."

I heard the shuffling of the phone and Millie Johnson came on the line.

"I want to thank you for finding my boy," she said, her voice filled with sorrow. I could feel her pain over the telephone.

I didn't know what to say; I was my most awkward self at moments like this. Every tragedy in my life was like the one Mrs. Johnson was experiencing. Someone died before their time, without explanation, or answers. Why them? Why now? Why, God? With me, it was my parents' death when I was just a kid; years later, my grandfather's senseless murder. If there were words for times like this, I didn't know them.

"When you outlive your child," Millie Johnson said, "it's like living in hell while you're here on this earth. And that's where I am. I'm sunk as deep as Lucifer's pit as I sit here thinking about my Jamal. I already knew in my heart something bad happened to him, but it don't make it easier to find out for sure."

"Is there anything I can do for you, Mrs. Johnson?" I asked.

"Find out who did this to my baby."

"Mrs. Johnson, with Teddy Crane dead, we may never know for sure. Maybe the police will find out one day."

"The police the one's told me Jamal run away. What they gonna' tell me now?"

She probably had a right to mistrust the police, based on their efforts so far, but they could still do things that I couldn't.

"I'll do what I can, Mrs. Johnson. Even if it's only staying on the cops' case to make sure they don't stop trying to prove who did this."

She broke down sobbing. Alvin came back on the line. "Taylor wants to talk to you, too."

I could hear Taylor's respirator working in the background when he spoke.

"You found Jamal . . . like you promised."

"I just wish we'd found him alive," I said.

"Thank you . . . J.D.. Will you go to . . . Jamal's funeral for me? Mama's only . . . got Alvin and . . . she needs all the support . . . she can get. You can go . . . in my place. You always were . . . like one of her boys . . . anyway . . . It's Thursday . . . at Gowensville . . . Baptist Church."

"Of course, I'll be there, Taylor," I said.

Alvin got the phone back. "So what do we do now?" he asked.

"I guess we wait and see where the cops come out in their investigations with Jamal and Teddy and Natasha. I'll stay in touch with them. What I learn, you'll learn."

I didn't tell Alvin the wild news that Agent Mosely Smith was looking at Teddy as the Carolina Stalker serial killer, and it wasn't because I didn't trust him. I'd wait until Smith completed his search of Teddy's house, so I could tell Alvin with more certainty Teddy was a worse guy than even we suspected. I told Alvin I'd see him at Jamal's funeral and hung up.

I went through my phone messages. The cops took my phone while they questioned me, and when they gave it back, I didn't check my calls. I'd missed two: one from Kelly, wondering when I was coming home, and one from Ronnie Dill, saying he'd found Jamal's journal.

CHAPTER FORTY-SIX

I called Ronnie on the number attached to his messages and got his father. He bluntly told me that "Ronnie's at fuckin' school—or he goddam better be," and slammed down the phone. What a guy.

Then I called the office at Ronnie's high school to see if they would let me talk to him, thinking maybe I could drive over and pick up the journal if he had it with him. An assistant principal told me in no uncertain terms that she could not get Ronnie out of class for any reason other than a family emergency. The lady I was speaking to said she knew Ronnie's father's voice, and I was *not* him. I told her, "And thank God for that," and hung up.

I took out Agent Moseley Smith's card and called him. He must have seen my name on his caller I.D. because he didn't wait for me to tell him who was calling.

"You're not going to be calling me every fifteen minutes, are you?" he said. "We're still at it, so you'll have to give us a little time, Mr. Bragg."

"You don't sound happy," I said.

It was a moment before he spoke again. "Sorry I barked at you. You're right; I'm not happy. I'm disappointed. I think I let you get my hopes up. We've found no masks, no polo mallets, no two-gallon zip bags, and no keepsake jewelry. The only thing of interest so far are a couple of cowboy hats and two of those long coats, cowboy dusters, you called them. Two different colors, a light one, and a dark one. They're in the lab with our people who are combing them for blood, or hairs, or anything that can tie Crane to the murdered girls. So far, no luck. We're checking behind walls now, hoping he had a secret hidey-hole somewhere. Maybe he knows he was seen and threw it all away."

"How about his car?"

"There was nothing in it, either. There are several dents and scrapes on the front end, but they only show paint scrapings from other cars, or walls or whatever. No blood or hair. So far, all we've got on him is that he was a terrible driver."

I was beginning to feel like "the boy who cried wolf," but my memory of the masked rider, coattails flying was still vivid. It had to be Teddy. What the guy wore and his physical appearance fit Teddy too well.

"If there's nothing else, let me get back to work," he said. "If anything turns up, I'll call."

With nothing to do until Ronnie Dill got out of school, I followed Kelly into the *Clarion*. I spent time with Eloise, while Kelly went to work on this week's edition, which would cover the murders in North Greenville County. She would best the large Greenville daily paper with a more detailed account based on what I could tell her. No one had interviewed me over there, and Kelly would be the only one with a first-hand viewpoint of both events.

Kelly would stop every so often, and come to quiz me about some detail regarding the crime scenes, the state of the victims, and so on. I'd told her my suspicions of who I thought did it, but she couldn't (and wouldn't print) guesses. She, like me, would have to rely on police work to reveal that. Perhaps with my new connections with the FBI and Greenville County Sheriff's department, I could soon deliver her another "scoop," not to mention an ending for my own "horse country" story, which I had yet to write. I told her she couldn't use my name and to refer to me as either a reliable witness, or just "a witness." She was good at what she did, and I didn't try to read over her shoulder or tell her how to write it, nor would she let me if I'd tried.

Later, Kelly, Eloise, and I had lunch at a restaurant in the nearby town of Easley which served Cajun food, including fried alligator bites, which I'd had in Florida once, but was very drunk at the time, and remembered little about it. The waitress told me it tasted like chicken. I had the chicken and told *her* it tasted like alligator. She didn't think I was funny.

Finally, it was time to head for the Dark Corner and Ronnie Dill's house. I wanted to get there in time to catch him as he got off the school bus if that proved to be his transportation home, and I guessed it was.

I parked the Jeep on the shoulder down the road from his house, not wanting to risk running into his father. A half-hour later a yellow school bus came down the road and stopped in front of Ronnie's house. I got out of the Jeep and stood at the front fender. When I saw Ronnie get off, I gave him my best ballpark whistle. He saw me, glanced in the direction of his house, and came hurrying over to me.

"So you found it?" I said.

"Yes I did," he said. He pulled the backpack from his shoulders and took out a small hard-bound book with a blue cover, and handed it to me.

"I ain't read it," he said, as if that's what was expected of him.

"You heard about Jamal?" I asked.

He stared at the ground between his feet and looked like he was about to cry. "They announced it this morning at home room. They're going to close the school Wednesday, in memory of him. And anybody wants to go to his funeral on Thursday, can."

"I'm sorry Ronnie," I said. "I know what good friends you guys were."

He looked up at me. "I'll never have another friend as good as him."

I didn't say anything. Perhaps he was right, but I hoped not. Ronnie was a good kid, and with a daddy like his, he at least deserved a few good friends.

I opened Jamal's journal and looked at it. It was filled almost cover to cover with cursive writing in a neat hand, but with a lot of abbreviations and acronyms.

"Where'd you find it?" I asked.

"In our old secret hiding place," he said. "A place Jamal and me used to keep secret stuff when we were kids. I hadn't thought about it in years. It's an old hollow tree out behind Jamal's house—a big old poplar. The book was wrapped in a plastic garbage bag and stuck down among a bunch of acorns squirrels had stored there, and some matchbook cars I found a long time ago in a ditch by a house down the road." His eyes stared into the distance as he recalled the memories.

"I ain't seen them cars since we were nine years old," he said. "Jamal wanted me to take them back, saying they belonged to some other kid, not us. He wouldn't even play with them. I put them in our hidey-hole and never did get around to taking them back."

"Well, you've done a good deed here, Ronnie. Maybe it will help us discover who killed Jamal."

"I'd like that," he said, "but I'd like it better if he was still alive."

"Me, too," I said and suddenly had a thought. "Do you have any ambition about going to college?"

"Ain't no way I can go to college," the kid said. "We can't afford it."

'How are your grades?" I asked.

"Not too bad. Specially math and science. Why?"

"I'll tell you what," I said, thinking about the college fund Natasha had set up for Jamal Johnson. "If you'll bear down at school, hit the books and get your grades up as high as you can, maybe we can do something about that."

I assumed that Natasha's parents would take charge of that trust now, and might not be opposed to helping this kid, who needed all the help he could get. Jamal and Mrs. Johnson would approve, I thought. I told him about it. "Don't get your hopes up just yet," I said, "but I'll speak to them about it."

"For real?" he said, and again looked like he was about to cry.

"I'll do what I can if you will too. Deal?"

He gave me an earnest look and stuck out a thin hand. I shook it.

"I'm going somewhere to read this," I said, holding up Jamal's journal. "I'll let you know what I learn. Thanks again, Ronnie. You're a good guy."

I left Ronnie standing on the side of the road and walked to my Jeep. A cup of coffee always made a good companion for reading, so I headed into Landrum looking for that, along with a quiet table for one.

CHAPTER FORTY-SEVEN

A place named Southern Delights didn't sound like a coffee shop to me, but the lady behind the counter at the gas station where I filled up the Jeep's tank said it had the best cup of coffee in town. I took her word for it and found the place in downtown Landrum. Not only was the coffee as good as advertised, but also the freshly made warm cinnamon bun I ordered to go with it was out of this world tasty.

I grabbed a small table by the window, got comfortable, and opened Jamal's journal. There was the typical teenage stuff, a lot of it about school, teachers, classmates, and training tips to himself about running track, with quotes from someone I assumed was his track coach. Much of the narrative was in bits and pieces, personal notes to himself that would help him remember more later. Many entries were about his girlfriend Monique, a lot of them cryptic and in a code completely beyond my ability to decipher. It was easy to see which things he didn't want anyone else to read—like his mother. I gathered from these entries that he and Monique had gone well beyond the kissing and making out stage. He was a good kid, but he wasn't a saint. I scanned past most of this.

The more I read, the more I learned that Jamal had big dreams for the future. His narrative left me feeling like I knew him, which made me regret his death even more.

There was an entry of him overhearing Kroll and his vet Sam Squires talking about Emperor's infertility. He thought neither Mr. Kroll or his vet were aware that he heard them. They were in the hall of the stable, and he was working in a closed stall. Jamal sounded certain about what he heard. If that got him killed, Kroll would have had to know somehow that Jamal overheard them. Did

Monique talk to someone about it? Or did Wilson Kroll or Sam Squires catch him eavesdropping and Jamal didn't know?

A few pages later, Jamal included the account of his losing his job. He simply wrote, "laid off," and didn't call it a firing. Jamal sounded more confused than angry about it, puzzled over the whole thing, believing that he was a good worker doing a good job. Overall, Jamal didn't seem too upset. Nothing was said about an argument, harsh words, threats, or Kroll's infertile horse. Jamal must have been just the most viable scapegoat for Kroll to blame for the shooting. Who would believe Jamal over him? That part had worked.

I was almost to the end, beginning to think there was nothing more of interest. Then I saw the last entry, dated the Saturday Jamal went missing. It read:

"Old Mrs. N. came morning. Went with. Move boxes to rm. in stable loft. $25. Trunk in storage rm. always locked. Trunk open today. Looked in. Weird stuff. Halloween masks. Women jewelry. Broken polo mallets. TC came in. Caught me. Accused stealing. Yelled. Don't like him. Finished wk. Mrs. N. took home."

Was *TC* Teddy Crane? And *Mrs. N,* Chuck Norman's mother? At lunch Wednesday with Teddy and Chuck, Teddy said he boarded his horses at the Norman's stables. What else did he keep there? The trunk Jamal found? This was why Agent Smith didn't find anything at Teddy's house. *Teddy didn't keep it there, he kept it at the stable where his horses were!*

I left money on the table for the coffee and cinnamon roll and headed to my Jeep. Chuck said he lived in one of the big old barns on Hunting Country Road, and with a little help from Google and GPS, I found the address. It was west toward Tryon a mile from Natasha's place.

I called Detective Mosely Smith, but it went directly to his voicemail. At the beep, I said, "Detective Smith, this is J.D. Bragg. I think I know why you didn't find anything tying Teddy Crane to the serial killings at his house. He doesn't keep it there. He hides it in an old trunk at the stables where he boards his horses." I gave him the address, and added, "I'm not waiting until you get a search warrant, I'm on my way there now."

Smith wouldn't like it, but I wanted to see it for myself. My brain was spinning. What if Jamal wasn't killed because he knew Emperor was infertile? What if Teddy killed him because he caught him looking in the trunk? Jamal didn't know the significance of what was in there, but Teddy couldn't risk him even telling anyone. The mask hadn't made the news, but Teddy must know it eventually would since he was seen by a witness leaving the scene of one of his murders. Why he didn't just throw it away, I didn't know, but he still had it when he hit me at the track, and when he was looking into the window at Kroll's party. The mask must hold some significant meaning to him, but who knew what went on in his deranged mind. He was a serial killer.

CHAPTER FORTY-EIGHT

I found a place just out of sight of the Norman's huge home and parked along the shoulder. I got out and climbed over a rail fence and went into the woods that circumvented a picturesque green pasture. I came out behind the stables, which were to the side and behind the Tudor-style house. No one saw me—or at least I didn't think so. But there were enough windows in the big house that someone could have been looking out of one of them, but I'd take that chance. The worst that could happen was a trespassing charge, now that I didn't have to worry about Teddy hitting me in the head with a polo mallet again.

The doors were closed on the four-car garage on the side of the house, so I had no idea who was home. I went in through the rear of the stables and passed two stalls with horses in them, Teddy's, I assumed. One of them gave me a horse raspberry as I walked by. The other stalls, except for one filled with hay, were empty and looked like they had been for some time. I remembered Chuck saying they sold their horses after his father died, and these stalls had been without animals so long, they no longer smelled of them.

I climbed a narrow set of stairs up to the loft and found a huge room that had held hay and other silage when more horses were stabled there. Now it was bare. As I'd seen, Teddy kept his horses' fodder in one of the stalls below.

There was an open area in the middle of the floor for pitching hay down below, and a door off to one side, which I assumed was the storage room. I walked over and opened it. Inside was a smaller room filled with old cast-off furniture large and small, covered with clear plastic or bed sheets, and stacks of cardboard moving boxes of various sizes. The result of Jamal's labor on that Saturday, probably. In a corner were a couple of old saddles and tack, and against a far wall, an old wooden trunk, the lid padlocked.

In for a penny, in for a pound, the old cliché went. I went back down the stairs, found a pitchfork, and brought it back. I inserted the tines between the lock and the latch and put my weight behind it. The latch broke, the wood splintered, and the padlock fell to the floor.

I raised the trunk lid and found just what Jamal described. There was not one, but two identical Guy Fawkes' masks. Teddy kept a spare, I thought. There were also two of what Jamal described as broken polo mallets—but they weren't broken, the handles on them were just shortened, one sawed off to about two feet, the other shorter, about hammer size. These mallets weren't meant to reach a ball on the ground from horseback. They were used to smash in the teeth and lips of Teddy's victims. A large plastic zip bag contained items of women's jewelry and accessories; bracelets, necklaces, and rings, mostly flashy cheap things like a prostitute would wear. Teddy's souvenirs.

I used the pitchfork to move things around so I wouldn't get my fingerprints on anything. Underneath the masks and mallets, I found a box of the plastic zip bags—2-gallon size. There were plenty left in the box, so Teddy had well supplied himself for the future. One side of the trunk held a stack of folded clothing, an Aussie drover's slouch hat on top. I moved the hat and unfolded what turned out to be a long cowboy duster, like the ones I'd seen Teddy wear. Agent Smith said he'd found two of them at Teddy's house. I guess one as stylish as Teddy just couldn't have too many cool threads.

Then I saw the award ribbons. There were about a dozen at the bottom of the trunk, all awards for Junior equine events and competitions. There were a couple of 2nd and 3rd places, but most of them were for 1st place. They were for polo, dressage, jumping events, and riding competitions. Childhood memories, I thought. Even serial killers were children once. There was also a packet of clippings, tied together by a length of string. I took it off and looked at them. They were old enough to have turned a faded yellow. They were all stories about a junior rider that one headline called the "child prodigy of the horse world." I looked at a photograph. It showed a kid dressed in the shirt, helmet and boots of a polo player. The caption underneath gave his name, but I'd already recognized him. It was a young Chuck Norman.

What the hell? I thought. *Why were these in here?*

Suddenly I heard the floorboards creak behind me.

I turned to see Chuck Norman standing in the doorway pointing a gun at me.

Then it hit me as if the roof had fallen in on me.

"It's *you*, not Teddy," I said.

Before I could say another word, he shot me.

He got me just under my collarbone near my right shoulder, and it knocked me flat on my back. Don't let anybody ever tell you it doesn't hurt to get shot. It hurts like hell. My first thought was that at least the bullet missed my lung; the pain was higher than that, and I seemed to be breathing okay. My second thought was that he was going to shoot me again.

He was making his way toward me in a stiff-legged gait; the gun pointed directly at my head. He wore a determined look that said his next shot wouldn't just wound.

I held out my good arm toward him, palm outward as if I were superman, able to stop a speeding bullet. But I had no super powers, my Glock was in the Jeep, and I needed a real world way to stop him, and quick. The only thought I had was to get him talking. I gritted my teeth against the pain and said, "Why did you kill Teddy and Natasha? They were your best friends."

It worked. He stopped suddenly, his eyes doing a slow refocus like his mind had slipped into some other spatial dimension, and he was fighting hard to get back.

"Teddy knew I was being *him*," he finally said, his face morphing into an angry pout, his voice almost child-like. He lowered the gun when he said that, lost in the thought.

"How were you *him*?" I asked, saying anything to keep him talking before he shot me again. I could only hope Detective Smith got my message and was pulling into Chuck's drive right now, a cadre of cops behind him.

"I was being strong. Like Teddy."

My shoulder was going numb. The good news was the pain was subsiding, the bad news was I might be bleeding to death. "You admired Teddy, didn't you?" I said.

"Teddy would never have put up with *Mother*. He would smash her in the mouth if she talked to him like she talks to me."

Smash her in the mouth. Interesting choice of words, I thought.

"You admire those 'occupy' protestors, too, don't you? That's what the 'Anonymous' mask is all about, right?"

"The mask represents my fight for justice and retribution."

"These women are substitutes for your mother, aren't they? You're shutting her up by shutting them up."

"Don't try to psychoanalyze me!" he yelled, spittle flying from his mouth. He took a quick step toward me, raising the gun again. "I don't like that . . . *I don't like that*! Do you understand? Do you know what it's like to listen to the things that come out of my mother's mouth—the brow-beatings, the criticisms, the terrible, cruel things she says to me? I wanted to shut her up. I *had* to shut her up. But, how could I? She's my *mother*!"

"I'm not trying to psychoanalyze you, Chuck, I'm just trying to understand you, and why you killed Teddy, when you admired him so much."

"He turned on me. He was going to tell," he said and nodded to the open trunk behind me. "He saw . . . what's in there."

"When was that?" I asked.

"When that nigger boy saw it."

His face had gone very red, and the wild look was back in his eyes. "Teddy wasn't my friend anymore. He was yelling at me. Just like Mother."

"Why was he yelling at you?" I asked.

"Because you accused him of looking through Mr. Kroll's windows at his party, and you thought he was the one who hit you on the track that night. He knew it was me. He'd seen the mask, too. And sooner or later he would learn about the *women*. I was seen *being him*, and it would come out."

"What about Natasha? I said. "Did she walk in on you?"

"She wasn't supposed to be there. She just barged in and left me no choice."

I didn't see any regret in his face. "You killed Jamal Johnson, too, didn't you?" I asked.

"*Can you not hear*? I just told you he saw who I was, too. He had no right looking at my things. My mother caused that. She hired him. Once again, she was trying to destroy my life like she did when she sold the horses. And then there the boy was, right in my headlights. I was in Mother's big SUV, and it was easy. But I should have buried him deeper. I won't make that same mistake with you. I should have hit you harder at the track. You're like Mother. Everything you do is against me."

I saw the intensity grow in his eyes as he stiffened his arm and pointed the gun between my eyes. I tried to roll away but there was nowhere to go. I gritted my teeth waiting for the shot, then suddenly his face exploded, a mist of blood spraying over me, and he went down in a crumble of elbows, knees, and legs.

Behind him, his mother stood in the doorway, holding a smoking pistol almost as big as she was. I couldn't believe she made it up the stairs without either Chuck or me hearing her.

She slowly opened her fingers and let the gun fall to the floor. I jumped at the sound it made when it hit.

"I should have done that years ago," she said, in a calm voice. "Charles was a sick boy, but I ignored it.

"I need to call an ambulance," I said, trying to get my phone out of my pocket with my good arm. I dialed nine-one-one, said I'd been shot and gave my name and location. I hung up as they started asking questions.

If Mrs. Norman heard me, she didn't act like it. She slid down the wall until she was sitting on the floor, still talking.

"As a child, Charles was quite the horseman," she said. "After Robert, my husband died, I sold the horses because Charles had begun to abuse them, hurting them when they didn't perform to his standards. He was furious with me when I did that. Afterward, he seemed to fold in upon himself. He lost interest in everything, going into a shell and never coming out."

She sighed at the thought and continued.

"I have never known what goes on in that head of his. He has never forgiven me for getting rid of the horses—yet he never mentions it."

I was beginning to feel weak and dizzy and closed my eyes. I don't think she noticed.

"You may not know this," she said, "but Robert, my husband, was kicked in the head and killed by a horse he was shoeing. Or so the authorities determined. I must confess that I have never been comfortable with that conclusion. Charles was with him when it happened, but he didn't seem to show the shock and grief I expected from a fourteen-year-old who just witnessed his father killed. Later, we found a blacksmith hammer buried in the hay in the stall. It had blood on it. Now, there were obviously legitimate ways for blood to get on that hammer as the accident would have caused blood to splatter everywhere, but there was only one way the hammer could have been buried that deep in the hay: someone placed it there."

I opened my eyes and looked at her. "Mrs. Norman, are you saying Chuck killed his father with that hammer, buried it in the hay, and blamed it on the horse?" I managed to say.

She looked at me with tired eyes. "In hindsight, I wish I'd told someone. But to be honest, I didn't want to know the truth. So I've kept it secret all these years, and turned a blind eye to the sickness in Charles, hoping it would never surface again if I could just keep a tight rein on him."

With all the strength I had, I pushed myself back against the trunk and leaned against it. The room was spinning, but the pain in my shoulder seemed to be keeping me alert. I saw Mrs. Norman staring at the open trunk.

"I've known about that chest for some time," she said, "and the effort Charles made to keep it secret. "But I couldn't marshal the nerve to look. Perhaps I didn't want to know what was in there. But from what he was about to do to you, I don't think I made the right decision. Once again, I should have told someone."

Over the sound of her voice, I heard approaching sirens. She stopped talking and was listening now. We could hear car doors slamming out in the yard. Mrs. Norman sighed audibly, and gave me a look that held a lot of things in it: sadness, anger, defensiveness—but I didn't see remorse.

I looked down at Chuck Norman lying dead on the floor and thought of Jamal, Natasha, Teddy, and all those dead prostitutes I never met. I wondered if Mrs. Norman had sought psychiatric help for him all those years ago, rather than burying her concern about him and spending the rest of his and her life punishing him verbally for what he was, they would all be alive, and he wouldn't be lying there.

They had Mrs. Norman in the back of a squad car, and me in the back of an ambulance. Twice in less than a week. The paramedics patched me up as best as they could and readied me for another trip to the hospital in Columbus.

Thanks to a shot of something a paramedic gave me, I wasn't in much pain.

Smith came over just as they were about to shut the ambulance doors on me and said, “I don’t know whether to arrest you for coming here without waiting for me, or kick your butt for being so stupid.”

“I’ll settle for a ‘thank you,” I said. “I solved your big case for you.”

He gave me a thoughtful look. “You came to the Dark Corner to write a story about these people,” he said. “I'd say you got a humdinger.”

“Everything but a happy ending,” I said.

EPILOGUE

Eloise, Mackenzie, and Kelly had all come with me to visit Taylor Johnson in the medical facility in Greenville he called home. Millie Johnson and Alvin Brown were there, too. It was my first time back since Jamal's funeral service. As much as I hated funerals, I attended because Taylor had asked me too. Alvin and I had kept Millie Johnson company, and gave her our arms to lean on—my good one since the other one was in a sling.

It was a beautiful day outside, and Mrs. Johnson opened the blinds to let the sunshine stream into the room. She had brought a large tin of her incredible peanut butter cookies and we all sat in chairs surrounding Taylor's bed, munching on the cookies and talking.

Chuck Norman now lay buried in a Tryon Cemetery, and ironically, Teddy and Natasha rested not far from him. They didn't charge Chuck's mother for shooting her son, an act that was generally thought to have saved my life. She still lived in her big home on Hunting Country Road, ostracized by her neighbors. I heard that she was in failing health, attended around the clock by a live-in nurse she brought down from somewhere up north.

There was reputed to be a for-sale sign in front of Wilson Kroll's castle, although the bets were that he would buy his way out of his legal troubles. But his stud business and reputation in the community—and probably with his Cleveland friends—was irreparably damaged.

Alvin pretended he was disappointed he didn't get his licks in with Chuck, but that was Alvin. In general, we were all working hard on our personal versions of closure.

Natasha's family had taken over her education trust, and transferred the recipient award from Jamal to Ronnie Dill. I was proud of myself for playing a small part in that.

Millie Johnson had wholly supported the decision to offer Jamal's financial aid for college to Ronnie Dill. In fact, between the Ladds and Mrs. Johnson, they helped Ronnie Dill's mother serve her worthless, abusive, husband divorce papers and got him kicked out with a restraining order to keep him from coming back. The Ladds also helped Mrs. Dill find a good-paying job as a maid for another family on Hunting Club Road.

"So how is the Dill boy doing?" I asked Mrs. Johnson.

"That boy's already improving his grades, with a whole nother' year to go. He's bound and determined to get into a first-rate college. I'm so proud of him. He's even stopped saying 'ain't,' and words like that. I heard from Mrs. Dill that he's even gained some weight."

As to my relationship with Kelly, we had slid back into our long-distance relationship and shoved our respective phobias under the rug. A voice in my head said, *to be continued.*

I noticed Taylor looking at me.

"It wasn't . . . your fault . . . J.D.," he said.

"I know that Taylor, but Jamal didn't deserve what he got. He was a good kid. Everybody said so."

"Not that. *I'm* not . . . your fault. Stop blaming yourself . . . for me."

I stared at him lying there, unable to move, hooked up to the lines and tubes that kept him alive, overwhelmed that he was concerned about *me* and *my* feelings. No words could describe how much I admired Taylor Johnson's courage and character.

I'd told Agent Smith that the story I would write about the Dark Corner didn't have a happy ending. I was wrong. Just knowing Taylor and the rest of the people in this room was my happy ending. These were my friends. This was my family.

I HAVE A FAVOR TO ASK.

Thank you for reading DARK CORNER. I hope you enjoyed it. Please help me bring this book to the attention of other readers by reviewing it on Amazon. Reviews are the only way I can compete with the giant New York Publishers who have a lot more money to spend on advertising than I do. The review process only takes a couple of minutes. Just go to Amazon.com, search DARK CORNER and scroll down to Customer Reviews. You will be striking a blow for the little guy, and I would much appreciate it. – Ron Fisher

ABOUT THE AUTHOR

Ron Fisher has been a creative director and writer for several of the top advertising agencies in the country, including his own, and has won numerous awards including a Gold Lion at Cannes. Originally from South Carolina, he's lived in San Francisco, Dallas, and now Atlanta, where he can be found happily writing more J.D. Bragg mysteries.

BOOKS BY RON FISHER

CADILLAC TRACKS (J.D. Bragg Mystery #1)

DARK CORNER (J.D. Bragg Mystery #2)

COMING SOON

THE JUNKYARD (J.D. Bragg Mystery #3)

FIND OUT WHERE IT ALL STARTED. Read the first book in the J.D. Bragg series and follow Atlanta investigative journalist J.D. Bragg as he chases a story back to the small town environs of upstate South Carolina where he grew up, only to find that it places him, and his whole family, in mortal danger.

www.ingramcontent.com/pod-product-compliance
Lightning Source LLC
Chambersburg PA
CBHW030428310726
48979CB00009B/1671/J

* 9 7 8 1 9 4 9 0 7 3 0 7 2 *